Love From Scratch

A Laugh Out Loud Romantic Comedy

Summer Dowell

To Quin (I love you, I'm sure one day you'll read this)

Table of Contents

Prologue

A good first impression could make or break a relationship. It was an image the other person would forever have of you. Something they might stow away in the back of their mind, but never truly forget. That was why my first impression on Luke Bradley was so unfortunate.

"Alright you little troublemaker, if you fall flat again I'm done with you. This is your last chance so don't screw it up." I was attempting a challah bread recipe for the third time that week. And yes, I was speaking to a pile of dough.

Unfortunately I didn't hear my roommate Jessica walk in the door at that moment, so she heard a good 30 seconds of me talking to myself. That wasn't the bad part actually. She was used to me talking to my food. The real unfortunate thing was she wasn't alone.

"Jenn!" Jessica's shoulders were shaking, "who in the world are you talking to?"

I looked up to see Jessica walking in, hand in hand with the most attractive man I'd ever seen.

"I, uh... was just... um," I was doing a great rendition of a star-struck fangirl. My mouth had dropped open when I'd noticed them. My stuttering only reinforced the composed vibe I was sure I was putting off.

"I'm messing with you girl." Jessica's eyes scanned the room, searching for our kitchen hidden under my current mess. She turned and smiled at the Ken Doll standing next to her. "Luke this is my roommate, one of the coolest girls you'll ever meet—Jenn Harvey!" She presented me with a sweep of her arm.

Branding me as one of the coolest people she knows probably wasn't doing her any favors at that point.

While I had put on makeup that morning, I was pretty sure my sweat had turned my mascara against me as it was now smudged like black raccoon circles around my eyes. My hair, one of my best features normally, was tied up in a bun Chewbacca would have been proud of. My neon purple sweats were only slightly enhanced by the white spattering of flour that decorated them.

The beautiful man reached out for a handshake despite it all. "Hey, I'm Luke Bradley, nice to meet you." Noticing my hands were preoccupied he pulled back. "Maybe we'll shake next time."

I managed to pull myself together by then.

"Oh yes, excuse my mess! I'm testing out a new recipe for my blog." I tried to motion to the mess with my head since my hands were still stuck in the dough. "I'm struggling with it, hence the disaster." I finished with what I hoped was one of my winning smiles (since the rest of my good features had obviously failed me this morning).

"What are you making today?" I wasn't sure if Jessica was asking me or Luke's oversized bicep she was nuzzling.

"Um, some challah bread." I was trying to discreetly check out this Luke fellow without seeming too obvious. So far I'd noticed his hair was a dark brown that was borderline black. He had a matching set of chestnut brown eyes. I was just admiring the fact that his weathered T-shirt was straining to contain his shoulders when Jessica's answer brought me back to reality.

"Challah bread? Never heard of it. I'll bet you get it this time, nobody bakes like you Jenn."

Both of them smiled and nodded as Jessica dragged Mr. Beautiful off to our adjoining living room. They settled into the white leather loveseat (Side note, our apartment came pre-furnished. I would never in my wildest dreams buy white couches. Talk about a pain to clean). The two lovebirds settled in for a nice cuddling session while I awkwardly debated what to do.

If I was being honest, I felt a desperate need to go spend the next hour showering and putting on makeup. This Luke fellow probably thought Jessica roomed with a troll. However I was also on my third version of this bread and there was no way I was messing this one up by stopping halfway through.

Instead, I tried to discreetly fix my bun into more of a stylish mess than a bird's nest mess. I even found a spare paper towel to wipe away my smeared mascara. That was about as good as it was going to get though. I had more important things to worry about, like the egg whites that needed to be whipped for my glaze.

Jessica and her man were ignoring me at that point anyway. They were in their own world over on the couch, oblivious to everything else.

And that was the first impression I left on Luke Bradley.

*****

I started this out wrong. My name was Jenn, I was a 26-year-old female of average height (5'5") and average weight (I wasn't disclosing that information). I was around a size 8, with aspirations to one day be a size 4. My best feature had to be my smile. I dedicated this to a solid four years in braces, a detriment to my middle school days but I was thankful for them now.

Despite my striking good looks and winning personality, I was still single. To be honest, I hadn't had a serious relationship since my sophomore year of college. And that one wasn't worth mentioning. The guy was a biochemist major and I think every conversation we had revolved around the chemical makeup of our world.

Clearly dating had taken a back seat in my life the last few years. Not exactly by choice, but I was perfectly fine with my singleness.

Valentine's Day was a little rough, and my mom ended every phone conversation asking if I was seeing anyone, but other than that it wasn't too bad. I wasn't tied down to anyone or anything.

And that was where all my problems with Luke Bradley began.

Chapter 1

Beep! Beep! Beep!

There was nothing like being woken up at 4 AM by your alarm clock. It was a habit I wouldn't wish on anyone. Such was the life of a baker.

My senior year of college I realized that I had no idea what one did with a bachelor's degree in communications. My choice of major. You'd think the school guidance counselors would have mentioned something about that to me.

I got a rude awakening after graduation when I spent six months filling out job applications with zero responses. It got to the point that I was applying anywhere for anything. My first and last interview was at a local bakery called Bread & Butter. Despite the fact that I had no baking experience I got the job. It was an entry level position that barely paid the bills. But I was happy to have it.

Initially I planned on working there until I could find something more permanent. What I didn't realize was how much I'd love baking. Let's just say it'd been four years and I'd never looked back.

With my usual groan, I reached over and flailed for my alarm clock button. For whatever reason, people loved buying bread between the hours of 6 AM and noon. This meant I had to be at work by about 4:30 every morning.

As I pulled up that morning I could see lights on inside. Ann was there. Ann was the bakery's owner and the one who had hired me that fateful day four years ago.

I pulled into the empty lot and shut off the shuttering engine of my eight-year-old blue Toyota Corolla.

I hopped out of my car and as I walked through the front door I inhaled my favorite smell in the world: baking bread.

That smell was what hit you every time you stepped into Bread & Butter. Regardless of the time of day, there was a lingering scent of fresh bread.

There was no one behind the front counter but I heard Ann call out, "In the back!" and knew she had already begun the day's work.

She looked up at me when I walked in. "Jenn! You're here, perfect. I started on the wheat and sourdough loaves. You want to get going on the chocolate chip pumpkin bread?" She motioned to the counter where several economy sized cans of pumpkin sat waiting.

"Good morning to you too." I mumbled, tightening the hair tie holding my ponytail in place.

Ann was already busy pulling out yeast starters from the previous day. Ann was like a little energizer bunny in the early mornings.

I grabbed the cans of pumpkin and started gathering the other ingredients I'd need.

Our chocolate chip pumpkin bread was the number one seller through the months of September, October, and November. It was like fall hit and everybody automatically went pumpkin crazy. Although I couldn't complain too much, it was one of my favorites as well.

Ann and I worked alongside each other, keeping a constant chatter going.

"So what'd you do this weekend?" She was adding ingredients to one of the mixers and the air turned hazy with all the flour flying through the air.

I tried to think how I could make updating my blog and doing my laundry sound interesting. About two years ago I started my own baking blog that had become surprisingly successful. Apparently there were others out there that loved butter and sugar as much as I did.

"Oh nothing much," I responded. "Ran some errands and took care of some housework. How about you? Anything fun?"

"Hank and I tried a new restaurant on Saturday night. It was a barbeque place. Hank thought it was overpriced but I thought the clam chowder had been worth it." She let out a short laugh and brushed a strand of curly hair from her eyes. "But considering they're a barbeque place and I thought their soup was their best offering, I guess I wouldn't recommend it."

"Well, I'm glad I can mark it off my list then."

I considered telling her about my experience of meeting Jessica's new boyfriend. Being caught as a total mess in the kitchen was something Ann would understand. Baking was not the most glamorous work.

But as I was about to start on my story I heard the telltale tingling from the front doorbell. Customers were arriving and it was show time.

*****

When I first began working at Bread & Butter, I actually didn't do any of the baking or prep work. As I said before, I didn't have any actual baking experience. I started out answering phone orders, running the register, or washing dishes.

It wasn't until a solid 2-3 months into my dishwashing career that she allowed me to help with the bread. And that was a game changer.

I knew I was hooked when I stopped spending my free time looking through job listings and instead looking through library cookbooks. I was addicted. And it was safe to say I still was.

The first recipe I learned was Ann's buttermilk bread loaf. A yeast-based bread.

I soon learned yeast was a fickle friend. Yeast liked to be coddled and pampered. It was like the prima donna of leavening tools. Baking soda and baking powder—those things would take what you gave them. Not yeast though.

The easy part was mixing all the ingredients together. After that the real work began: the kneading.

I had to go an entire month of hand kneading before Ann let me pass that job off to the stand mixers. She said it was character building, but I think she was just trying to help me develop my biceps.

But when that perfect loaf came out of the oven smelling like heaven, it was all worth it.

Basic Buttermilk Bread Recipe

· 1 1/2 cups warm buttermilk
· 2 TBSP melted butter
· 3 TBSP sugar
· 1 tsp salt
· 3 1/2 cups bread flour
· 1 TBSP yeast

1.) Combine the warm buttermilk, melted butter, sugar, and yeast in a mixing bowl. Allow to sit until yeast becomes bubbly, about 10 minutes.
2.) In a separate bowl, whisk together dry ingredients until combined. Slowly add dry ingredients to buttermilk mixture until combined.
3.) Using a stand mixer fitted with a dough hook knead for 7-8 minutes. (Or knead by hand about 10 minutes.)
4.) Place dough in large lightly greased bowl and cover. Let it rise in a warm place for 40 to 50 minutes until doubled in size.
5.) Punch dough down and knead by hand several times. Roll dough into a log and tuck the ends under. Place in a greased bread loaf pan and let rest in the warm spot for another 30-45 minutes.
6.) Preheat the oven to 350 degrees F. Bake dough for about 30-35 minutes or until top is golden brown. Let cool and slice.

Chapter 2

During my break later that morning, I took the time to call my mom. She'd left me three voice messages over the last 24 hours so either the house burnt down or it was something important like she couldn't remember her password to her email account.

She always left very cryptic voicemails like, "Jenn, call me!" or "I need to talk to you soon!" I think she did it on purpose. She knew I'd fear it was something important and would finally call her back.

Clearly, she never read the book The Boy Who Cried Wolf.

"Hey Mom, how are you?"

"Oh Jenn I'm so glad you called! I need your help!"

If this were anyone else I'd be expecting something urgent, but since it was my mom I knew I didn't need to be too concerned. "Okay, what's going on?"

"Oh the church is doing a social this weekend and I'm supposed to bring a dessert large enough to feed ten people. I don't know what to make and I knew you would have an idea."

While I appreciated my mom's awe for my late-blooming baking skills, I was not sure why she depended on me for new recipes. Literally, there had to be at least 1 million chocolate chip cookie recipes available online.

But I humored her anyways.

"Well, what are you thinking of making? A bar, a cake, some cookies?"

"Something for a crowd. Not a cake though, all the cutting gets too messy in a buffet line."

"How about oatmeal cookies? That's always a winner."

She humphed. "Cheryl Williams always brings oatmeal cookies to every event. She insists she has the best recipe on the planet but of course she won't share it. I don't want to get into a cookie contest with her."

"How about some peanut butter bars?"

"Last month there was a big pow wow about whether we should allow peanut dishes to church events. Apparently there is a new family whose son has a peanut allergy. I'm not sure if a decision was ever reached but I don't want to chance it."

"Okaaaay…" who knew there were such politics at the church social?

After a few more minutes of debating, we decided on a pumpkin pie/sugar cookie crossover I happened to post on my blog last week. It was a winner; I wasn't just tooting my own horn.

From there we moved on to the usual topics like the well-being of my siblings. I had two younger brothers who were both in college. There was realistically only a five year difference between me and my youngest brother, but to hear my mom talk about them you'd think they were still babies. Total mama's boys.

We also chatted about my dad's job, my work/blog, and ultimately... my dating life. Everyone knows any conversation with their mom would end by discussing their relationship status. It was just a fact of life.

"Oh honey I know there are no good men where you live. If only you could come home for a bit and meet someone here." My mom was always trying to convince me to come back to the motherland (aka Colorado) where she had a wealth of connections to good-looking, hard-working, rich, family oriented, single men. I always told her if that was the case she should consider opening her own matchmaking company because that was a very rare breed of man. She had never taken me up on the suggestion.

"Mom, there are plenty of men here in California. I've just been so busy with work and my blog that I haven't had time to meet them." We both knew I was lying.

"Work smirk! Jenny dear, there will always be time for work. But some things in life have an age limit." She didn't say it out loud, but what she clearly meant was it was my ovaries and digressing egg production I should be worried about. In her mind, my best fertility years (and her chances of becoming a grandma) were quickly falling behind me.

"Don't worry mom, I know what I'm doing! I still have plenty of time to find the right guy. Trust me!" While this conversation was very uplifting and motivating, I did my best to end it soon. I had hoped to run by the drugstore before my lunch break was over and time was ticking. I was in serious need of a new tube of mascara and had finished the last of my deodorant that morning.

When I finally hung up (after promising I'd be sure to go out and socialize this weekend) I checked my watch and estimated I had 15 minutes left. If I didn't get distracted I'd be fine. I sprinted across the street to the pharmacy kitty corner to Bread & Butter.

As I entered the store the teenage cashier threw out the customary "welcome!" and I lifted my hand in an equally half hearted greeting.

First I perused the 1,243 mascara options every makeup section had.

There were two types of makeup women in this world. First, those that found something they liked and stuck with it until they died or the product was discontinued. Second, those that couldn't' make up their mind if their life depended on it.

I obviously fell into the second category since I didn't think I'd ever bought the same mascara twice. There was always a new one to try! And don't get me started on eyeshadow colors. Variety is the spice of life, right?

After I picked my mascara of the month and grabbed a new stick of deodorant, I headed to the front of the store. I looked longingly at the rows of nail polish colors, but my mascara research took too long and I needed to get back to work. I'd have to try out that magenta purple color next week.

After I checked out, I hurried out through the doors. Ann would never be angry with me for being late, but I'd feel bad taking advantage of her.

As I reached the curb I heard a light honk from the Black Mercedes waiting at the stop light in front of me. I peered through the window to see who it was. And what do you know... it was Jessica's Mr. Smoking Hot man (aka Luke) smiling his dental award-winning smile at me.

I went to my cool knee-jerk reaction of waving frantically like a five-year-old. It was only after a couple seconds that I realized I was waving my stick of deodorant at him.

He didn't seem to be too bothered by it though because he called out, "How's it going Jenn? What are you up to?"

I was so dumbfounded that he remembered my name I just stared at him for a second. Those beautiful dark brown eyes that a girl could get lost in...

"I uh, I'm buying myself some deodorant," I stuttered. Awesome. I mean I'm glad he knows I am hygienic (he might've questioned it after our last encounter), however it probably wasn't the thing I wanted to emphasize about myself.

He gave me a crooked grin in response. I was pretty sure he was trying not to laugh. "Oh yeah? That's cool, are you off of work now?"

I stepped closer to the beautiful car that matched its beautiful driver (wait, did I just think that? Pull yourself together Jenn) and leaned closer to the window. "Sorta, I'm on my break. Gotta eat and all that... you know...keep my energy levels up." If I could somehow be given the gift to rewind time at this moment that would be awesome.

He grabbed a fast food bag sitting on his passenger chair and said, "I too am a responsible adult and keep a close eye on my energy levels. Although an egg mcmuffin probably isn't the healthiest option." His smile could melt butter.

"Nah, you're good. Those eggs are full of protein and that cheese has got to have some calcium in it. You're basically a walking health ad." The good thing about being a sarcastic person was it could pull you through awkward situations. Fingers crossed it would pull me through this one.

He snickered and looked like he was about to reply when a horn honked from behind him. The light had turned green and he was holding up traffic. He simply yelled, "Thanks for the pep talk! I'll see you later!" and took off in his super expensive yet tasteful car. Okay yes, I was idolizing him too much and needed to take a step back.

I tried not to think about my social awkwardness as I jaywalked back to work. Why couldn't I have been smooth and natural? Why did I turn everything into a weird situation?

Lost in my own thoughts I almost didn't see Carly as I walked through the door.

Carly. I didn't want to sound dramatic, but if I had an adversary, it was Carly. Let's just say from the moment we met, she disliked me. And I was still not sure why. I think it was because I was her only competition at Bread & Butter.

The only reason Ann hired Carly was because she was Ann's goddaughter. Therefore Ann had a moral obligation to support Carly in all her endeavors. Even if she wasn't exactly qualified for the task. Because to be honest, Carly was a terrible baker. I couldn't tell you how many loaves of hers I've had to toss.

Ann did her best to hide this fact from Carly by having her run the cash register most days.

Carly barely glanced at me from her position behind the counter, despite the fact that the store was empty and she was doing nothing. I gave the side of her head a nod and said, "Hey Carly, how's it going?"

She replied with a grunt. That was about the extent of most of our conversations.

Shrugging my shoulders I pushed through to the back kitchen where I saw Ann pulling out hot rolls from the ovens.

"Did I miss anything exciting?" I asked.

Ann looked up and gave me a smile. "Nope just finishing off the last of the day's loaves. Here, you can pull these off the pan and get them out front."

I gave her an okay sign and went to work. And I did my best not to spend the rest of the day daydreaming about those brown eyes in the black Mercedes.

*****

I worked on my blog calendar that evening. This weekend I planned to bake and photograph a cinnamon roll recipe with a pumpkin filling as well as a gingerbread snickerdoodle.

I flipped through the cookbook I was using for inspiration one more time. I loved cookbooks. I loved the endless inspiration they gave me. One day I hoped to see my own name on a cookbook cover.

I snapped out of my daydream with a yawn and rechecked my ingredient list to make sure I had everything.

Just then Jessica popped her head in my door. I jumped a little and she laughed. "Caught you looking at dirty pictures again?" She motioned to my laptop.

"Yep, if that's what you call images of pies and ice cream sundaes, then you got me," I replied. "We both know I'm addicted to food porn."

Jessica stepped fully into my room and said, "Well I'm headed to bed. I have a late event in LA tomorrow so I won't see you. Make sure you call me if you die or anything exciting."

Jessica and I had initially met in college. We were randomly placed together as roommates our freshman year and hadn't separated since. We'd upgraded from our college apartment slums to a nice place in Irvine, the heart of Orange County.

Jessica had gotten a business management degree and currently worked as a PR consultant for fashion merchandisers. To be honest, I don't know what that entails, but she seems to enjoy it.

I nodded my head. "Alright, how was work today?" I considered telling her about my run in with Luke, but I was still trying to pretend it never happened.

"Eh, nothing too exciting." Jessica fiddled with the clip holding her ice blonde hair. Jessica could have been a Victoria's Secret model with her figure. She was a 5'10" size 2 blonde bombshell with the blonde hair and tan to match. At least I knew her highlights were from a bottle. No one could be that naturally perfect.

"I had a little 14 year old diva and her mom come in to check out our services today. I was pretty sure they're going to go with another company, I did my best to disinterest them."

I held back a smile. "I thought you were supposed to be bringing in clients, not turning them away."

"Oh no," the hand not holding the hair clip covered her eyes, "I can't tell you what a pain these two would be. The mom is 100% sure her daughter is the next Beyonce and the girl is 14 going on 25. She asked me if our water was organic. Is there even such a thing as organic water?"

"Geez, well I hope you at least got her autograph. You know, just in case she does become the next Beyonce."

She chucked her hair clip at me while I busted up laughing.

Even though I was trying to avoid the topic of Luke, I had to find out how things were going between them.

"So, how's the current boy toy?" I tried to sound nonchalant as I asked. It had been a week since our awkward encounter in the kitchen, and Jessica had told me little to nothing about him since.

"Luke? Oh, he's good." She suddenly wouldn't meet my eye and I swear I saw a blush hinting at her cheeks.

"Wait, wait, wait. You can't leave it at that. Tell me more. Are you guys a thing already? I thought that was your first date with him on Saturday."

"I guess it was technically our first date. But I met him the weekend before at that work convention I went to. I know one of his coworkers so we all went to lunch together. At some point his coworker was joking that Luke should take me out and next thing I knew we had a date scheduled." She was playing with her hair as she spoke. "We had so much fun, at least I did. Clearly Luke must have too because we had lunch again on Wednesday."

I tried to bite back the jealousy. "Well that's exciting. You think things are going somewhere?"

She shrugged noncommittally. "We'll see. So far I really like him. He's different than the guys I normally date, he's less self centered I guess."

Jessica did tend to attract the narcissistic guys. Men that were more worried about having a trophy girlfriend than anything else.

"Well, fingers crossed," I responded.

"Thanks, good night." she smiled as she shuffled back to her bedroom.

I yawned one more time and reached out in a big stretch. Looking back at my computer I sighed. I loved my blog. I really did. However, it was time-consuming and exhausting some weeks. There were endless hours coming up with recipes, photographing them, editing them, managing my website, responding to reader's questions, etc... it was a beast. But I loved it.

I checked my clock, it was 9 PM, bedtime for this girl. Early mornings meant early nights.

Jessica shuffled back in a minute later wanting her hair clip back. But after that it was lights out.

Chapter 3

The rest of the week passed uneventfully. Ann decided to roll out some of her fall recipes early, so I'd been mixing up gingerbread and pumpkin bread batters like there was no tomorrow.

Carly had been helping with the additional flavors at the beginning of the week. However, on Tuesday she accidentally switched the measurements for the ginger and the cinnamon, creating an entire batch of gingerbread that came out so spicy we had to toss it. Then on Wednesday she managed to flip an entire bowl of cream cheese frosting on my shoes. After that Ann placed her permanently on front counter duty.

Jessica had evening work events three nights that week, so her time hanging out with Mr. Beautiful had been limited. Meaning I hadn't had to face him again since our awkward interaction on Monday.

And by our awkward interaction, I meant my awkward interaction. I'd run through the scenario at least 87 times in my head and how I could have reacted differently. None of them included waiving a stick of deodorant in the air.

Oh well, I didn't know why I cared so much. He was taken. And taken by one of my best friends at that. Talk about unavailable.

I'd sworn to put him out of my mind, which was what I was doing on the following Saturday morning as I worked up a sweat in our kitchen. It was baking day and I was making the most of it.

I decided to start with the pumpkin cinnamon rolls. I had gotten the dough mixed up and it was on its first rise in the corner.

While I waited for that I mixed the pumpkin spice filling. Although I was sure to use a light hand with the ginger, I think I was a little gun shy after Carly's mistake earlier that week.

I was deep in thought, mixing up my butter/sugar concoction when Jessica strode in the door from her early morning run.

I eyed her black leggings jealously. Why did my leggings never look that way? Mine pointed out my flaws rather than enhance my assets. Although I also never wore mine to work out which could have been my problem. I preferred to wear them during one of my couch Netflix marathons, surrounded by Oreos and ice cream.

Jessica was on the phone when she walked in, her giggling, high pitched tone indicated she was talking to a man. I was assuming it was Luke. Lucky girl.

She giggled "Ha ha, you're too cute. Let's plan on Monday night then. Ha ha... You're ridiculous... All right babe. Talk to you later." She hung up the phone in a contented daze. I was not even sure she'd realized she walked in the door.

"Sooo... things heating up between you and the boy toy?" I asked, going for nonchalance.

She started at my words and glanced over at me. "Ah, I didn't see you there Jenn!" She looked a little sheepish. "Wha—what are you making this morning?"

I laughed and pointed my finger. "Don't try and sidestep my question Jess?"

"Oh things are good," She bit her lip to hide a smile before dropping into a stretch with the limberness of a gymnast.

I couldn't remember the last time I'd got that close to touching my toes.

"Okay, better than good. Jenn, I'm into this guy, like *really* into him." I could see a flush rise up her cheeks. "Am I being ridiculous? We've only been dating for maybe two weeks. But he is amazing..."

(I swear I could see stars in her eyes at this point.)

"...he's attentive, and nice, and funny..."

"Wow," I interrupted before she could list off all the enviable qualities of Ken doll, "so you think he's the one?"

See this was the problem with girls. We immediately jumped to marriage. You liked him? Well then you were probably going to marry him, right? We just skipped the whole dating part of the relationship. Straight to marriage. I blamed Jane Austen books.

"Yes! No. Well, that's ridiculous I couldn't say that."

I wasn't sure if Jessica was arguing with me or with her running shoe. She had somehow managed to contort her body into something that resembled a figure eight.

"I don't know Jenn, at this point I'm going to go with my gut feeling that I like him and I hope he feels the same way about me."

I snorted. Jessica was the type of girl that had never been dumped. So I wasn't sure why she was acting nervous or concerned." Jessica, you know there's no way he's going to dump you. So if you're into it, then he's into it." I tapped my whisk on the counter for emphasis.

"Thanks for the pep talk, although you're a little surer than I am."

"So tell me more about Luke. So far all I know is he's super nice and you think you're going to marry him and have his children."

She gave me a hard stare.

"Okay, maybe just marry him. We'll hold off on the children part."

She gave a deep sigh. "He is 30 years old and he loves sports and traveling. His favorite food is Mexican…". She paused.

"Well, you basically just described about 50% of the male population. How about the important stuff like yearly income, how many kids he wants, inheritable family diseases…"

"Jenn you are ridiculous. He is a mechanical engineer. I know he works with airplanes but I have no idea how much he makes or any family diseases he might have."

"Do you need me to do some background checks for you?"

"Stop!" she said as she tried to bite back a snort of laughter.

I went back to my mixing and she studied her fingernails for a moment. I was lighthearted and joking on the outside, but on the inside I was still trying to push back the twinge of jealousy I felt when talking about Luke. Which really was ridiculous. I couldn't understand why I had such a draw to this man I barely even knew.

"Do you think we could have a girl's night tonight? Invite Bree and Christie? I could use some girl talk to get myself out of my head."

I pretended to consult my mental calendar, although I knew my Saturday night was wide open. "Yeah, I'm free tonight. Give the girls a call and see what they're up to."

She squealed and gave me a tight hug. I pretended to wave her off, plugging my nose. "Whew, you need a shower."

"What would I do without you Jenn, you're the best." She glanced down at my mixing bowl. "And what are you making? It smells heavenly."

I gave a dramatic sweep of my arm. "I am making the most delicious pumpkin cinnamon rolls you've ever had." I paused. "At least I hope. I'll let you know in about four hours."

She snickered as she walked towards the bathroom. "Save one for me!"

I turned back to my pumpkin concoction, adding one last dash of ginger. One could never have too much spice in their life after all.

*****

Turned out both Bree and Christie were free. Christie would do anything for a night out away from her kids, so she was an easy sell. Bree was a little trickier. We had to convince her that spending a Saturday night at her office was nowhere near as beneficial as dinner out with her girls. Lawyers.

The four of us met back in college our freshman year. Bree and Christie were our next door neighbors on our dorm floor. We'd quickly become a foursome.

Christie had been the mother hen to us all. She made the chicken noodle soup when someone got sick, sympathized during rough breakups, and reminded us not to wash our whites and darks together. It was only fitting that Christie was the first to get engaged and tie the knot of our crew four years ago. She now had a set of boy twins, and was pregnant with a little girl. Such an overachiever.

Then there was Bree. Our nickname for her during college was Brainy Bree (we meant it lovingly). She knew from day one she was going to be a lawyer and never veered off course. We often had to remind her to get her nose out of her books and eat. Now she worked for a big-name law firm up in LA. Not only that, but she was engaged to another successful lawyer who shared her ambitions. They were the perfect match. (Note to self: cut Ben and Jerry's from diet so I can fit into my bridesmaid dress)

We decided to meet at 7 PM that night at our usual spot. Actually, we didn't discuss it; it was just assumed we would meet at our usual spot. That was the great thing about being lifelong buds. Some things never changed.

Now I know a group of classy girls like ourselves would most likely be dining at some hip, upscale restaurant right? But not us. Our spot originated back in our college days. Back when we were all broke and living from one packet of Top Ramen to the next. Our go-to spot? Gijorno's.

Gijorno's was your classic, hole-in-the-wall Italian place. It had an impenetrable smell of garlic and grease that literally seeped out of all corners of the building. It was heaven.

The moment you walked in you'd hear a chorus of "Ciao!" "Signorinas!" "Buona sera!" I didn't speak Italian but you'd think we were long-lost relatives with the greeting they'd give us. I used to feel pretty special because of it until I realized they did that with everyone.

We always started out with a giant plate of their classic garlic bread. I was pretty sure there was more butter then actual bread in this dish, but that's what made it good. Next (because contrary to popular belief, a girl could never have too many carbs), we'd follow it up with one of their extra large specialty pizzas.

Back in the good old college days, we couldn't afford their specialty pizzas. We had to make do with a straight cheese or pepperoni. Now that we were all in a higher tax bracket, we were willing to dish out for the extra goodies like artichokes and sausage.

Then the waiters would dangle the idea of dessert in front of us and you know we couldn't resist.

Well, at least I couldn't. Jessica usually had a little self-restraint but she eventually caved once the rest of us started biting into our cream-filled cannolis.

Tonight was no different. By the time we got through the garlic bread, everybody had dished out the most recent details of their life.

Bree had given us all the details of wedding planning. As expected, everything had its own spreadsheet and a pro and con list.

"I booked the photographers for only a half day because the florist isn't scheduled to deliver the flowers until noon.

Why pay for four hours of photography when I won't even have my bouquet yet?"

We all nodded regardless of the fact that she wasn't paying attention to our reaction.

"I'm just glad we double checked that the company making our wedding cake has both gluten free and dairy free options. We have family members on both sides with particular needs so each layer will have to be different."

I had no idea how Bree found time to sleep in between wedding planning and her rigorous work schedule.

When she finished updating us on all things wedding, Christie gave us some comedic relief with her never-ending twin stories.

"I kid you not, this morning I caught them trying to flush all their super heros down our upstairs toilet." She inhaled deeply as if trying to calm herself. "Jack insisted they were doing a rescue mission to save the spider I'd flushed earlier that morning—against their wishes obviously."

We were all busting up laughing at this.

"Christie, you seriously need to write a book about raising twins. If you just wrote down all these stories you'd have a best seller!" Jessica said, using her pizza slice to emphasize her words.

Christie shook her head. "If I had enough time to do something like that I would. At this point I'm struggling to take a shower every day!"

I believed her. It seemed she simply went from one disaster to another.

"So," Bree cut in, a meaningful glance directed towards Jessica and me, "anyone dating anyone new? I need some juicy gossip. Being engaged is a tad boring now."

"Just wait until you're married," Christie cut in. "If I want any hint of drama in my life it comes solely from tabloids or The Bachelor reruns."

"I have nothing new or interesting. But Jessica..." I took a giant bite of my sausage loaded pizza, letting the sentence hang in the air for Jessica to fill.

Jessica rolled her eyes at me. "Okay, yes I am dating someone new, but it's nothing serious so don't get excited!"

Regardless of her insistence, Bree and Christie both squealed with enthusiasm.

Jessica gave them the basic details, his career, his likes/dislikes, and his general appearance. I personally thought that she underrated how good looking the man was, but I might have been biased. I clearly had a ridiculous crush on him.

"So are you going to marry this guy?" Christie asked with obvious glee.

"No! I mean, I don't know," Jessica was flustered, a very unusual trait for her. "I mean we've only been dating two, maybe three weeks. It's way too soon to get into that stuff." She tried to look nonchalant as she sipped her water but her flushed face told a different story.

Bree, ever the efficient and organized one butted in. "Well if you think it's serious you might start considering your timeline. I'll be the first to tell you that booking wedding venues, photographers, etc. is a nightmare." You could see the wheels in Bree's head turning. "You have to know at least a year out for the good ones, otherwise they're all booked. You're way better off if you can get in early."

Like the knight in armor I was, (and the only reasonable one in our group at that moment) I came to Jessica's rescue.

"We all know the guy likely wants to marry Jess right now," I said, giving her a tight squeeze, "it's just up to Jessica to decide if he's good enough for her. No need to stress about it." I tried to change the subject. "Anyway—."

Christie jumped in before I could though. "Girl, all I know is you need to *enjoy* this time. This dating period? Live It Up." She emphasized each word with the napkin she was using to wipe up some spilled pizza sauce. "The attention, the compliments, the thoughtfulness, it doesn't get any better than this." She leaned back and held her hands up defensively. "Don't get me wrong, marriage is great. Marriage is wonderful. You should all get married ASAP and start having babies. But marriage is way different than dating is." She tapped her temple with one finger. "I can't remember the last time Chad and I had an evening to ourselves. It's just going to get crazier in a few months," she added as she rubbed her ever growing belly. Given that she was the only one actually married, Christie knew what she was talking about.

"Christie you know I've told you countless times if you need a babysitter I'm here for you!" I exclaimed. And I meant it. I liked kids a lot. Growing up I was surrounded by endless family and cousins. Kids everywhere. I missed that part of life. One day I'd be there too I told myself.

Christine grinned. "I know, I know... but the twins are so nuts I'd feel terrible leaving them with anyone sometimes."

Bree wasn't ready to let the topic go. "So honestly Jessica, how serious are things between you guys?"

"I don't know I've never been so into anyone before. It's a new feeling for me," she said sheepishly.

I got what she was saying. Jessica was modest, but I was pretty sure she'd ever dnated a guy that didn't like her way more than she liked him. This situation with Luke might be a first for her.

As a side note, I'd like to point out how well I'd been taking all this. Right? Somebody needed to give me a gold star or something. I mean it was pretty hard having a discussion with your best girlfriends about one of their boyfriends that you totally had a crush on. This was something from a Jerry Springer show.

I mean I was happy for Jessica, really I was. I wanted her to find her true love and get married and have lots of babies. I just didn't want her to necessarily do it with Luke. Was that asking too much?

We spent the remainder of the evening discussing the latest movies, recent tabloid gossip, and other meaningless things we all loved.

Sometime around nine we all rolled out of the restaurant, completely bloated and satisfied. We said our goodbyes with promises from Jessica to keep everyone updated on her boy.

"I'm going over to Luke's for a bit," Jessica said when there was only me and her left in the parking lot.

"Sounds good, I'm probably going to bed. Maybe I'll be able to sleep off some of these calories I just consumed." It was a Saturday night, so I didn't have work in the morning, but I still liked my early bedtimes.

"Right? I'm pretty sure all my clothes smell like garlic." Jessica took an involuntary sniff of her shirt then shrugged. "Eh, oh well."

I laughed and waved goodbye.

It wasn't until I was sitting in my car and turning the key that I realized I was the only one of our group going home to nobody. There was no spouse, fiancé, or significant other waiting for me anywhere. Instead, I was going home to check on a bowl of yeast to see if it had risen properly. Something had to change.

Chapter 4

Fall flavors were beginning everywhere which added a boost to the store's traffic the following week. No one could have had a successful holiday season if they hadn't consumed their weight in pumpkin scones, cinnamon bread, and spicy gingerbread. It was a fact. So our ovens were roaring nonstop.

Ann was going to give me some creative liberties this year. I wanted to add pies to the menu and she agreed to try them out.

The flavors I suggested were fairly traditional, apple and pumpkin pie, however, I was going to add my own special twist to them. Instead of making plain crusts, I wanted to jazz them up a bit. So after work on Tuesday I started recipe testing.

First I was working on the pumpkin pie crust. I was going to substitute some of the flour with ground graham crackers and add cinnamon to the dough. Fingers crossed it worked.

With the apple pie, I was going for a riskier approach. I was hoping to infuse some more savory herbs (think

Thanksgiving Day) into the crust to create a contrasting note to the sweet apple filling.

I started cutting my shortening into my flour, quick sharp movements so the fat didn't warm up. Ten minutes later I was elbow deep in a bowl of pie crust that I swiftly divided into five sections, two for each recipe variation and one for a control version.

I was wrapping them up to chill in the fridge when there was a sharp knock on the door. I checked the clock, it was 5 PM. The only person I could imagine it being was the FedEx guy. He made regular appearances to our apartment due to Jessica and my united addiction to Amazon. I briskly brushed off my hands as I made my way to the door.

I turned the knob and started my usual greeting of, "Hey, you can just leave it—." But it wasn't the FedEx guy. It was Luke. Dreamboat Luke.

He had the audacity to look freshly showered and put together in contrast to my disheveled appearance once again. The punk. I was pretty sure he had yet to see me wearing anything but an apron around my waist and flour in my hair since we'd met.

"Uh—hi, I mean—sorry I thought you were the FedEx guy," I mumbled.

He gave me a sly grin and said, "Sorry, just me." He stared at me for a second then seemed to snap out of his daydream. "Is Jessica ready?" He peered around me.

I glanced over my shoulder as if I too anticipated her to walk out any second. I turned back to him. "No, she's not even here. Were you expecting her?"

"Yeah, we're supposed to grab dinner tonight. I'm pretty sure she said five." He pulled out his phone and seemed to be flipping through text messages.

"I know she had an event luncheon today," I offered him. "Maybe it ran late or there was traffic?" I decided I should offer a little hospitality to the man so I opened the door wide. "Come in, maybe she'll show up in a minute."

Luke glanced at me and smiled, "Thanks, I'll give her a call and see where she's at."

He strode past with the phone to his ear and a faint woodsy smelling cologne hit me. He would smell as good as he looked I thought irritably as I shut the door with slightly more force than necessary.

Luke went into the living room and perched on the edge of the couch, fiddling with the fringe on our coral colored throw pillows as he held the phone to his ear.

That was one of the beauties of living with just girls, you could have feminine decor like purple and coral pillows and there was no guy around to complain.

Jessica apparently answered his call because he said, "Hey pretty lady, where are you at?"

Jessica obviously started in some sort of explanation because he spent the next minute or two nodding and mumbling "uh huh... mmm..." He eventually looked up and winked at me and I realized I should stop staring at him like a lovesick schoolgirl.

I shuffled into the kitchen and tried to check my reflection in the microwave. Yup, I was as big of a mess as I thought. I finished wrapping up my dough segments and placed them in the fridge. They would need to chill for at least 30 minutes so the shortening could get cold again. I wasn't kidding when I said pie crusts were tricky things.

Luke popped his head around the corner as I finished scrubbing out my mixing bowls. "What are you up to?" His eyes roamed my kitchen.

"Pie crust," I answered with a flourish of my arms. It wasn't until after I struck my pose that I realized my crusts were in the fridge and he couldn't see them. "Well I actually just finished them; they're in the fridge." I cracked open the fridge so he could take a glance.

"Cool. So you're a baker, right? Jessica said that's your thing." He stepped further into the kitchen and leaned on one of the few clean spots on the counter.

Did they talk about me? For a moment I felt butterflies in my stomach and then realized how dumb that was. Of course they talked about me, I was Jessica's roommate. Just like they probably talked about his friends, coworkers, and anyone else in their lives like a normal person would.

"Yeah, I guess I am. I work for a bakery called Bread & Butter. We specialize in bread, but we also do just about every other baked good too. Ever heard of it?"

"I think I have. It's near where I saw you the other day right?" He seemed genuinely interested to my surprise.

"Yep, that's the one," I answered while secretly thinking how unfortunate it was that he hadn't forgotten that day.

"So how did you get that job? Did you go to culinary school or something?"

"Ha ha—nope." He was probably imagining some sort of Le Cordon Bleu experience, with the white chef's hat and all. "Unfortunately, I wasn't smart enough to go that route." I gave him the quick version of my culinary history.

"No way," he replied after I was done. "So you were never formally trained or anything? How about growing up? Did you bake all the time with your mom?"

I bit my lip, holding back an unladylike snort. "I wish, but I was a pure novice. Five years ago I could barely tell the difference between flour and sugar."

He laughed out loud, a nice hearty laugh that made me feel better about my stifled snort. "Well that's the point I'm at now so I won't judge. You must enjoy it. Otherwise you would've quit long ago."

I realized I was bouncing slightly on my toes and stopped myself, nothing got me excited quite like talking about baking. "Yes, as a matter fact I do love it. I can't believe I've only been baking for five years, I feel like it's a part of who I am now." I indicated towards the flour dusting my hair, "As you can see, I take my baking with me everywhere I go."

He smiled and dusted off the top of my hair; I was surprised by the intimacy of the gesture and froze like a statue.

Luckily Luke didn't notice. "It suits you though. You seem happy here in your kitchen. What is your favorite thing to bake?"

"I don't think I could tell you. It would be like choosing a favorite child." I said, trying to relax the tension out of my shoulders. "But right now I am trying to master a new pie crust recipe."

He folded his arms in a condescending manner. "I don't want to brag, but in the seventh grade I won my city's 4th of July pie eating contest. I managed to eat two whole pies in eight and a half minutes."

I stared at him. "Are you serious? Two pies? How old were you?" I mean I felt like I could hold my sugar quite well. I had no problem finishing a carton of ice cream, a batch of cookies, etc. But I didn't think even I could eat a whole pie by myself, let alone two.

"Fourteen. And to be honest, I don't think I could perform to the same level today. It was those growing years that gave me an endless appetite." He stood straight. "However my fine taste in pie flavors hasn't left me. So if you're looking for a professional taste tester, I'm your guy." I wasn't able to hold back my snort this time. "So that was your angle. Well, today is your lucky day. I'm always looking for new subjects to taste my food. Since Jessica's not here I am definitely in need of another taste tester."

"However," I said, getting a stern look in my eye, "you're going to have to work for your food if that's the case."

I pulled out two baking sheets and my ultimate weapon, another pink apron.

*****

We spent the next half hour side-by-side rolling out dough (well technically I was rolling the dough, I made Luke hand over his rolling pin when he destroyed my first batch) and swapping stories.

I told him about some of my best culinary successes as well as my biggest flops. As much as I wanted them to succeed, my jalapeño cinnamon scones never panned out.

He told me a bit more about his history. I learned more from him in 20 minutes than I did from Jessica in the three weeks of them dating.

Luke grew up in the suburbs of San Diego and was the oldest of three boys. His parents still lived in the house he grew up in. One of his brothers lived in Chicago as a lawyer and the other was finishing up medical school in Illinois. Luke had gone to school at USC and gotten a masters degree in mechanical engineering which led to his current job of working with airplanes.

"So basically I'm the bottom of the totem pole compared to my brothers. You'd think an engineering degree would put me at the top but those two had to outdo me with their law and medical degrees."

I adjusted the angle of my rolling pin. It kept getting stuck on one side of the dough. "But just think, at least they probably ride the airplanes you designed when they take their luxurious vacations and business trips."

He gave me a dark stare that eventually broke into a laugh.

"So tell me what exactly you design on airplanes." I'd given up on my sticky rolling pin and was re-flouring my countertop.

"Have you ever had a bad airplane landing? One where you weren't sure if you were going to live through?"

I thought for a minute about my past flights. "I've definitely had one or two bouncy ones."

"Well, that's what I'm trying to eliminate. To be specific, I work with engine vibrator sensors. I'm developing a system to..."

I might have dazed a little when he got into the technical jargon. I did take the opportunity to stare at his beautiful face though. The man had some of the darkest brown eyes I'd ever seen. My own eyes moved lower to his mouth. I was mesmerized by its movement. I swear he had a dimple in his right cheek when he said certain words...

I realized that he had stopped talking and was staring at me with his arms folded.

"You weren't listening to anything I was saying were you?"

"Wh-ha... no! I was totally listening. The airplane sensors you know, they test the vibrations of the engine... and..." I had nothing.

"Hmm, it must have just been the glazed over look you had on your eyes. I'm assuming that's your concentrating look." He let out a dramatic sigh, and I considered suggesting he try out for a local theater production. "It's okay, everyone zones me out when I start talking about my work."

"I wasn't trying to zone you out," I said apologetically. This discussion did make me realize how intelligent Luke was. You'd never guess it by how down to earth he was. I clearly had spent too much time assessing his looks and not enough time assessing his intelligence. (Note to self: work on not being so shallow)

"So," he said poking at the edge of one of the crusts I'd rolled out, "explain to me exactly what we're testing this afternoon?" (I loved how he said "we" like he was an integral part of this).

"We are testing how my pie crusts are affected when I add other ingredients to them," I answered simply while motioning wildly with my hands. Had I mentioned I was a hand talker? "I am trying to give the crust extra pizzazz and flavor. So when you bite into them you think to yourself 'what makes this amazing pie so unbelievably delicious?"

I said this all with a smile and luckily he caught on to my joking.

"I see," he squinted his eyes as if in deep thought. "They'll say to themselves, who is this Jenn that created such a masterpiece? It's a whole other level of amazingness. She is a genius."

Despite the fact that he was mocking me I grinned. "Exactly."

I finished placing my rolled strips of pie crust on a baking sheet. Normally I would put them in an actual pie pan to be filled, but I wanted to test their flavor and texture without other distractions. The oven was already preheated to a perfect 375° so I popped them in and set the timer for 25 minutes.

"And now, we wait," I said with another arm flourish. (I really needed to stop doing that)

He fiddled with the ties on his pink apron. I didn't think he'd actually wear it but apparently he was very secure with his masculinity. "So, are these pie crusts for your shop or your blog?"

"They're for the shop, although it's not actually my shop. The owner is a woman named Ann—I work for her." I stopped and drummed my fingers on the counter, feeling the flour still caked under my nails. "But she's given me some creative reign lately and is letting me introduce some pies for the holiday season." I let out a rush of air through my cheeks. "However it's on a trial basis. She wants to taste them first and make sure they're up to par."

"Hmmm," he said, rubbing his hands vigorously together, "so this taste testing is serious business."

"More or less." I walked around the counter towards the living room. "Here, let's relax, I can't deal with all the stress while standing up,"

I flopped down on the couch and tried not to notice that he chose to sit on the same one as I did. It seemed like he should have chosen to sit on the loveseat by himself... but then he would have had to walk around the coffee table so maybe that would have been awkward... but more awkward than sitting next to me? I gave my head a shake and tried to stop over analyzing the situation.

"So," he leaned forward, his elbows resting on his knees, "how much longer are you planning on working at the bakery?"

"What?" I was confused.

"Well, you're clearly a go-getter," he motioned with his hands (good at least I'm not the only one that used their hands too much). "You worked your way up in this bakery and you've got your own blog going. I just assumed the next step was to open your own place, right?" He looked at me with raised eyebrows.

"Well, ah, I couldn't do that... Ann needs me," I finished, wanting to roll my eyes at my own excuse.

But he had hit on my secret dream. I mean, I had several dreams in terms of my baking future. Obviously I wanted to take my blog to the next level and become one of the real superstars of the food blogging world. I also wanted to publish my own cookbook one day.

The one dream I kept deep was the dream of opening my own bakery. I hid this for several reasons, but the main one was fear. Fear of it being too hard. Fear of others laughing at my ambition. Fear of failing.

Luke was still staring, waiting for my answer to evolve.

"It's just that Ann started me in this business. I feel a strong sense of loyalty to her," I continued trying to make my answer sound reasonable. "It's like if I branched out on my own, I would be saying I thought I was better than her or something." I shrunk back into the couch.

He nodded, seeming to accept my answer. "I can see that, but don't you think she'd rather you achieve your own dreams?" His serious tone held my attention. "I mean, I've had lots of people help me in my career, but I don't think any of them feel entitled to my entire future just because they assisted along the way."

He was right. Ann would love for me to start my own shop if I wanted to. There was no way she would have any hard feelings. I still tried to hold onto her as my excuse. "Maybe, but I don't think I could leave her. She taught me everything I know and we make a good team."

Luke didn't argue after that, instead he leaned back with his eyes closed. "Well, if you're not going to open your own bakery, what are your goals with your blog?"

"What are you? Some kind of life coach?"

He cracked one eye open and looked at me, "I have been known for my sage wisdom. I'll also be billing you for my services after this."

I laughed out loud, but mentally I was thinking about how easy it was to talk to him. Despite that until an hour ago we'd never said more than ten words to each other, we now felt like old friends.

Just then the oven timer beeped. It's loud ding brought me out of my trance.

"All right." I jumped up. "Enough chit chat, time for some serious business."

I walked into the kitchen and slipped on some oven mitts. The smell wafting from the oven was heavenly. I lowered the oven door and slowly slid out the two cookie sheets. The crusts were a light golden color, the edges slightly darker than the center. My pumpkin crusts had these beautiful brown flecks of cinnamon. Meanwhile, the apple crusts were dotted with flecks of green from the rosemary and thyme.

Luke walked up beside me and stared down at the crusts. "Well, they certainly look delicious." He lowered his face to the pans and took a deep breath in. "And they smell delicious as well. So far they have a five-star rating from me."

I turned away to set the pans on the counter, and to hide my smile. "So here's what I want you to specifically look for when you taste these. Usually we'd start with appearance, but since this isn't really the finished product, I'm not too worried about that. So first," I raised a single finger, "you need to assess the flavor. What specifically can you taste? Are there any overriding flavors? Is it too salty, too cinnamony, to rosemary-ey?"

"I'm pretty sure that's not a word," he cut in.

"Shush, no interrupting the boss," I admonished. I lifted a second finger, "Next I want you to think about the texture. Remember a good pie crust is very flaky but it should also melt in your mouth." My hands were going in dramatic circular motions again. "It's best if you eat with your eyes closed. Limiting the other senses lets you focus more on your mouth and everything going on inside it."

"Is that scientifically proven?"

"Yes. I am basically a doctor so don't question me." I scooped the pumpkin pie crust off the pan with a flat spatula. I gave the crusts another 2 minutes to cool, then I cut each one into three pieces—one for me, one for Luke, and one for Jessica (for whenever she got home). I'd learned it was good to get multiple opinions.

"All right," I said as I presented the plate to him. "I want you to try these two versions and tell me which you like better. Remember: eyes closed, focus on flavor and texture."

Luke already had both eyes closed and he was reaching out blindly for the plate.

"You can open your eyes while you pick up the crust," I told him dryly.

He peeked one eye open. "I didn't want to break the rules." He grabbed the two versions, one in each hand. I watched him as he took a bite of the first.

The main difference between the two versions was the amount of graham cracker crumbs I put in it. I was trying to reach a balance of having enough graham flavor, but not disrupting the normal pie crust texture.

Luke made a low "mmmm" sound as he finished his bite of the first one. Next he took a bite of the second, the more graham crackery one. He had a similar response to it. He went back and forth between the two crusts, taking minuscule bites of either one until they were both gone.

When he was finished he opened his eyes and brushed his hands off. "All right, I've collected my findings." He looked at me wide eyed, "Are you going to write this down?"

I rested my forehead in my hand. "Look Luke, this isn't that technical, just tell me what you thought."

He huffed, "Well so much for the scientific method. Okay, the first one I liked. It kind of reminded me of my mom's pies, maybe a little sweeter. But the second one really stood out. I could tell there was something different in the crust, something unique. And while it might've been less flaky, I think the flavor made up for it." He looked at me as if waiting for my approval.

I nodded at him and took a piece of each crust for myself. I did a similar taste test and had to agree with his analysis. The second one stood out more. The only thing it needed was a little more nutmeg, the cinnamon was too overpowering.

"Perfect," I said as I finished off my samples. "I think I'll hire you full-time. I agree with your thoughts—the second one for sure."

He smiled broadly at my conclusion, reminding me of a young boy who had been praised for doing a good job.

"Ready for round two?" I asked, holding up the second tray of pie crusts. The tasting of the second ones went similar to the first. This time we both decided to use the version with fewer seasonings though. That parsley came in just a little too strong.

I was putting the pans into a sink of soapy water when Jessica burst through the door. "Holy cow, that was the longest drive of my life!" she exclaimed chucking her purse on the counter with a flourish.

Luke walked over and planted a kiss on her head. I could feel the green monster creep up inside me as I watched. It was hard to come back to the reality after the last hour we just spent together. Luke was Jessica's boyfriend.

"Sorry Jess, lots of traffic?" He gave her shoulders a slight massage.

"Yesss." She covered her eyes with her hand. "There was an accident going across two of the left lanes and cars were backed up for miles. I didn't think I would ever get home."

I walked over to her with the plate of leftover pie crust in hand. "The good news is I have some pie crust for you to try, that should soothe your sorrows."

Jessica smiled at me. "Jenn you're the best. I don't know what I would do without you." She eyed the plate of pie crusts. "Although I do have to ask where is the rest of the pie? How come I'm just getting crusts?"

I laughed. "Because that's what we're testing." I put the plate back and set it on the counter. "You can come back and do a test for me after you're more relaxed. I wouldn't want your opinions to be affected by your grumpy mood."

Luke was still standing behind her, one hand massaging her shoulder. "You still want to go out tonight or are you too tired?" he asked.

"Ehh," Jessica made a sort of moaning sound. "Do you mind if we scratch dinner tonight? I don't think I can do anything except go soak in a hot bath and go to bed." She turned and leaned into his shoulder. "Today was rough beside the traffic. I had the most demanding group of divas at the conference today."

Luke smiled at me over the top of her head. "I'm sorry, that doesn't sound like much fun." He leaned back and propped Jessica's face up with a finger under her chin. "You go rest. We can hang out another night this week. Besides, Jenn has filled my stomach with enough crust to count for dinner."

She reached up for a kiss and it was at this point that I started feeling like the third wheel I was. Luckily they limited their PDA and two minutes later Luke was gone.

Jessica promised she'd come to try my pie crust after her bath and then she was off down the hallway.

And once again it was me, alone in my kitchen.

Basic Pie Crust Recipe

· 1 1/4 cups all-purpose flour
· 1/4 teaspoon salt
· 1/2 cup butter flavored shortening
· 1 tsp vinegar
· 3 tablespoons ice water

1.) Whisk the flour and salt together. With a pastry blender, cut in cold shortening until the mixture resembles coarse crumbs. Drizzle vinegar and 2 to 3 tablespoons ice water over flour. Toss mixture with a fork to moisten, adding more water until dough comes together.
2.) Gently gather dough particles together into a ball. Wrap in plastic wrap, flatten into a disk, and chill for at least 30 minutes.
3.) Roll out dough on a floured surface and use as needed.

Chapter 5

I couldn't get Luke's question out of my head the rest of the week.

What did I really want in life? Did I want to continue working at Bread & Butter forever? Would my blog continue to be my sole creative outlet? Or would I shoot for more? The ideas kept circling in my head.

Thursday morning it was just Ann and me wrapping things up in the kitchen. We usually finished our last batch of bread around 10 AM, and after that spent a good hour cleaning up the mess. Carly was working the front desk so Ann and I were elbow to elbow at the sinks scrubbing down pots. There was a soft hum of music coming from the front of the store, but other than that we worked in an easy silence.

"Ann, what was it that made you open this place?" I finally asked out of the blue.

"Open what place? Bread & Butter?" she replied, not taking her eyes off the pan she was working on.

"Yeah, what made you think opening a bakery was a good idea, or would even work?" I tried to sound nonchalant in my questioning.

"Well first off I had no idea if it would work," she began. She let out a quick laugh. "I had no idea what I was getting myself into. I didn't and still don't really have a head for business." Her hands had stilled as if thinking about the past was all she could process at the moment.

"Hank was the one that made me go for it. He believed in me, in a way no one else ever had." She got this starry eyed look in her eyes, despite the fact that she was staring at a dirty dish towel.

Hank, was the sweetest guy ever. I'd smile like that too if I was married to him.

"He knew how much I loved baking, the thrill I got every time I pulled a fresh loaf from the oven. He said I should just do it, stop dreaming about it. I'll never forget when he said 'you might regret it if you try... but you'll for sure regret it if you don't'." She paused and looked at me.

"Sometimes we stop ourselves from doing things in life because we aren't sure of the outcome. We like to play it safe. Stay in our little comfort zones." The stillness in the air was palpable. "But sometimes we need to shake off our fears and take the leap. It's been hard in more ways than one, but I never regret taking this chance. Even if Bread & Butter had turned into a total failure, I don't think I'd regret trying."

She turned back to scrubbing her pan and the stillness was broken.

I wasn't ready to move on yet. "But what if you didn't have Hank? What if you didn't have someone to tell you that you could do it and be there for you when things got tough?" We both knew I was talking about myself at this point.

"Oh Jenn," she turned and wrapped me up in a tight hug, sudsy hands and all. "You've always got me. No matter what you decide to do in life, I will support and help you in any way I can."

I blinked back tears and hugged her back. "Thanks Ann. That means more than you know." I stepped away and wiped my eyes with the back of my hands, simultaneously getting bubbles in my hair. "But don't worry; you're not going to be rid of me anytime soon."

"That's good," she said, swatting at the bubbles framing my face, "because you still have the rest of these pans to scrub out."

*****

I decided that afternoon I was going to stop living my life without a plan. Living like I was scared of what the future would bring.

One thing for sure had to change. I needed some sort of a companion in my life. Someone I could talk to besides my yeast at night.

On my way home I stopped at a pet shop.

I oohed and ahhed over the puppies in the front of the store, I knew that was unrealistic. Way too much time and effort went into puppies. But they sure were cute.

Kittens fell into that same category so I drifted by them as well.

The center of the store had a huge sign hanging from the ceiling that said 'Birds'. I'd never considered having a pet bird so I headed that way. There were three large cages full of blue and green squawking parakeets. They were pretty adorable actually. I wondered if I could teach them to talk back to me. I knew parrots had great mimicking abilities. I began reading the display case. Parakeets were known for being extremely loud animals and very social. They needed several hours a day outside the cage interacting with their owners. Maybe a bird wasn't for me. I could get used to the noise but I bet Jessica wouldn't appreciate it. Let alone our neighbors.

I spent a few more minutes reading before I decided to move on. On the left side in the back was a large sign that said 'Reptiles'. I didn't even bother going in that direction. If there was one animal group I would gladly remove from the earth, it would be reptiles.

On the right side in the back, there was a large sign that said 'Fish'. Now that was something I could get on board with.

The wall was lined with glass aquariums from the floor to the ceiling. The blue aquarium lights gave an eerie glow to the area. There was every fish you could imagine. Freshwater fish, saltwater fish, glowing fish, miniature sharks, sea snails, goldfish that were sure to die within 24 hours...

I scanned the rows, contemplating what level of dedication I was going to put into my new roommate. After a few minutes of reading the different display cases, I flagged down a store employee who was unpacking some boxes an aisle away.

He was a younger looking guy, somewhere around his early 20s, with tattoos up and down each arm and piercings in both eyebrows. His hair was probably shoulder length, but he had spiked it up in a large mohawk. And it was dyed purple. I had to give him props for individuality.

"Hi," I said hoping he didn't realize how much his appearance intimidated me. "I was wondering if you could tell me which of these fish is the easiest to take care of. Like hypothetically speaking, if I were to accidentally forget about it for a weekend, which of these fish would still be alive?"

He broke into a smile, which changed his entire appearance. Instead of the bad boy look I believed he was going for, he looked like he could be my next-door neighbor.

"Well miss," (can I say how grateful I was that he didn't call me ma'am, at least he assumed I was young), "if that's the case I suggest you start with a betta fish."

He turned away from the wall of aquariums to the shelf behind us. It was holding a row of cups full of individual fish. Each cup was about 3/4ths full of water and was topped with a plastic lid.

"These are betta fish." He motioned to them. "They are some of the hardiest fish we have. They can go for days without food and are best kept separate from other fish. Just in case you're worried about your pet's social life," he said with a wink. (Did Mr. Purple Mohawk wink at me?)

"Awesome!" I said perhaps a little too cheerfully. "Not that I'm planning on forgetting to feed my future fish." Hopefully, there wasn't some sort of future pet owner screening test you had to go through. I was failing if there was.

He continued on. "The great thing is they thrive well without an air-filtered tank. Most of these other fish need to have oxygen pumped into their water to remain healthy. Betta fish are made of sterner stuff. A simple fish bowl should work fine." Purple Mohawk scrutinized me closely.

"You do have to occasionally change the water and make sure the pH level is okay. Do you think you can handle that?"

I nodded my head vehemently. I still feared that I might be failing some sort of undercover screening test.

"Well, then I guess you better pick out your newest friend." He turned back to the boxes he had been unpacking.

I looked at all the little plastic cups lined in a row. This was an important decision. I was basically choosing a new family member, how would I know which was the right one?

I got down low and studied each fish. The majority of them were a dark blue color, with strands of green running along their sides. For the most part they all ignored me and floated almost listlessly in their water. However, towards the end of the row, there was one little fish that stood out.

In contrast to all the blues and greens, this one was a deep red color. And she was staring me down hard. (Yes, I assumed it was a she) I know it sounded ridiculous, but I swear she didn't take her eyes off me.

I put my face up close to her and she started swishing her tail back-and-forth, almost as in a challenge. If she could speak she would be saying "who do you think you're looking at?"

I picked up the cup and eyed her from all angles. She was still now, almost cautious as to what I was going to do with her.

"Hello little miss," I began, "you are apparently a fighter, which is just what I need. Someone to motivate me to make some changes. You're coming home with me."

I walked to the display of aquariums and glass bowls. I passed up all the fancy ones. I wasn't ready to drop a hundred bucks on her quite yet.

I decided on a nice globe-shaped bowl. For decoration I grabbed some sea green rocks. I held her up to see if she was partial to any of the plastic plants. She stared down a yellow algae one so I grabbed it. "I like your taste," I told her.

I checked out the betta food options next. Betta fish didn't eat very much, a little pellet about the size of a mustard seed was all they required.

"I'm going to be the best betta fish owner there ever was," I told myself as I headed towards the cash register in front.

In front of the line was an old woman buying what looked like a year's worth of cat food. She must've been a regular though because the girl checking her stuff out referred to her by name and asked about her cats.

Alarms rang out in my mind as I studied the woman. I needed to be careful. I had a high probability of becoming a cat lady if I didn't change my ways.

Finally, the girl was ringing me up. Just as she was handing me my receipt, Mohawk guy walked up to the cash register.

"Hey," he began, reaching out to me with a pamphlet in his hand. "Here's some information on betta fish. I thought you might need it. This should tell you all you need to know about caring for them."

I thanked him and was genuinely surprised by his thoughtfulness. You never knew about people, appearances weren't all they were cracked up to be. He waved off my thanks and headed towards the back of the store again. The girl gave me a final smile and I was off with my new companion.

I was a little uncertain what to do with her in the car—did you buckle up a fish? Luckily her cup fit nicely in one of my cup holders, so I figured that was secure enough.

I kept up a running one-sided conversation with her the whole way home. I needed a good name for her, something unique and strong.

Sunny, Ariel, Coco, Elsa, Dory, Bubbles...

Nothing seemed right.

As I stopped at a red light I looked over and noticed a poster advertising a local high school's theater production being put on by the drama club. They were doing a series of Greek mythology stories. One name caught my eye on the list.

Athena.

I wasn't much of a scholar in my high school years, but there was one topic I always loved: Greek mythologies. Something about those gods and their ridiculous tiffs and battles with each other always interested me. Athena, the goddess of war, was the perfect role model for my little fish.

Satisfied I had solved that problem, I turned on some music and we jammed the rest of the way home.

*****

That night I decided it was time to make a plan. A life roadmap for myself of what I wanted and planned to achieve.

I got out a purple spiral notebook and a hot pink jelly roll pen, like the 13-year-old I was, and snuggled into the pillows on my bed. I titled my page "Life Plan" because clearly, originality was my strong suit.

"All right Athena, how should we start this?" I asked turning to look at my new roommate. I had given her bowl a very prominent spot in my room, on top of my dresser, right next to the floor length mirror. I figured I needed to keep her close so I had somebody to discuss my life calamities with.

"I think I should probably focus on my career goals first," I began, "since they're the reason I'm having this quarter-life crisis."

I sat and thought about what I wanted. Did I want to run my own bakery like Ann? Or would I rather run some sort of café style place? Maybe even a catering business? When I thought about it, there were so many options. I didn't have to do a bread shop like Ann. What did I truly love about baking?

While I did love bread, it wasn't my favorite thing to bake. If I could make anything it would hands-down be the sweet side of baking. I was talking the cookies, the pies, the pastries, etc. Those were the things you could really have fun with, things you could put creative spins on.

There were only so many ways to make a sourdough loaf or rosemary bread. But cookies? There were probably about 20,000 different cookie variations out there. Pies? Muffins? The options were limitless.

So at the top of my page I put in all capitals: OPEN A SWEETS BAKERY.

That felt good. It felt good to visually see something specific instead of just vague ideas. Now came the hard part. How to do it?

I spent the next 15 minutes bullet pointing some main thoughts about what I'd need to accomplish before this would happen.

Financing was a big issue. I'd need to get a bank loan to start out.

Next, was location. Location was one of the biggest determiners of a shop's success/failure. I'd have to find somewhere convenient for shoppers yet also affordable. I made a note to research business real estate agents.

Next up was the whole branding/marketing issue. Nothing like a good marketing campaign to get my shop started off on the right foot. I'd have to discuss this with Jessica, she dealt with a lot of this in her job.

Finally came the fun part: the menu. Now this was my expertise, the reason I was even considering opening the shop.

I spent a solid 30 minutes coming up with different flavors and menu options. Things I'd like to focus on, and directions I'd take during different seasons.

Athena gave me her two cents by blowing a few bubbles occasionally. It was funny how comforting the presence of another living thing could be.

After a solid hour I leaned back and stretched. I'd gotten a crick in my neck, but it was worth it. I felt energized and excited. The first time I'd really felt this way in a while.

I looked down and re-read my planning outline. I'd covered 5 sheets of notebook paper with my ideas. Realistically I knew this was at least a 1-year plan. You didn't just decide to open a bakery and have it all work out in a week. But I had to start somewhere.

*****

The next morning, Friday, Ann was in a frenzied state when I rolled into the bakery at my usual hour.

"Jenn, you're here. Oh good!" She grabbed my arm and dragged me into the kitchen. "I have done something terrible!" She covered her eyes with her free hand. "I totally forgot about the farmers market benefit tomorrow!"

"The what?" I asked, a little confused. Farmers markets were definitely not in our wheelhouse. Some bakeries thrived on them but Ann had never made it a usual part of her business model.

"Ugh, yes. About a month ago I promised the Irvine Farmers Market Association I'd bring five dozen loaves to sell during their benefit sale this weekend. It's a fundraiser for the local food bank I believe. I didn't get the details when I agreed to it." She was mumbling at this point.

"Last night I got a voicemail reminding me that the loaves need to be dropped off tomorrow morning by 7 AM at the front table." She slumped over the counter, clearly overwhelmed. "Let's just say we have a very full day ahead of us."

I went over to the big whiteboard where we kept track of the day's orders and items we were baking. We already were booked to deliver a large order to a business reception this afternoon, in addition to the normal everyday items we sold in store.

Ann was still hyperventilating on the counter so I decided to take charge.

"Okay, the first priority is to finish up the loaves for the catering event this afternoon. Once those are done we can work on today's normal orders. We'll have plenty of time this afternoon to finish the farmer's market items."

I started grouping things in a flow chart on the whiteboard.

"This is why I don't do charity work. I'm unreliable," Ann was muttering to herself.

"Did you promise any specific flavors?" I asked, ignoring her self-deprecation. While we probably had enough stock to make about any of the bread we offered, some recipes were more time-consuming than others. If we didn't have any special requests, we could focus on making simpler flavors.

"No," she said, beginning to get a grip on the situation, "they didn't request anything special, just the number amount."

"Okay then," I turned and began writing on the board again. "We'll give them our basic fan favorites. Let's do a dozen buttermilk loves, a dozen seven-grain loaves, a dozen sun-dried tomato loaves, and two dozen rosemary garlic loaves." I surveyed my chicken scratch with a critical eye. (Note to self: work on penmanship)

Ann was nodding her head. "Yes, that looks good. Except let's switch the sun-dried tomato to Tuscan herb. I'm using most of our sun-dried tomatoes for the event today."

I made the change and we begin divvying up who would do what. I began on the orders for the catering event and Ann began prepping the yeast mixtures for this afternoon.

That was the nice thing about baking, once you got into the rhythm, everything went smoothly. It was almost like a dance.

By the time Carly pulled in around 8 AM we were well on our way to getting things done. I took a break for a moment to give Jessica a call. We'd planned to meet for lunch today, but I knew it wasn't going to happen.

She answered on the second ring, sounding a little groggy.

"Hey Jess," I said, "sorry, did I wake you up?"

"Ugh, yes you little she-devil. I decided to skip my workout and sleep in since I didn't have a meeting until this afternoon." She let out a big yawn. "But now that I'm awake what's up?"

"Sorry, I figured you'd have been up and ran a marathon by now," I said, biting my lip to keep from laughing. Jessica's unnatural love for exercise had always been a running joke between us. "Anyway, I don't think I can meet you for lunch today. We had a couple unexpected orders come up so I'll be skipping lunch."

"Ah bummer." Her voice dropped. "We haven't hung out for a while. Tell Ann to stop working you so hard."

"Someone's got to bring home the bacon, at least until I marry my sugar daddy." Although we both knew I'd probably never stop working. I loved it too much. "Maybe we can do it tomorrow? I should be free if you are."

"Eh, I am up in LA again tomorrow," she paused and seemed to be thinking. "Let's just order takeout at home tonight and watch a movie. I'll blow off Luke, he won't care."

"You sure? I hate taking away time from you two lovebirds." Although I swear they were together 24/7. That was part of the reason I hadn't seen Jessica much lately. Whenever she was free she was with Luke. The lucky girl.

"Yep, no biggie. Let's plan on it."

We said our goodbyes and I turned back to the kitchen to attack the next batch of rosemary bread.

Chapter 6

When I left that afternoon I told Ann I'd deliver the bread to the farmers market in the morning. She looked so exhausted I figured I could give her this break, even though Saturday morning was technically my day to sleep in.

As I got home I texted Jessica and asked what she wanted to eat. We had two places we got takeout from.

One was a Mexican restaurant that had the best burritos you'd ever tried. I was not kidding. First, the burritos were about the size of my head. Second, they were made with these amazing homemade tortillas that were basically nectar of the gods. Third, they were stuffed to the brim with every delicious ingredient you could possibly want: Spicy shredded pork, cheese, green rice, cheese, avocado, cheese, pico de gallo, did I mention cheese? They were not exactly healthy, but they were delicious.

Our second go-to place was an Indian restaurant. Their tiki masala was to die for but one of my favorite things was this sautéed spinach dish that I couldn't pronounce. I always was the awkward American ordering over the phone saying, "that one sautéed spinach dish with the chunks of cheese in it?" Then they would quickly respond with a beautiful pronunciation of "Saag Paneer?" and I'd say "yeah, that one!" It was pathetic but you do what you have to for good food.

By the time I walked in our door Jessica had already responded to my text.

INDIAN!

Since she clearly had a strong preference I didn't question her and simply called in our order. You had a problem when you had your roommate's takeout order memorized.

Jessica always got tikka masala and tandoori chicken combo while I preferred the tikka masala and saag paneer combo. Of course I get a side of their garlic naan bread as well, because when in doubt, always order more bread.

I paid for it with my credit card and scheduled it to be picked up in half an hour. That was just enough time for Jessica to grab it on her way home. I texted her back.

Food Ordered. Ready for pickup in 20.

(I had to say 20 minutes because Jessica was notoriously late. If I said 30 minutes she wouldn't get there for 45).

That done, I made my way to my bedroom to check on Athena. There she was, bubbling happily in her little bowl. I dropped two fish pellets in, all the while feeling sorry for her pathetic meal options.

I always wanted to give her more, but the pamphlet Mohawk Guy gave me was very strict about not overfeeding betta fish. Supposedly they could die from it. Whatever, I was always happiest when overfed. I dropped in one more pellet just out of spite. My fish was a warrior, she needed her energy.

Precisely 38 minutes later Jessica walked in the door, the smell of Indian spices wafting in with her.

"I don't think I've ever loved you as much as I do at this moment," I said, reaching for the bags of steaming food.

"You know I almost said those exact words to the guy working behind the counter when I picked this up." She handed me one of the bags and kept the other for herself. "But then I thought Luke might get mad if he heard about it so I refrained."

We made our way unceremoniously to the couches and dropped down on them.

"Are you guys using the L-word now?" I asked, trying to stamp down the jealousy in my voice.

I know it was ridiculous, Jessica and Luke had been dating for over a month, you'd think I'd have gotten over my little crush by now. I was a grown woman for goodness sake. There was just something about Luke I was so drawn to, in spite of the fact that he wasn't available.

The afternoon I'd hung out with him in my kitchen had been so fun. Our conversation was so natural and easy going. That was what I wanted in a relationship. A friend. I think I was jealous that Luke and Jessica were so happy together. I wanted to be with someone who made me so happy.

It also wouldn't hurt if he was ridiculously good looking like Luke.

Luckily for me Jessica couldn't read my thoughts and had no idea I was crushing on her boyfriend. Her boyfriend she might be using the L-word with.

"No," she began as she pulled out her plastic fork, "we actually haven't said 'I love you' to each other. I mean you know me; I'm never the first to say that or get serious in a relationship. I feel like it's always the guy who wants to move forward to the next step." She dug through the container and came out with that giant forkful of chicken. "I feel like I'm ready to get to that point now, but I'm scared. I don't know what it's like to make the first move. What do you think?"

She shoved the chicken into her mouth and started chewing. Meanwhile I was trying to swallow the bite that had lodged its way in my throat midway through her speech. It was time to pull myself together. I was the rational roommate who was here to give moral support.

"Well, I don't think there's anything wrong with letting him know how you feel. If nothing else, it might clear things up for you." I shrugged my shoulders. "For all you know maybe he's just shy when it comes to talking about his feelings. Maybe he's used to more aggressive girls."

Jessica looked at me thoughtfully.

"I mean the way I see it," I rationalized as I speared a cube of paneer cheese, "what could happen? He's clearly into you. I think the worst case scenario would be he's not ready to say it back yet. I don't think he'd be sad hearing you say it to him though."

"But that would be so embarrassing!" she said emphatically. Poor Jessica. The girl had never been turned down in her life. It would be a rude awakening if he didn't say it back to her.

"Welllll.... yeah, I mean that would stink but it's not *that* embarrassing is it? I mean wouldn't it be worse dating him for another month only to find out he didn't really like you?" I didn't think she was buying my rationalization.

"I mean that would stink too, but at least I wouldn't have totally opened my heart to him and said I love you. If he didn't say it back that would be a total rejection."

We had both made our way to the naan bread by now and there was an impressive amount of garlic floating through the air. Poor Athena must have been so jealous with her boring dinner of pellets.

"Okay then, so what's your relationship plan?"

"I don't know Jenn, I guess we're just going to keep dating like we are and see where it goes." She looked unconvinced herself.

I decided to be the supportive roommate. "That sounds great. If that makes you happy and comfortable then go with it, don't complicate things." I broke off another strip of bread and put it in my mouth. "But I don't think you should avoid telling him your feelings just because you're scared," I said around the bite of bread in my cheek.

She nodded reluctantly. "You're right. But I think I'm going to wait a little longer. I don't want to scare him off with how deep my feelings are now. I mean he's such a great guy; I've never dated anyone like him."

Jessica lifted her shoulders. "It's like he genuinely cares about me. He's always interested in my work, and what I'm doing." She rolled her eyes. "I'm not as dumb as most guys like to think. I know half the time they're just interested in me because of my looks. I feel like no one's ever appreciated me for anything else."

I felt sorry for her, I really did. As hard as it was to have a roommate who looked like a real-life Barbie, I realized it had to be tough always attracting shallow guys. I'd seen it in her past boyfriends too many times. Even though I was jealous of her and Luke, I wanted it to work out for them if he made her happy.

We spent another 15 minutes discussing how awesome Luke was. She told me all the nice things he'd done for her, the texts he'd sent her, the flowers he'd sent to her work. He did sound amazing compared to the other losers she'd dated.

All I knew was by the time we were done I'd earned some more roommate brownie points. It was hard to sit and listen to your friend gush about how the guy you were secretly crushing on (I know it's illogical) was so into her. Serious brownie points.

By then we'd finished our grease-filled dinners and began what Friday nights were made for: vegging out in front of the TV. At least until we decided we'd stayed up late enough to regret it tomorrow.

*****

I definitely regretted the late night when my alarm went off Saturday morning. I promised to deliver the bread for Ann though so I had no choice but to get out of bed. The farmers market was located on the outskirts of Irvine, a giant park that was actually called the "Great Park". I figured I could make it there in about 15 minutes since there would be no traffic on a Saturday morning.

I'd had the foresight to load all the bread into my car the night before. So my 6:40 alarm gave me approximately five minutes to get ready. I threw on a pair of jeans and a loose T-shirt. My hair went up in a ponytail and I figured sunglasses could take the place of makeup this morning. Luckily I was only going to be there for about five minutes to drop off the bread. No one cared how the delivery girl looked.

After I brushed my teeth and grabbed my keys, I headed out.

Before I got in the car I popped the trunk to make sure the bread was still there. Sure enough, they were all perfectly nestled in their boxes. Each loaf was individually wrapped, stamped with a Bread & Butter logo, and labeled with the type of bread it was.

I hopped in and was off.

When I pulled up, I could see the farmers market was just a skeleton of what it would be in a few hours. There were rows of white pop-up tents with tables set up underneath. Every so often there was an early bird merchant, already setting up their storefront. However for the most part the place was deserted.

I parked the car and headed towards the biggest tent in the front. I assumed this was the check in spot. Hopefully they would know where the bread was supposed to go. There were two girls standing next to the table with clipboards in hand discussing something.

One was tall and lanky with fiery red hair that framed her face with curls. She wore beige slacks and a loose white blouse.

The girl next to her was darker in coloring and had her black hair pulled back in a tight bun. She was wearing black slacks and a navy button-down which matched her no-nonsense look.

There was a guy standing a few feet off from them, his cargo shorts and neon green T-shirt a humorous contrast to their business attire. He was talking into a walkie-talkie, something about an electrical problem from what I could hear.

I hesitantly approached the girls with a slight wave. The redhead noticed me first and her face broke into a wide grin. I liked her immediately. You could always trust somebody who had a smile that showed all their teeth. The dark-haired girl glanced over at me and gave me a nod before looking back at her clipboard.

"Hi," said the redhead, "how can we help you?"

"I'm here to deliver some bread for the fundraiser." I motioned towards the parking lot where my car was parked. I wasn't sure if I was supposed to have formal paperwork or something. I told her the name of the bakery and Ann's information.

The redhead flipped through a stack of papers sitting on the table before brightening. "Yes, here you are! Thank you so much for your donation, we really appreciate it!"

The dark haired girl once again looked up and gave me another slight nod. I hoped for her sake she was on the financial team, not the PR team. Her people skills were a little subpar.

"I'm Meg," the redhead said chattily, reaching her hand out to shake mine. "Let me ask Peter where he wants your stuff." She turned to cargo shorts man and motioned him over.

"Where are we putting the donated baked items?" She asked him.

Peter apparently, stopped talking into his walkie-talkie and walked over to the table. He gave me a little wave in greeting and looked down at a map in the center of the table.

"I think we're putting the baked items in tents C30 and C31." He pointed his finger toward the location.

I glanced down and noticed the tents he mentioned were at the far end of the market. Bummer. I wished I'd had a wagon or something to carry all the boxes.

He looked back at me. "Is it just you or do you have some help?"

"It's just me, but don't worry I'm pretty buff." I flexed my nonexistent muscles.

Luckily he laughed before speaking into his walkie-talkie. "Hey Jeff, send me someone to help carry some bread to a tent will you?" The person on the other end commented in an affirmative.

He turned back to me. "While you obviously have some guns on you, I'm sending someone over to help. Just in case." With a departing wink, he was off, probably to deliver more orders to his walkie-talkie crew.

Meg took charge again. "Great, while we're waiting for your helper I have a couple waivers for you to sign." She slid a few notices over to me with a ballpoint pen. I signed my name with the dramatic flourish I'd mastered in the seventh grade and slid them back to her.

With nothing else to do, I began to study the farmers market again.

I could do this one day, I thought to myself. Maybe it would be a good way to start my own store. This would be like a soft opening to test how people liked my products.

A familiar voice startled me out of my deep thoughts. "You needed help carrying some stuff?"

I spun on my heel and came face-to-face with Luke.

Luke. Why did he always catch me when I looked my worst? Why couldn't I run into him one day after I'd spent a couple hours getting a professional blowout? Or at least when I was wearing a decent outfit? I shoved my sunglasses firmly in place. At least these hid my sleep deprived eyes.

"Luke!" I said, a little giddy despite my resolve to play it cool, "What are you doing here?"

His dark eyes crinkled in a grin when he recognized me. "Jenn! A better question is what are you doing here? You sell your stuff at the farmers market?"

There was something about a cute guy joking with you that made everything better. "No, I'm just dropping off some bread we donated for a benefit sale going on today." I should've known a bit more about this donation we were making, but honestly, I had no idea what the sale proceeds were even for.

"I didn't realize you were such a philanthropist," he said wryly. He motioned towards the parking lot. "So is this stuff in your car?"

"Oh, yeah," I nodded and sprung into action. I began a quick walk towards the parking lot, then slowed down when I realized it wasn't a race. Luckily Luke managed to match me stride for stride.

"So," I began, trying to cover the momentary silence (Anyone else hate awkward pauses? They were the bane of my existence), "what exactly are *you* doing here?"

"Well, it just so happens that I have a little Good Samaritan in myself too." I wasn't sure if he was making fun of me but I went along with it.

"Oh do you now?"

His eyes turned sheepish. "Well, that and my cousin might be on the board managing the fundraiser today. She may or may not have coerced me into helping out."

"Family. You can't live with them, you can't live without them." I pointed out my little Corolla in front of us. "Here she is."

"This is where the goods are?" he asked as I popped the trunk. "I kind of feel like we're doing a drug deal out here or something."

"Yep, I only deal in the hard stuff." I motioned at my boxes. "What'll it be? Wheat or white?"

He kept a straight face but I could see him biting his cheek trying not to laugh. He hefted two of the boxes in his arms as if they weighed nothing. Well technically, they were full of bread. So they were pretty light. I was just trying to give him bonus points for manliness at that point.

I chose to only grab one box. I didn't want to overexert myself, and it would also force him to make a second trip back to the car with me. I felt like it was a win-win decision.

"So, do you guys do things like this often?" He asked as we walked across the parking lot.

"Uh... do what often?" I was still lost in my own thoughts about having more face time with him. Well, actually not face time. Maybe just more time together... looking indirectly in my vicinity. At least until I showered.

"Donate your bakery items to fundraisers," he answered.

"Oh! "I was very grateful that he couldn't read my thoughts at that moment. "We do occasionally—we should do more of it though. I think Ann, the owner, was roped into this unexpectedly."

I realized that made her sound callous so I tried to restate myself.

"Not that she wouldn't normally volunteer—I just think it was something she agreed to on the fly. She's an awesome woman and she would love to donate like this more often. We don't have connections to many charities though. I mean not that you need connections to help out a charity or anything..." I realized I was rambling so I shut my mouth.

Luke seemed to take it all in stride. "Yeah, before my cousin got involved with her current position I didn't volunteer too often myself. But the last few months she's emailed me every weekend with a charity event, fundraiser, or 5K that she could use help with." He quirked his mouth skeptically. "Sometimes I think she's just using me because I'm family, but it does make me feel good to help out."

I nodded in agreement. It did feel good even though I technically didn't know who I was helping. "So, who or what is this charity for anyway? I wasn't given too many details."

He laughed, "Wow you truly are altruistic. You don't even know who you're helping but you're still helping."

I giggled along with him, "I guess that's one way to look at it."

"I believe the proceeds are going to help out with local homeless shelters. Not all the booths are for the charity, but I think about half of them are donating their profits. I bet they come out with a good earning by the end of the day."

By this point we'd reached the tents. Luke weaved his way through a few empty booths and I followed, hoping he knew where he was going. There was apparently some sort of system to the madness because we finally stopped at a row of empty tents near the far back corner.

I saw three long tables covered with wide white tablecloths. Two of them still sat empty, but one was full of what looked like freshly baked pies.

We placed our boxes on the middle table and started pulling the loaves out.

"Here," Luke said handing me two loaves, "I'll pull them out of the boxes and you arrange them how you like on the table. Girls are better at making things look pretty." He pulled two more from the box.

"I'm not sure if I should be flattered or if I should pull out a feminist protest at that comment," I replied, taking the next two loaves from him.

"Ha ha, are you a feminist?" He asked.

I thought for a moment. "No, but I've still got a little girl power in me."

He smiled. "Good for you, I like it when somebody has things they'll stand up for."

"What about you?" I asked, deciding to pry a little.

"I've got a little girl power in me too."

I swatted him. "I meant, what's something you'd stand up for?"

"I believe in lots of things, like treating everyone equally and being kind to all... I also believe that pizza should be considered its own food group and that a man has the right to go multiple weeks without washing his sheets or making his bed." He pulled out the last of the bread while he finished his speech. "I also believe Taco Tuesdays shouldn't be limited only to Tuesdays and that the trash man shouldn't be allowed to come pick up trash cans before 7 AM—they are way too loud."

He had me snickering at this point, despite my effort to stay stoic. "Wow, those are pretty important topics. I'm glad you're taking a stand on these kinds of things. The world needs more Lukes don't we?"

He gave me a wink as he stacked the empty boxes. "Well, I figure being real is better than fake. I could tell you my life goal was to end war and save all the orphans but then I'd be lying."

I finally laughed out loud. "I guess you're right. Glad you're at least doing your part as far as tacos are concerned." I turned and started walking back to my car. "You can help me with the last load—that might win you a few more Good Samaritan points."

It took us another 10 minutes to bring the last of the bread over to the table.

At that point, a blond girl with a high ponytail and thick-rimmed glasses showed up. She was holding a clipboard, which apparently was the token symbol of someone in charge around here.

"Luke, I brought you here to work, will you stop spending all your time flirting with girls!" She said this with a rebuking tone but there was a glimpse of a smile in her eyes.

I thought Luke would laugh but there was a surprising flush in his cheeks that confused me. Obviously I knew he wasn't flirting with me. Despite the fact that I had unacceptable feelings towards him, I would never act on them. Most importantly he had never considered me in that way. Had he?

"Ha ha, you caught me Eden," he said, wrapping his arm around the blonde's shoulder. "Jenn, this is my cousin Eden, the catalyst to all my humanitarian acts. Eden this is my friend Jenn."

Friend? Technically I was just his girlfriend's roommate. I guess we were friends too now…

I ignored the thoughts racing through my head and reached out my hand. "Hi, nice to meet you."

Eden took my hand with a friendly shake. "Thanks for your donation, you're from...," she looked at the notes on her clipboard, "Bread & Butter bakery right?"

"Yep, five dozen loaves of the best bread you can buy," I added, sounding like a human tagline. There was a reason I never became a saleswoman. Just not my forte.

"Awesome, we appreciate your help! We couldn't do this without people like you." While that little spiel probably came straight out of a handbook, she said it so genuinely I had to believe her.

"It's not a problem at all! We really just wish we could do more!" I may have been getting a little too into character at this point. Rein it in sister.

"Ah, thank you, well if you'd like to stick around I'm sure we could use you once the market opens today!" She responded brightly.

Crap. I knew I'd gone too far with that "wish we could do more" part.

"Oh, sure... anything specific you need help with?" I hoped she'd take back her suggestion.

She flipped through her clipboard and hummed for a minute. "Hmm... let's see..."

"She can help me out."

We both looked over at Luke, surprised.

He shrugged his shoulders sheepishly. "I mean unless you have something else for her to do. I am going to be helping at this section once the place opens. She's the best one to sell her own bread, right?" He looked at me. "You can win everybody over with your baking expertise."

Suddenly all this volunteering didn't seem like such a bad idea.

"Great!" Eden said. She jotted something down on a piece of paper and then capped her pen. "Well, everything opens in about 45 minutes. The group leader for this section should be over in about 20 to brief you on all the details about collecting payments and what not."

She looked around for a moment then added, "There's not much else to do so I guess just sit tight and the rest of the donations should come in soon."

"All right cuz, we'll let you know how things go." Luke gave Eden a quick hug before she jogged off. He then turned to me as he leaned against one of the tables. "Well, thanks for offering your help, hope you didn't have anything else planned this morning."

I could tell he was trying to hold back a laugh. He probably knew I didn't want to stay and help. What he didn't know was working with him made the deal much more enticing. "Well, you know me, Miss Do-gooder." I sat on the corner of the table opposite of him. "So have you ever worked at one of these before? How complicated is it?"

"Considering you run a bakery, I don't imagine it's much different than working the front counter there. People come up, stare at everything for a few minutes, you try and sell them on how wonderful your goodies are. If they're not buying it then you try and guilt trip them into the fact that's it's for the needy and hopefully win them over. Pretty basic." He sat fiddling with a leftover zip tie from the bags of bread. I'd started to notice that about him, he always seemed to fidget when he was sitting still.

What was I doing? If I'd hung out with Jessica's boyfriend enough times to notice little nuances like that, was I crossing some sort of line? It felt like the times we had hung out had been accidental but was it still inappropriate?

Maybe I should beg off from helping this morning. Fake sick or something. I'd hate for Jessica to think I was after her man. I'd never do that to her, no matter how much of a crush I had on him.

"So what were your plans for this morning before you got roped into volunteering?" He asked, interrupting the beginnings of my personal intervention.

I looked over at him, leaning against the table fiddling with his zip tie, and decided it was all in my head. He clearly thought of me as nothing more than a friend. Stop looking for drama when there was none I told myself.

"I was actually planning on going back to bed. Hence the minimal effort I put into my appearance." I made a sweeping motion with my hand over my outfit and sunglasses.

He let out his familiar deep laugh. "I can appreciate a good casual Saturday. Some girls spend way too much time on their appearance in my opinion. What's going to happen when they settle down with a guy and let him see them without all the makeup and big hair." He made a shocked face. "The guy's not going to know who he's with anymore."

I had to agree. I'd seen one too many girls who were a slave to their makeup and beauty routine. However, I was a born contrarian. "Whatever, girls have it rough. It's such a double standard. Guys can just roll out of bed and no one cares. But if a girl doesn't have her mascara perfect and her hair blown out," I did a dramatic demonstration of this with my hands over my face and hair, "she's not given a second glance by most men."

He nodded when I finished my soapbox speech. "You're right, it's not fair. I'm sorry; if it makes you feel any better I think you look great in jeans and a t-shirt."

I could feel my face heat up with this comment.

He continued on without noticing. "I'm sure there are lots of guys that'd give you a second glance. They probably all wonder what's behind those Hollywood sized sunglasses." He said this last part with a smirk.

I stuck my nose up in the air. "There's nothing behind these glasses but puffy eyes from staying up too late last night with Jessica."

At the mention of Jessica's name the humor in his eyes suddenly disappeared and he became more serious. "That's good. Di—did you guys have fun last night? I was meaning to call her but—"

Before he could finish his sentence a large woman bustled up to the table pulling a wagon behind her.

I didn't mean this in a bad way, but if you could imagine what Mrs. Santa Claus might look like, this was her. Fluffy white hair topped a rosy-cheeked, round face. She had squinty little eyes framed with endless laugh lines and a perfect little bow-shaped mouth. I instantly started smiling when I saw her.

She walked toward us on her short little legs. "Oh good," she exclaimed "I found you! I assume this is where all the baked items are being sold."

It sounded like a statement more than a question as she stopped in front of us.

"Yep, I think you're at the right place," I answered her non-question question.

"Perfect, would you dears mind giving me a hand and unloading all this?" She waved her hand at the wagon. It was fully loaded with boxes of what appeared to be cookies. Maybe she actually was Mrs. Claus.

"Yes ma'am, certainly!" Luke hopped off the table and started unloading boxes for her. "Where would you like these?"

"Let's see," she peered at the three tables. "I'll take the third one over there; it seems to have the most space."

It was a good choice with the number of boxes she had. This woman was out to feed America with cookies.

"Now if you don't mind arranging them by cookie type." She helped grab a box. "They're labeled on the top with what's inside." She pointed to the name on her box which read "snickerdoodles".

It turned out she had brought an arsenal of flavors with her. Along with the snickerdoodles, there were classic chocolate chip cookies, chocolate chip oatmeal, raisin oatmeal, peanut butter, chocolate peanut butter, white chocolate macadamia nut, and even a vegan chocolate chip option. This woman had covered her bases.

She let us take care of the unloading while she arranged the boxes on the table. Once we were done the woman stepped back to survey our work. "Perfect! It looks lovely." She turned to both of us with a big smile. "Now for introductions. I am Beverly Hinds, and I work on the PR side of the Irvine Farmers Market Association. Although in my former years I ran a moderately successful catering company, hence the cookies." She somehow managed to say all this in one breath. "Now tell me about yourselves!"

Luke recovered first and began, "Nice to meet you Beverly. I'm Luke, I'm cousins with Eden who is helping run the show today. I unfortunately have no baking skills, I'm just here for my muscles and good looks."

This last part had Beverly in giggles, her eyes almost disappearing into the sea of laugh lines around them.

I hoped to be like that when I got old. To be someone who looked like they spent their days smiling and laughing. This woman clearly had life figured out.

"Ha ha, Luke you are a hoot! And that's great; we love it when the family gets involved." She turned to me, still smiling. "And are you with him?"

I smiled awkwardly, a slight blush at my cheeks again. There were two kinds of people in this world: those who never blushed or showed their emotions and those of us who turned pink at the slightest touch of discomfort. It drove me nuts.

"No, no we're just friends. I came with my own delivery of bread for the sale. I work at a bakery called Bread & Butter."

She seemed to think for a minute, and then her face lit up with recognition. "Oh yes, that's Ann's place isn't it?" She clasped her hands together. "Such a lovely lady, I met her several years ago at an event like this. We've gotten together several times over the years to keep up. She always was a whiz with bread. I never could master it quite like her! I might have to buy one of her loaves myself today!"

You couldn't help but smile continuously when you were near Beverly. "I agree she is a whiz at making bread. I'm hoping some of her expertise rubs off on me someday."

"Well you're in the best hands." She gave Luke a side-eye glance. "And don't turn this guy down too fast, even if he is a little full of himself. I've always said a man who can make you laugh is one you shouldn't let go of." She gave me a knowing look.

"Oh, no," I swear my face must have been flaming red by now, "you don't understand, he's actually dating my roommate. So we're—there's nothing between us. Absolutely nothing, nothing at all. Totally platonic friendship here. That's us."

For the love, stop talking Jenn!

Luke gave me a strange glance then added, "Yep, we are strictly farmer's market business partners."

I think I loved him a little more for turning this moment into a joke. Did I just say love? Someone help me.

"Young people these days." Beverly turned to pull a lock box out of her wagon. "So, I am actually the boss of you two today." She gave us both a stern look. "I run a tight ship here so I expect you both to pull your weight."

I covered my mouth with my hand to hide my grin. I couldn't imagine Beverly running anything close to a tight ship. A tiki-lit party boat seemed more her style.

She spent the next 10 minutes briefing us on how to collect payments, the prices charged for each item, and how to deal with credit card payments. It was straightforward but she still wanted us to role play once or twice.

Luke offered to be the customer first so I agreed to show off my sales expertise.

True to form, Luke got fully into character. He informed me he was a grandfather here to buy cookies for his three beautiful granddaughters. He insisted one was allergic to peanuts, one hated raisins, and the other was gluten-free.

I almost kicked him after this absurd description, but since Beverly was watching I played along.

"Well sir, today is your lucky day because we have an assortment of delicious cookies here to choose from. I think a classic chocolate chip cookie would fill all your needs.

Let's do two normal chocolate chip cookies for the first two granddaughters, and one of our gluten-free specialties for the third." I bagged and handed him his imaginary cookies. He patted my head like the grandfatherly figure he was pretending to be. "Thank you dear, you are such a sweetheart. My little granddaughters will love these." He pulled out his wallet and started rifling through it before finally handing me a $50 bill. "Keep the change," he said.

I rolled my eyes at him. "Thank you sir, it's been a pleasure."

Beverly clapped her hands and said, "Excellent! Quite a solid act there you two. Have you ever considered drama as a second career?" She smiled broadly at her own joke. "We can forgo any more trial runs. You seem to have it under control."

I pulled Luke's $50 bill out of my pocket and slipped it into his hand. "Who carries around $50 bills these days? You really are a grandpa."

"One can never be too prepared! You might hit a big charity bake sale and need some cash on hand!" He shoved the money into his wallet and put it in his back pocket.

Sometimes I wished I was a guy. So I could do things like keep my wallet in my pocket. Girl's pants just didn't have pockets big enough to keep a wallet in. I could barely fit my keys in my pocket let alone a wallet or phone.

We sat chatting with Beverly for another ten minutes until she got buzzed on her walkie-talkie that the doors were opening.

We each decided to man a separate table. Luke took over the pie section, I of course, was in charge of the bread, and Beverly took over her cookie display. It took a good 15 minutes before we saw our first clients, but come they did.

I thought I was going to need some sales skills but I swear these people were basically begging us to take their money. I'll chalk it up to their enthusiasm for charity, although the smell wafting from our tables was pretty delicious.

Beverly had the smart idea to offer samples of our goodies, I decided to sacrifice one of my rosemary garlic loaves for the task.

People loved it. We were out of rosemary garlic within 15 minutes. Luke's pie table wasn't doing so bad either. By the time the hour was up he only had two apple pies and one lemon meringues. I had two loaves of wheat bread left and Beverly was down to her last two boxes of gluten-free cookies.

We high-fived and congratulated each other on our success. Beverly gave us each a gluten-free cookie to celebrate and I cut into one of the wheat loaves on my table.

I was pleasantly surprised at how good her gluten-free cookie was. Every gluten-free product I'd tried thus far tasted either extremely dry or gummy. I didn't even miss the gluten in this one.

"Wow," I told her, "these cookies are amazing. How did you do that?"

Beverly smiled at me. "My best friend's daughter has a gluten intolerance. She realized it when the girl was about ten months old. I made it my mission to discover some of the best gluten-free recipes so she could enjoy the good things in life too."

She picked up one of the cookies and took a giant bite out of it. "This cookie took me two years to perfect, but I finally did it. I'll send you the recipe as long as you promise not to share it with anyone else." She said this last part with a questioning glance.

I nodded my head, still not sure if she was joking or serious.

"I'm amazed at this bread," Luke said through a mouthful of wheat bread. "I thought I'd never like anything but white bread until this moment. I was always a trial for my mom. I think she spent the better part of her life trying to get me to embrace multi-grain bread." He took another bite. "She never could do it. But I think you might have won the battle!"

I laughed at him, "Well I can teach you to make it if you love it that much."—

Wait, why did I say that?

"Really? Could you teach me to make this? Will it taste as good as yours?" He asked with skepticism.

"Well," I drawled with false modesty, "it obviously won't taste as good as mine does... but maybe can come close."

"It's a date then, you name the place and time and I'll be there to learn these bread making skills you have." He popped the last piece into his mouth and chewed it happily.

Beverly looked back-and-forth between the two of us her eyebrows raised. I could've sworn I heard her mutter, "Girlfriend, smirlfriend..."

Beverly's Gluten Free Chocolate Chip Cookies

· 2 1/4 cups all-purpose gluten-free flour blend
· 1 tsp. baking soda
· 1 tsp. salt
· 2 ounces cream cheese, room temp
· 3/4 cups melted butter
· 1 ½ cup packed brown sugar
· 2 tsp. vanilla extract
· 2 egg yolks
· 2 cups chocolate chips

1.) In a medium bowl, mix together flour, baking soda and salt. Set aside.

2.) In another bowl place the cream cheese, melted butter, and brown sugar and beat on medium speed for 2 minutes.

3.) Add vanilla extract and egg yolks beating on low-medium speed until well mixed.

4.) Add the flour mixture and beat until just combined. Mix in the chocolate chips by hand.

5.) Line cookie sheets with sheets of parchment paper and scoop heaping tablespoon mounds of cookie dough spaced 3 inches apart.

6.) Cover and refrigerate dough 4-6 hours.

7.) Preheat oven to 375°. Bake the cookies for 11-12 minutes. Remove when edges are slightly browning.

Chapter 7

I was a little unsettled on Sunday morning by the time
Luke and I had spent together on Saturday morning. I
couldn't figure him out. Was he that chatty and borderline
flirtatious with all girls? Or was it something about me that
made him act that way?

The worst part about it all was my own treacherous
feelings. I was not that kind of girl. I would never, in a
million years try to steal my best friend's boyfriend... It was
basically the law. Any friend's guy was off-limits now and
forever.

This was why I was up at 6 AM making an unplanned
recipe for my blog instead of spending my Sunday morning
sleeping in. A girl could only toss and turn in bed for so
long.

I had decided to make cream puffs for no reason other
than they sounded delicious and I needed a sugar binge.

I found my usual recipe for them from one of my
favorite cookbooks, one by Gaston Lenotre. He was an
amazing pastry chef, one I adamantly admired.

Cream puffs had this glamorous reputation of being
really difficult. To be honest though, they were one of the

easiest desserts to master. There were three basic parts to them:

    1.) The choux pastry. This was the actual bread part that made up the bulk of a creampuff.

    2.) The cream filling. Yes. The more of this stuff the merrier.

    3.) The chocolate glaze. Some people forgo this step but I felt like it was a necessary element.

I was working on the pastry part first. It was made by cooking your ingredients in a saucepan. It was strange for a baked good, but that was how it was done.

The buttermilk and flour were cooked over the stove until they became a sticky mound of dough. Then came the tricky part. Eggs had to be beaten in one at a time until they were fully incorporated. The key was to not scramble the eggs in the hot mixture.

And that was where I was at, beating eggs into my dough like a mad woman when there was a brisk knock at our door. You'd think I'd get used to being caught unexpectedly in my kitchen by now.

"Who the heck is knocking at my door at 6 AM on a Sunday morning," I muttered to myself as I walked to the door with saucepan in hand, still beating my eggs. I opened the door and of course, there was Luke, looking fresh as a daisy in workout gear.

I gave him the stink eye and swung the door open for him to enter. "Why don't you just get a dang key to our place since you're always around," I stated ungraciously as I continued to beat the eggs in our doorway.

"Well good morning to you too sunshine," he said brightly and patted my shoulder as he walked past.

I kicked the door close and followed him back towards the kitchen.

"May I ask—why—you are here—so early this—morning?" I started to lose breath with the effort of stirring. Sometimes I think my baking could count as a workout. I wasn't kidding when I said the bicep in my right arm was significantly stronger than my left.

"Jessica and I are supposed to go for a run this morning." He looked at me huffing and puffing and bit back a grin. "Maybe I should've offered to help you and got my workout that way." He was much too happy for 6 AM on a Sunday.

I peered into my pan to check on the batter. Satisfied that the eggs were incorporated I set it down on the countertop. "You should've. Does Jessica know she's going on this run with you? I'm pretty sure I haven't heard a peep from her room yet."

Luke looked surprised. "Well she sent me a text last night asking if I want to go on one, so I figure she knows about it." He looked down the hallways where our bedrooms were. "Would you mind checking on her for me? I doubt she wants me barreling into her room if she's asleep."

I nodded and brushed past him. "The things I do for you Luke. You owe me." I caught a whiff of his cologne as I slid past, and tried to ignore the butterflies his nearness stirred up in my stomach.

I found Jessica under a Mt. Everest sized pile of blankets. "Jessica? Jess? Hey Jess, get up!" I finally yelled while ripping blankets off the mound.

"Hmmm...? Whhhhat?" She moaned from somewhere under the mountain.

"Luke's here. He said you're supposed to go on a run with him." I saw her eyes peek over a blanket.

"Ah, crud. Did my alarm not go off?" An arm snaked out from under the blanket, fumbling on her dresser for her phone.

She was missing it by about three inches so I reached over and grabbed it... "Well you have an alarm set for 5:45, but it's for 5:45 PM, not 5:45 AM."

"Ughhh..." the moan was back under the blankets now.

"So do you want me to tell Luke you're coming or no?" I asked after another minute of silence. I wasn't sure if she'd fallen back asleep or not.

"Yeah, I'm coming." This time she actually sat up. Her blonde hair was a mass of tangles and there was mascara smudged under both eyes.

"Are you sure you don't want me to send Luke in here? He told me once he likes girls who aren't ashamed of their natural beauty."

She peered at me through squinty eyes. "What?"

"Never mind. I'll tell him you'll be out in ten minutes." I chucked her phone back on the dresser and closed the door behind me.

Luke was lounging on our couch, scrolling through his phone. He looked up when I came out. "Is she coming?"

I nodded. "Yeah, her alarm didn't go off. Give her ten minutes and she'll be out."

He ran his fingers through his hair, mussing it. "I mean I can just go for a jog alone. It doesn't really matter to me."

I was surprised by that comment. I knew they hadn't hung out all weekend, it seemed like he'd be anxious to spend time with her. I shrugged, "I think she's planning on coming, but if you don't want her to I can stop her?"

"No no, I'll wait. That's great." He leaned back on the couch and I decided to go back to my cream puffs.

Two minutes later he wandered into the kitchen. "So, what are you making this time?"

"Cream puffs," I said, not looking up from the pastry bag I was filling with choux dough.

"Cream puffs! Those are my favorite, my grandma used to make them when I was a kid. We used to play a game to see how many we could sneak before she'd notice."

His running shoes made a squeaky noise on the tile floor as he leaned against the door jam. "Although looking back I'm sure she knew to the very last creampuff how many we'd eaten."

I gave up on my attempt to ignore his presence. "Grandmas usually do. I'm sure she made them with the expectation you guys would eat them all."

"So is this for your blog? Or is this a recipe for the future Jenn's bakery?" He wiggled his eyebrows in mock suspense.

I blushed a little; embarrassed for some reason that he even knew about my bakery goals. "No, this is for the blog. I doubt 'Jenn's Bakery' will ever happen."

He dropped his joking tone and asked, "Why? I thought you said it was something you'd always dreamed of doing?"

"Yeah, well I've also always dreamed of owning a pony and that probably won't happen either," I was being a little snappier than I intended, but I wanted to get him off my back. For some reason him thinking I could do it made it all seem more possible. And that scared me.

"Jenn, I'm serious. I don't see why you shouldn't try and start your own bakery. I was checking out your blog the other day and it's awesome. Your recipes are legit." He reddened a little, but he hurried on. "Not that I actually know anything about baking, but they look good and you seem to be getting a lot of comments."

I was shocked he'd taken the time to look through some of my posts.

It was at that moment Jessica came into the kitchen. She had tied her messy hair up in a high ponytail and thrown on some black running clothes. She had a pair of pink neon socks on her feet and her running shoes in one hand.

"Hey," she said, looking at Luke sheepishly, "sorry about that. I didn't set my alarm right and so I slept in." She plopped on the floor and began putting on her shoes.

"No problem, Jenn was entertaining me with her baking skills," Luke gave me a wink.

"Well, we all know Jenn is the master baker." Jessica stood, her shoes securely tied to her feet. "What are you making?"

"Cream puffs." I waved my pastry bag full of the dough over my prepped baking sheets. "Just about to bake the shells up."

"Mmm, one of these days you're going to have to teach me how to make those." Jessica pointed with her finger.

Luke jumped into the conversation. "Yeah, you promised you'd teach me to make wheat bread too. I seriously want to learn. When is that going to happen?"

I'd assumed that promise was more of a hypothetical one. I was trying to spend less time with Luke, not more. Moving on from this silly crush meant no more hanging out with him.

"Oh... well I don't know..."

"Any night this week works for me," Luke said, cutting me off.

"Well, the bread would have to be a two-day thing. One day to make the dough. Then we'd need to give it time to rise, so another day to actually bake it, probably too much time to commit—."

"Okay, how about Tuesday and Wednesday nights? I can make it work if you can."

Dang, he was being difficult. Didn't he realize I was doing this for him and Jessica? Wait—that was my answer. Jessica could join us. It would be less awkward if Jessica was there, right?

"Sure, that'd work fine. How about you Jessica," I looked over at her, "you think you could make it those nights?"

Jessica seemed to be mentally considering her calendar. "I could do Tuesday night. But on Wednesday I have an event scheduled. You'll have to do that part without me."

"Okay," said Luke, "let's make the dough all together Tuesday night. Then Jenn and I will bake it Wednesday night and you can try it when you get home from work."

Jessica gave him with a lovesick smile. "Perfect, you do the work and I'll enjoy the benefits. Sounds like a great arrangement."

Luke put his arm around her. "All right, let's go for that run you promised me." He looked back at me in the kitchen, "Good luck with the cream puffs Jenn. I'll see you on Tuesday night for our lesson!"

I gave them a halfhearted bye before noticing the hole my clenched fingers had made in my pastry bag.

*****

I spent the next 20 minute scraping all my pastry out of the bag and trying to refill another one, muttering to myself the whole time. The bad vibes from my lack of a love life were seeping into my baking. I finished up my cream puffs by early morning and then spent a good 30 minutes photographing them.

One of the good things about our apartment was the large bay window in our living room. Food photos, at least good ones, could only be done in natural light. So that window was a life saver.

This time I stacked three cream puffs on a blue china plate I got at a flea market. I had an old wooden spoon and a white embroidered towel angled in the background as accent pieces. Overall it was a lovely setting that made me want to go have a tea party at a garden cottage somewhere.

But I settled for scarfing down a couple cream puffs in front of my laptop.

I can honestly say editing photos was my least favorite part about being a food blogger. I obviously loved making the recipes, I didn't even mind staging and photographing them, but the hours I spent editing always felt like a waste. I'd considered outsourcing my photo editing, but I couldn't justify the cost.

So here I was, adjusting lighting and shadows, smudging out unplanned crumbs, cropping and tilting. I was pretty good at it now and could edit a batch within a half hour. Those first days of blogging were pretty rough though.

I saved the new photos to a file named "Cream Puffs" with the date. Then I turned my focus to my emails. I hadn't given my blog tons of attention last week and emails were beginning to pile up, full of recipe questions and collaboration invites.

I often got offers from various food companies for small sponsorships. They'd ask me to use their product and blog about it. Anything from unique flour types, to specialty dairy products, to premade baking kits... you name it. I tried to be pretty selective on the requests I accepted.

Along with the emails were all the unanswered comments on my blog posts themselves. I did my best to reply to all recipe questions and even the reviews. It could be a little overwhelming though.

But enough complaining, I was glad I did it and it was something I loved. Even if I hadn't been as focused on it lately. I mean I had things like Luke Bradley popping in at all hours of the day to worry about.

After a few hours playing catch-up with my blog, I stood and stretched. I should go on a run like Jessica and Luke, I thought to myself. Like every other female on the planet, making fitness a priority in my life was always a goal. One I rarely achieved, but a goal nonetheless.

I didn't have the energy for a run, so I settled for a 20-minute yoga video I found on YouTube. I probably didn't burn as many calories but it did relax me. Nothing like a little Warrior One and Warrior Two to save the day.

I showered, and then cleaned up the mess I'd made in the kitchen. I put the leftover cream puffs in a large Tupperware in the fridge for Jessica later on. There were some serious perks to being roommates with a baking blogger.

After that, I figured I'd better call my mom. It'd been two weeks since I last talked to her and she tended to worry if I didn't keep in touch regularly.

"Hey Mom," I said when she picked up on the second ring.

"Jenny! I was thinking of calling you today, I haven't heard from you for a while. How are you honey?"

No one else but my mom could get away with calling me Jenny. Considering she grew me in her body for nine months she had that right. We chatted about the usual for a few minutes. She updated me about my brothers, my dad, the neighbors... nothing like some good family gossip.

"So what are you doing for your anniversary next week?" I expected the usual dinner and a movie answer, so I was surprised when she said they were thinking of doing an overnight trip to Vegas.

"Dad's been talking about doing it for a couple months now. I'm not really sure why. He won't admit it but I think he just wants to try out some of their buffets. Neither one of us are big gamblers."

"Well that sounds fun! You guys never go do anything big, it'll be good for you."

"Yes, I told dad as long as we get to go see Celine Dion perform I'm fine with it. I'm also hoping to convince him to go to Cirque du Soleil too."

My parents had been married 33 years now and their relationship was like a well oiled machine. They knew exactly when to give and take and rarely fought over anything bigger than the TV remote.

We chatted about my work and then, of course, we moved onto the standard dating discussion. "So have you met any fun guys lately?" My mom always started out this way. She liked to put out feelers to see where I was emotionally because some days I was not in the mood to talk about dating.

"No, I've been pretty busy with work and my blog." My usual lame answer. This was code for: no guy has asked me out.

"Oh Jenny, you work too hard. You need to make sure you give yourself time for a social life. Part of your problem is you never meet anybody where you work; you're always so isolated in that kitchen." She was silent for a moment then asked "How about Jessica? Is she dating anyone? I bet she meets a lot of nice guys at her job that she could introduce you to."

I smiled to myself. My mom always assumed Jessica was interacting with hundreds of attractive, successful young men at her work. What she didn't realize was the successful men Jessica did associate were usually in their late 50s to early 60s, happily married and balding. Not great potential for either of us.

"Yes, Jessica is dating someone." This shouldn't have come as a surprise since Jessica was always dating someone. "I think she really likes this one and he's pretty nice. I've hung out with them a couple times." I didn't mention that I had a ridiculously huge crush on him as well and was barely keeping the jealous green monster at bay.

"Well does he have any friends or roommates? You guys could go on a double date or something fun." Moms, always the hopeful ones.

"No mom, I'm not going to ask him to set me up," I'd done this before with a couple of Jessica's previous boyfriends. Often we doubled with a roommate or a buddy from work. They were usually okay dates, but I never got lasting relationships from them. More importantly, I couldn't bring myself to look that desperate in front of

Luke. There was something about begging for a date that made you feel dumb.

"Well don't be afraid to put yourself out there." I could tell she was wrapping up this part of the conversation for which I was glad. "These days everybody does. It's the only way to meet people."

She ended with her usual pep talk about how I was a beautiful girl and had so many talents any guy would be lucky to be with me speech. It was one I'd heard 100s times and I believe every mom was obligated to give to their kids.

We said our goodbyes, I promised to call her more often like I did every time before hanging up.

I contemplated my mom's words as I opened Facebook and scrolled through my friend's recent posts. I'd say at least half of them were in happy relationships. Maybe more. My mom had a point. Maybe I needed to focus more on my love life—or the lack of one. The question was, how to do it?

"Athena," I said as I picked up my little container of fish food and tapped a few pellets into her bowl. "We have some serious work cut out ahead of us." She blew me a few bubbles in response.

Cream Puff Recipe

SHELLS
· 1 cup water
· 1/2 cup butter
· 3/8 teaspoon salt
· 1 1/4 cups All-Purpose Flour
· 4 large eggs

CREAM PUFF FILLING
· 2 cups heavy or whipping cream
· 1/4 cup granulated sugar, or to taste
· 1 teaspoon vanilla extract

CHOCOLATE ICING
· 1 cup chopped semisweet chocolate
· 1/2 cup whipping cream

For the Shells:
1.) Preheat the oven to 425°F. Lightly grease two baking sheets. Combine the water, butter, and salt in a saucepan and heat until the butter has melted. Bring it to a rolling boil. Lower to medium heat and add the flour all at once, stirring quickly with a whisk. Continue stirring about another 30 seconds or until the mixture smoothes out.
2.) Remove the pan from the heat, and let the mixture cool for 5 Minutes. One at a time beat in the eggs. Beat vigorously for at least 2 minutes after adding the last egg.
3.) Drop large mounds onto the prepared baking sheets (3 to 4 tablespoons worth). Space the mounds about 3" apart.

4.) Bake the pastries for 15 minutes, then reduce the oven temperature to 350°F and bake for an additional 25 minutes, until they are a golden brown.

5.) Remove the pastries from the oven. Make a small slit in the top of each, and return them to the oven for 5 minutes, to allow the steam to escape. Place them on a rack to cool. When they're cool enough to handle, split each in half.

For the Filling:

1.) Pour the cream into a mixing bowl, and begin to whip it on high speed. Sprinkle in the sugar gradually. Whip until stiff and smooth.

2.) Fill the bottom halves of the puffs with whipped cream, then replace their tops.

For the Icing:

1.) Place the chocolate and cream in a microwave-safe bowl and heat for 30 second increments until the cream is very hot.

2.) Stir until the chocolate melts and the icing is smooth. Spoon over the shells. Serve immediately.

Chapter 8

I got through the rest of the weekend without much excitement. But Monday still came way too early.

"It's just another manic Monday!" Ann was belting out as I wandered into the kitchen that morning.

"Ugh," I responded when she glanced over at me.

"Ah, cheer up buttercup, I got some good news. We got a partnership request from the sandwich shop around the corner. They want to use us as their main bread provider for their menu." She said this with a little happy dance.

That was great news. Ann had been going after accounts like this for the last year, hoping to get a more regular income stream. The shop made great money, it just fluctuated more than she'd like.

"Oh my gosh, that's awesome. Congratulations!" I gave her a quick hug.

"I know, we've got to get all the details worked out first, but I think by the start of next month we'll be delivering regular shipments to them." She walked over to the radio and turned down the volume as the Bangles finished their last chorus of Manic Monday.

"So tell me how Saturday went. Did the delivery go fine for the farmers market?"

I gave her the rundown on delivering the bread and how I ended up staying and helping run the stand with Luke and Beverly Hinds.

"Beverly Hinds, I know her, I haven't spoken to her in years!" Ann slapped the counter. "Did she remember me?"

"Yes she did, she informed me that you make the best bread she's ever had!"

Ann let out a hearty laugh. "She always was a brown-noser."

"As I was leaving she actually gave me her phone number to pass along to you. She wanted to get together for lunch." I pulled out my phone and searched through my contacts. I sent Beverly's number to Ann and her phone made a little ding in the corner of the room.

"There you go; the ball is in your court. You guys can get together and reminisce about the good old days of baking."

"You're such a tart Jenn. I'm not that old you know," Ann grimaced.

I began washing my hands in the sink while she pulled out the yeast starts for the day.

"So you spent the morning with Luke?" She threw this in casually, but her tone was inquisitive. "Isn't he Jessica's boyfriend?"

I pretended to not catch her meaning. "Yes, he is, they've been dating for two months now."

"So you obviously don't have any interest in him or anything like that then," she said matter-of-factly.

I stopped drying my hands and looked at her. "Ann, I feel like you're fishing for something."

She looked at me innocently, "I only fish when there's something to catch. There's nothing here right?"

I sighed and set my towel down. "You want me to be honest? I might have a little crush on Luke. But I'd never do anything about it. I know he's off-limits."

"I know you, and I know you'd never do anything to hurt your friend. It does seem strange that you're hanging out with him one on one though. You just had to drop off the bread at the bake sale, how come you ended up staying all morning?"

"Wellll... they asked if I could help out for a few hours so I said yes."

"And that decision had nothing to do with Luke being there?"

"Um..." I stared down at my hands, not able to bring my gaze to Ann's.

Weren't you two together last week also?"

"Yes, but both times were totally by chance! Sort of. It's not like I'm looking for trouble." I finished defensively.

"Jenn, I'm not saying this to hurt your feelings. Because I know you. I know you'd never go after Jessica's boyfriend." She reached out and touched me on the shoulder. "But I also know that you're torturing yourself by continually hanging out with someone you could have feelings for. I think you need to stop dreaming about Jessica's guy, and start thinking about yourself."

My eyes were filling up with tears and I had to blink rapidly to keep them at bay. I stared up at the ceiling, "How? I've been out of the dating scene for so long, I don't know where to start anymore."

It was funny how saying things out loud could bring such a release of emotions. I didn't even realize I had this bottled up until now.

"Have you ever considered online dating?"

The sentence hung in the air. I hadn't. Online dating seemed like something people did when they were over 40 and desperate. Women whose ovaries were a ticking time bomb waiting to burn out. I wasn't there yet was I?

"No, not really. Is that something people my age even do?"

She looked amused. "Well, first off Jenn you're not exactly a baby yourself."

That one stung a little. I knew I wasn't fresh out of high school anymore but was I that old? It was amazing how years crept up on you.

She must've seen my expression because she followed it up quickly with, "I'm not saying you are old. I'm just saying you're an adult now. And yes online dating is something people your age do. As a matter of fact, I think it's getting more and more popular as the years go on. You should consider it."

I nodded slowly, it couldn't hurt. It wasn't like anybody would know about it. I think the shame of having to tell others I was online dating was my biggest hangup. But since it was online, I wouldn't have to discuss it with anyone.

"I might. Do you have any idea where I should start?" I couldn't believe I was asking for dating advice from my 50-year-old boss.

"I know my niece does it, I'll ask her which sites are the best. I think she has profiles on a couple of them." She looked at me closely. "Jenn you can't think of this as giving up. Just because you want to meet somebody and you are pursuing it doesn't mean you're desperate. It just means you're smart."

I smiled back at her. "You should be a saleswoman for one of these sites."

"Well first things first," she raised her eyebrows in mock seriousness, "you are going to need a good profile picture."

*****

I spent my lunch break sitting on a park bench scrolling through the different online dating options. It was borderline ridiculous how many websites there were dedicated to finding love. Our society was really getting desperate.

I decided to steer clear of any of the "swipe right" dating services. I figured a partner chosen solely on looks probably wasn't a lifelong commitment.

There were some very specific sites. Dating sites for Christians, dating sites for the rich and famous, dating sites for dog lovers, dating sites for different ethnicities, there was even a dating site for farmers. I couldn't find one dedicated to bakers however.

My best bet was to use one of the big websites that had been around for a while and had proven screening procedures. This was a huge drawback to online dating. For all I knew, I could be meeting a serial killer for my Friday night date. (Note to self: stop watching late-night murder mystery shows)

I pulled up Match.com on my laptop and clicked the "create new profile" option. I took a deep breath. "Okay, this is it; I'm going to do it." I was beginning to notice how often I talked out loud to myself. Yet another reason to get started with this dating stuff.

Some pigeons were picking at the ground nearby. A couple stopped and looked up at me. "Guys this is a big deal, if you want to be here for moral support I'd appreciate it." They gave me about another two seconds of their time then went back to pecking. Looked like I'd have to take this on solo.

The first thing the website had me do was create a profile name and password. I considered using something super juvenile like "hotb8kergirl" or "calilovingchick", but then I remembered I wasn't 12 years old anymore and simply typed in JennaH. I used my usual password of "bakethatcake".

The website sent me to a page with a questionnaire about myself. Ugh, personal questions. I guess I was glad they weren't requiring a photo at this point.

GENDER:

"Oh I got this," I said to myself as I typed in "Female".

WHAT GENDER ARE YOU LOOKING FOR?:

"Male". My confidence was rising.

ADDRESS:

This made sense since I wasn't looking for a long distance relationship.

BIRTHDAY: Again, I figured this was an appropriate question since I didn't want to date a 50-year-old male.

HEIGHT AND WEIGHT:

Well this was a little personal. I was about 5'5" on a good day, and I liked even numbers so I was going to round down to 130lbs.

BODY TYPE:

Body type? What kind of question was that? I mean I wouldn't call myself slender, but I wasn't heavyset. Saying I was an athletic build sounded a little presumptuous so I finally settled for "average".

CURRENT RELATIONSHIP STATUS:

I was just glad we'd moved on from discussing my body. "Single" and "Never Married". Check. Check.

KIDS:

This pretty much went over every possible question a person could have about kids. Did I have any kids? Did I want any kids? How many kids did I want? When did I want to have kids? I was surprised they didn't ask me what I planned to name them.

"I don't know when I want kids! You can't corner me like this Match.com!" Luckily only the pigeons were nearby to see my little outburst. This questionnaire was giving me anxiety.

I got through the kid questions along with the ethnicity, career, and salary questions. Finally, I was able to move on to the next page.

INTERESTS:

I was supposed to pick out five main interests from their list to highlight. They were all pretty broad categories and I was having a hard time narrowing them down to only five. I mean who wasn't interested in movies? And while I did like doing arts and crafts, I was not sure if that was necessarily something I'd need to have in common with a man. And volunteering? Really? Somebody was looking for brownie points if they checked that one.

I spent the next 15 minutes checking and unchecking the various categories until I was finally comfortable with five.

The final section was all about what I was specifically looking for in a partner. I was wondering if I could submit a photo of Luke because I'd determined that he was my ideal candidate. Clearly, the site wanted a bit more depth than just appearances. I was supposed to decide on things that were definite relationship deal breakers. Things like religion, education level, has kids, wants kids, salary, etc.

I spent about five minutes staring blankly at my screen until I snapped my laptop closed. This section was going to need some backup help.

*****

That night I roped Jessica into my online dating plan. She was surprised at first, but after a minute was all in.

"This is such a great idea Jenn, I don't know why you haven't done it sooner!"

We were sitting on the couch, my laptop open on the coffee table with my half-finished profile pulled up. Jessica was sipping a Diet Coke while I was stress eating a jar of peanut butter.

"You are such an amazing catch Jenn; your problem is you never meet people. You're always too busy working or spending time on your blog."

I didn't know if she was saying this to make me feel better, but it wasn't working. According to her, I was either a workaholic or a recluse.

"Yeah, I'm warming up to the idea," I said between spoonfuls of peanut butter. "I can't help but think online dating makes me sound desperate."

"You're not desperate, you're smart. You're an intelligent, driven woman who knows what she wants in life and is willing to do what it takes to get it. You need to see it from that angle." Jessica set her Coke on the table and put my laptop on her legs. "I like all your answers so far."

I was glad she liked my answers because basically all I'd answered were facts about me. I was a girl, I was caucasian, I was 5'5", and I weighed 130 pounds... if she didn't like those answers then our friendship had bigger issues.

"It's these next sections that we need to dig into," Jessica rubbed her hands together like she was about to devour a beast. "So, what are you looking for in a partner or spouse? What does he definitely have to have... or not have?" She asked. "We can start with the basics like he must make at least a six-figure salary."

We both burst into giggles.

"Considering I don't make six figures, I don't feel like I can make that a requirement." Not that I wouldn't appreciate it, I just didn't think I could make it a deal breaker.

Jessica wiggled her fingers above the keyboard. "Okay, let's get serious. I think kids should be a deal breaker."

"In what way? That he has to want them?"

"Well yeah," she began typing. "He has to want them, and I also think he can't have any kids. I feel like that's an extra dilemma you don't want right now."

I considered it. I didn't know if I'd mind dating a guy with a kid. I felt like men with children were much more dependable than those without. That also usually came with a previous relationship or marriage though.

"I'll agree with you for now. Must want kids in the future, and must have no kids currently."

"Okaaaaay," her fingers click-clacked on the keyboard. "What else? What level of school does he have to have?"

I thought about this, I didn't want to be snobbish, but I preferred dating somebody who graduated from college. Purely because he was more likely to have a steady job. "Let's say some sort of degree is necessary."

"Check, Check." She looked at me inquisitively. "Any physical features you're stuck on? Like he has to be above 5'8", has to have dark hair, has to be ripped, etc.?"

An image of Luke popped into my head and I mentally tried to shoo it away.

"No, I think I'll just stick with the kids and education deal breakers for now. If the floodgates open and I have hordes of men after me I'll get more selective." I said this with a smile, but Jessica looked at me seriously.

"It'll probably happen Jenn, like I said before, any guy would be lucky to date you."

I rolled my eyes. "Thanks mom. Let's move to the next section." The next part was my bio. This was the part where I tried to sell myself to people. I was not excited about it.

"Just put 'I'm your average girl in my late 20s who doesn't have time to meet people but wants a relationship. Message me if you're interested.'" I took another giant scoop of peanut butter.

Jessica grabbed the spoon out of my hand and shoved it back into the jar. "Jenn, you need to pull yourself together girl. You could literally meet your future husband on this site if you play your cards right." She turned back to the laptop. "So they have some examples. You could say something like 'I love to play sports and be outdoors', or 'I love traveling and having adventures', or 'I am a quiet person who loves a good book'."

"You might as well say 'I'm boring so don't ask me to have fun' if you're going to write that." My cynicism was high at this point.

"I think we should play to your humorous side." Jessica was ignoring my comment. "You use sarcasm as a defense mechanism, but you're actually pretty witty. We can even throw in something about your baking."

"Well thank you; I'm not sure whether to be flattered or offended." I quietly tried to sneak back my peanut butter and spoon from the coffee table.

"How about something like, 'if you like carbs I'm the girl for you'? Or maybe 'you'll never have to borrow a cup of sugar from your neighbor when you're with me'."

I didn't want to be rude, but Jessica clearly wasn't known for her bio writing skills. I reached for my laptop. "Give that thing to me."

I cracked my knuckles and let my fingers rest an inch above the keys. It took me another 15 minutes, but I was able to come up with a somewhat acceptable bio in the 500-word limit. There were some benefits to being a blogger. I was used to writing under a deadline.

Jessica read over what I had written, checking for spelling errors and the overall concept. "This is perfect, I'd ask you out if I was a guy."

"And if you were a guy I would accept your invite. Unfortunately for us, you're not and I'm just going to get responses from losers." I clicked the next button on my screen. "Oh crud, I forgot about the picture. I need to get a good picture of myself for my profile."

Jessica scrutinized me, "We can't do it now, we need natural lighting and it's too dark. Plus you're going need to do your hair, makeup, and find a cute outfit."

I looked down at my black T-shirt and ran my fingers through my messy bun. "I don't know, maybe I want to be real so the guy knows what he's getting into." I batted my eyelashes. "Plus who can resist this gorgeous 'baking woman' look?"

She rolled her eyes and grabbed the laptop back from me. "Okay," she said, in a voice that was way too chipper, "should we set up a profile on another site?"

"No."

Chapter 9

We decided I would take my picture the next afternoon. Jessica was going to be home early anyway since I was supposed to teach her and Luke how to make bread that night.

I was under strict instructions to make sure I had my hair and makeup done and a cute outfit picked out.

Was it slightly bizarre that half the reason I wanted to get all dolled up was because I knew Luke was coming over later? Wanting to look good for my profile picture was the main reason, looking good for Luke was just an added bonus. At least that was what I told myself.

At work I brought Ann up to date with how my online profile was going. She was very impressed at how quickly I had gotten the ball rolling.

"Good for you! Go get em' girl."

I felt like everybody around me was so hopeful for this online dating. Maybe I was a cynic, but I had a feeling I was just going to get responses from weirdos.

When I got home that afternoon I went in full prep mode. As they say, look good feel good. I was taking it to the max. I showered, did a hair conditioning treatment, a facial mask, and even shaved my legs past my knees. Serious dedication.

Next, I spent a ridiculous amount of time blow drying then curling my hair into effortless looking beach waves. (Yes, I see the irony in spending an hour trying to achieve an "effortless" look).

Finally, I began applying makeup, going heavier than normal since it was for a picture.

"Athena, you'd better be grateful you're a fish. We humans have way too high expectations." She looked at me through her glass bowl and blew a few bubbles. "What do you have to do to get a man, swim in a few circles and show him some fishy lips?" Again, the stare and bubbles. I needed to consider getting a more interactive pet.

After 20 minutes working on a smoldering smokey eye, I scratched it all and started over. I didn't know how some girls got the smokey look. I looked like someone had given me two black eyes.

The second time around I went for a more natural color palette. Light browns and tans, with a little gold accent. I gave myself a thick layer of mascara and finished with a light pink lip gloss.

There. Put together but not too over-the-top. A girl you could just have fun with. Right? Was that who I even was? I didn't know at that point. All I knew was Jessica was going to be home in about 15 minutes so this was what she got to work with.

I was still looking through my closet for a good outfit when I heard the front door open.

"I'm hereeeee!" She sang, skipping in through my bedroom door. "Oh Jenn, you look gorgeous, I love it when you do yourself up!"

I did a little shimmy and twirl for her. "What can I say; even I can look awesome if I spend two hours getting ready."

She missed my sarcasm. "Sometimes beauty is worth it. Have you decided what you're wearing?"

I picked up two shirts in the pile of clothes thrown on my bed. "I am thinking one of these two?" One was made out of forest green cotton material. It was a little casual but it had a flattering v-neckline so I thought it would be a good choice. The other was a navy collared shirt if I wanted to go for the more professional look.

"Eh, I think you need a little more color Jenn. You have a jazzy personality that screams color. These two shirts scream 'I'm boring, scroll past me'."

"Well tell me what you really think," I said. Sometimes having friends that told you the truth was a burden.

"Okay let's see what else you got." Jessica began rifling through my pile of clothes. She mumbled stuff like "hmmm", and "maybe", and "no not that one" to herself as she sorted through the mess. She finally came out with a purple scoop neck blouse and an emerald green v-neck that I'd forgotten I had.

"I think these two colors play up your hair and eyes. I'd normally always go with a v-neck, but you have such a long, slender neck you could pull off the scoop one pretty well too."

I had a long neck? I self consciously reached and fingered my apparent giraffe length neck. "Really? Like in a weird way?" I asked. Don't get me wrong, I like giraffes. I just didn't want to be a giraffe.

"Jenn don't start with me. I would kill to have a long neck like you. You can pull off any neckline and look awesome. If I had to choose I would probably pick the green one. But either would work." She held them both up for me to inspect.

I was pretty neutral so I decided to go with the v-neck like she said. "Okay, so what do I wear on the bottom half? Do I need to be fancy like slacks or can I wear jeans?" Suddenly I felt like a two-year-old who didn't know how to dress herself.

"It doesn't matter, this is just a photograph of your face and shoulders. You can wear your pajama pants for all I care."

I considered taking her up on that but I didn't want to push my luck. I threw on a pair of jeans and grabbed my camera. The good thing was I already had all the photography equipment since I used it for my blog.

I had a refurbished Nikon D3400 DSLR that I'd bought off Amazon about four years ago. I could probably do with an upgrade, but I felt too much loyalty to this camera to move on from it.

Borderline ridiculous? Yes. I know cameras don't have feelings. Moving on.

I also grabbed my tripod in case Jessica needed it. I wasn't sure what kind of pose she was planning. I followed her out the front door and we took the stairs down to the parking lot of our complex. We stopped there and looked around for a minute.

"We need something bright... something solid but not too busy... but eye-catching."

I wasn't sure if she was talking to me or to herself. I pointed to a little grass patch around the corner that the complex put in for dogs to pee on. "I can go stand by that tree."

"No too generic. We need something more." She started walking towards the direction of the main street. I followed silently behind her. We got to the corner and Jessica once again stopped and peered around.

Across the street was a strip mall with your basic necessities. A Thai restaurant, a Little Caesars ($5 Hot and Ready's were always a win), a dry cleaners, a frozen yogurt shop, and a dog groomers. On the far right of the strip was the city firehouse. They had four oversized garages, all of them painted, yes you guessed it, a firehouse red color.

"Ah! Perfect!" Jessica squealed. She grabbed my arm and pulled me to the crosswalk, hitting the cross button several times.

"You do know it doesn't matter how many times you push it," I said, not feeling particularly kind at the moment.

"This will be perfect, that bright red is the pop color we needed," she said to herself, once again ignoring me.

The light turned green and she started across at an amazingly quick pace.

"Don't you think the red is going to be a little bright? I feel like I'm more of a neutral beige kind of person. Can't we take a photo in front of this brown wall here?" I indicated to the side of the strip mall which was, as I said, painted a very neutral brown.

"Look Jenn, you might be a professional with food shots. But I am a professional at headshots. If you want this to be a good profile picture, you've got to have some color and some pizzazz to catch people's eyes."

We reached the giant red garage doors and Jessica propelled me forward next to one.

"Is this even legal? Are we allowed to be here?" I was feeling very self-conscious sitting in front of the fire station. I was just imagining the alarms going off and one of these giant doors opening. The newspaper cover story would be "Girl Gets Ran Over by Fire Truck While Posing for Dating Site Profile Picture".

"Yes, don't be ridiculous. All we're doing is taking a picture of you." She started turning my body in different directions, first angling me that way then another. Then she tried tilting my head several different ways. I felt like a Barbie doll.

Jessica finally got me into a position that was apparently what she was going for, although I didn't feel like I was doing the pose justice. I had my back slightly turned to her and my head angled so I was looking over my left shoulder. My right side was resting against the garage door.

"The key here is to act natural. Pretend like you're hanging out, having a good time." Jessica had picked up the camera and was looking at me through the lens.

"I don't want to point out the obvious, but there's nothing natural about hanging out front of a fire station. As a matter fact I can't remember the last time I felt this uncomfortable." Although to be fair, I did try to relax.

"Jenn, loosen up. I want you to think of something funny. Then I want you to look over your shoulder at me and smile as if someone's telling you a joke that you're laughing hysterically at."

I was not cut out to be a model.

I racked my brain for something funny. Nothing. So I just pulled out the best smile I could which I'm pretty sure looked more like a grimace.

"Um, okay... That's a good start. Maybe a little less of a strained look, try to look, um, happy?" She crouched to a low angle with the camera up to her face.

I tried again, this time I pictured the cute dog video my mom had tagged me in on Facebook this morning. (My mom was one of those people that tagged everyone she knew when she found cute pictures. Or funny videos. Or inspirational quotes... I'd tried asking her to stop tagging me in a roundabout way but she hadn't gotten the hint yet).

"Better, yes now look directly into the lens and pretend you're looking at someone you're really excited about seeing."

Was it bad that Luke was the first person that popped in my head? I tried to clear my thoughts and think of someone else.

"Wait—why are you shaking your head like that? You look like a dog. Come on Jenn this isn't that hard." I could tell she was getting frustrated with me. She stood and hopped on the raised planter to come at me from a higher angle.

"Yes, this is the perfect shot. Okay, pull it together Jenn. I want you to imagine you're seeing the hottest guy you know come up behind you and calling your name. Mr. Dreamboat himself."

Luke, that traitor, popped into my head again. I figured if it was to help me get another guy, it was okay to use his image just this once. I imagined him walking towards me with his little smirk and I let myself relax into a smile.

"Yes, yes! That's perfect, you're beautiful!" Jessica was shouting out praises as she clicked away rapid fire.

This was how it must feel to be famous I thought. I didn't envy them. The camera lens made me feel vulnerable.

Jessica stepped off the planter and walked towards me. "So this time I'm going to get a shot from the front. I want you to lean with one shoulder against the garage, and put your opposite arm on your hip. In a relaxed style."

Jessica and I clearly did not relax the same way. All the poses she put me in were very awkward. I tried my best though. We spent about another ten minutes trying out different shots.

We were finishing one where I was sitting and leaning back on my hands when the garage door next to me started opening with a loud "Brrrr". I jumped up like a scared cat and scampered to the edge of the sidewalk.

Have I ever mentioned I hated getting in trouble? I was always a borderline teacher's pet in school. Not because I truly wanted to be, but because I was always afraid of getting into trouble. I think my most rebellious moments of high school included toilet papering a friend's yard. Hard-core stuff.

Meanwhile there was Jessica, calm and cool as ever. She stood with her camera as two young, very attractive firemen strolled out. She gave them a little wave and called out, "Hi guys, just taking a photograph or two in front of your beautiful red garage."

One of them laughed and asked if she needed some models. His buddy struck a pose and Jess pulled out her camera and snapped a shot. "Got it. You guys are going to be famous!" She let out a burst of giggles before walking towards me.

I felt like such an idiot standing in the corner like a scared bunny. I was hoping the firemen hadn't noticed me, although I was sure they did.

"Good news, I think we've got some good ones to pick from." She gave me a sly smile. "But we better get home to look at them; you're apparently terrified of firemen."

I rolled my eyes. "Some of us were not born natural flirts like you."

She flipped her hair over her shoulder and simply said, "I'll take that as a compliment."

*****

I had to hand it to her, Jessica could take a good headshot. She got at least two decent ones of me in the first pose—I actually looked like I was having a great time. There was also a good one of me leaning against the garage with my arms crossed.

We eventually decided on one with me looking back— the picture with my arms crossed made me look a little defensive. I was so absorbed in picking out pictures that I forgot Luke was coming over.

A sharp knock on the door surprised both Jessica and me out of our photo trance.

"Oh, that's Luke!" Jessica jumped up and ran to the front door. She opened it and suddenly her demeanor turned all coy and flirtatious. "Hey there handsome, fancy meeting you here."

I heard a way too familiar laugh and then a response I wasn't able to make out.

What was I doing? Was I really going to be the third wheel tonight? Maybe I could bow out of this somehow, pretend to be feeling sick all of a sudden or something...

As I contemplated my possible escape routes, Jessica and Luke walked into the living room. Luke stumbled slightly when he saw me. If he wasn't standing next to his girlfriend, I would've said he was checking me out. That might have just been wishful thinking.

"Jenn, wow... you look, really nice!" I swear there was a slight blush to Luke's cheeks after he said this.

Jessica swatted him on the shoulder. "First off Luke, you never mention if a girl looks drastically different. It's like you're saying she doesn't normally look this fabulous." She turned and looked at me. "Because you do Jenn, even not all done up you always look fabulous."

Luke quickly replied, "What—I mean you always look great Jenn. That's not—I just meant you look extra nice tonight." He was fumbling for words.

I decided to be kind and put him out of his misery. "It's fine, I did put some extra effort into my appearance tonight." Then I realized that sounded like I'd gotten ready for him.

"Not that I got ready for our baking lesson—I had to take a picture for something... so I needed to look nice for it. That's all," I finished lamely. I didn't have the guts to tell him I was taking a profile picture for a dating website.

Luckily, Jessica took care of that embarrassing announcement for me.

"Jenn is going to start online dating! Don't you think it's a great idea?" she asked.

I wish I could've taken a picture of his split-second reaction. So I could stare at it and analyze for hours over what it meant. Yes, I know that is something a 14-year-old girl would do. But I swear he looked almost sick when she said that.

"Online dating? But—why?"

Jessica's looked at him dumbly for a second. "Uh because she wants to meet and date somebody?"

"Well, yeah, I know that... just... why online? Aren't there a lot of creepers and predators online?"

While I had to agree these were both secret fears of mine, even I thought his train of thought was a little weird. "Don't you think that's a little dramatic? There are thousands of people meeting on dating websites and probably like five cases of any predatory instances." Jessica was clearly annoyed by his lack of enthusiasm. "Don't come in here ruining all the progress we've made. Jenn is finally taking action in her love life—this is huge! Don't mess it up!"

Wow, I didn't realize she'd felt this way about my singleness.

Although looking back, Jessica had spent the last two years trying to set me up on endless blind dates and such. She'd introduced me to her boyfriend's roommates, "great guys" that worked in her building, the nice guy from the coffee shop... Poor thing, she'd probably worked so hard to get me to this point.

I tried to ease the tension with some humor. "Don't worry Jess, he's not going to talk me out of it. When I find Mr. Right you'll still have the honor of claiming you took the profile picture that brought us together."

Jessica threw a pillow at me. "You're darn right. I'd better get credit for that picture!" She turned back to Luke who was still looking unhappy but seemed to realize this wasn't a battle he should fight.

"Don't worry Luke, I'll keep tabs on her and make sure she's not dating any creepers. You can volunteer as her personal bodyguard on dates if you're that concerned."

He flexed his muscles. "I always knew these guns would come in handy one day."

"When you two are done discussing my future husband who's apparently an axe murderer we can get to work." I stood with my hands on my hips.

"Lead the way Betty Crocker," Jessica put her arms around Luke and leaned into him.

Oh crud, my third wheel nightmare was coming true.

For the next half hour we spent our time proofing the yeast and prepping our dough. I was amazed at how little Jessica knew about baking considering she'd been my roommate for the last four years.

"Yeast is amazing and yet so gross at the same time!" She said for what must've been the hundredth time as she stared at the bubbly organism in her bowl.

We spent the next 15 minutes learning how to knead. I could've had the mixer do it for us, but as I've said before, it's an essential part of learning to bake. Machine kneading was something you earned.

I was actually impressed by how well Luke was doing. He seemed to have a natural knack for the process.

Despite my apprehension, it was fun hanging out with them. They managed to keep their lovey boyfriend/girlfriend stuff to a limit. And I had to admit, they created the perfect picture together.

She was the beautiful bombshell and he was the tall dark and handsome Ken doll. Here they were working side-by-side in the kitchen. I could just see their little towheaded children running in the door from school. Chucking their backpacks on the ground, Jessica calling out "Hey kids how was school?" Then Luke would go throw a football with them in the backyard...

I snapped out of my daydream to Jessica's voice saying "Jenn, Jenn?"

"Huh, sorry what?"

"I asked how long do we have to knead this for? My arms are on fire."

I looked over at their dough and pinched off a piece to feel the elasticity of it.

Luke, ever the man, was still kneading vigorously next to her. "What do you mean Jess? I could—whew—could do this all day!"

I could be wrong, but I think he was sweating.

"Okay, that looks pretty good." I looked over Luke's dough as well. "They both look great. See how the dough almost springs back at you but it's still slightly tacky? That's perfect."

I brought two mixing bowls over and set them on the counter. "So you need to lightly oil these bowls then put your dough in them to rest. We'll cover them with some plastic wrap too."

"Oil them?"

It's funny how you forget that certain terms didn't make sense if you didn't cook frequently.

"Yeah so put a little oil, like a spoonful, in the bottom of your bowl and swirl it around so all the sides of the bowl are coated." I grabbed Luke's bowl and demonstrated it for them. "That way the dough doesn't stick as it's rising."

"Ah..." At least Luke got the concept, Jessica still seemed a little confused but she copied what I did anyway.

"Now the dough needs to rise. Usually we give it about an hour or two to rise in the bowl. Then we'd put it in the baking pan and give it a second rise." I looked pointedly at the clock. "But because I need my beauty sleep, and I don't want to be baking at midnight, we're going to do the overnight rise method."

I opened the fridge and placed the two bowls inside. "The cold temperature will make the dough rise slower, so by about this time tomorrow it'll be ready for baking."

"I can't believe I made bread today. I feel like a pioneer." Luke was staring at the flour-dusted countertop in awe.

"Ha ha, I don't know how to put this, but I think people have been baking bread for a lot longer than the pioneers." Jessica giggled into his shoulder and he looked down into her face smiling.

Uh oh. The couple stuff was coming out again. Any minute now there was bound to be some unfortunate PDA. I didn't want to be around for it.

"Wellll..." I began, clearing my throat loudly. "Looks like all that's left is the most important part of all." I dusted off my hands and slowly began backing out of the kitchen. "And it's a great two person job."

"What's that?" Jessica asked, looking perplexed.

"Dishes and clean up—good luck!" I called out over my shoulder as I dashed into my room.

The last thing I heard was a groan from Luke before my door clicked shut.

Wheat Bread Recipe

- · 1 Tbsp active dry yeast
- · 2 Tbsp sugar
- · 1 cup milk, heated to 110-120° F
- · 1 teaspoon salt
- · 2 Tablespoons oil
- · 1 egg
- · 2 cups whole wheat flour
- · 1/2-3/4 cup bread flour

1.) Place yeast, sugar, and warm milk in a large mixing bowl and let proof for about 5 minutes.

2.) Stir in oil, salt, and egg and beat on high for a minute.

3.) Add whole wheat flour and stir until it becomes a mound. With a dough hook attachment (or by hand), knead dough for 7-8 minutes, adding in bread flour 1/4 cup at a time until dough doesn't stick to your hands but is still tacky.

4.) Cover with a towel and let rest 1 hour.

5.) Punch dough down then shape into a loaf. Place in a greased loaf pan then cover and let rise again for 30 minutes.

6.) Preheat oven to 375° F. Bake loaf for 30 minutes.

7.) Remove immediately from pan onto a cooling rack. Let it cool at least 10 minutes before slicing.

Chapter 10

I got to work bright and early the next morning. Carly had gotten back from a week-long cruise with her girlfriends the day before, so we were able to enjoy her happy smiling countenance all morning. Read that as her sullen and grumpy looks.

The good part was that Ann let me off early due to the extra hours I'd worked covering for Carly the week before. I used the extra time at home very efficiently. AKA: scrolling mindlessly through men's profiles on Match.com.

I'd set my profile live last night after uploading my photo. I wasn't going to lie, it took me about 15 minutes to finally hit the submit button. The idea of putting myself out there for anyone to find was very daunting. I hated feeling vulnerable. But I did it. And now I was here to see what came of it.

Needless to say, not much.

According to my stats, I had two men who liked my profile and another who sent me a message via the website's internal service.

The message went like this:

"Hey babe saw that your into fitness. Working out is kinda my thang so sounds like we'd be a good match. Hit me up if you wanna meet. -Stan"

The fact that the only thing he'd noticed about me was that I was into fitness (which may or might not have been a total truth), did not inspire me to pursue this relationship. It could also have been his misuse of the word "your". A personal pet peeve of mine.

I moved to the two other men who liked my profile. I pulled up the first guy's page.

The guy had a mullet. A legit mullet in his profile picture. I literally spent two hours getting ready for my profile picture and I would question whether this guy brushed his teeth for his. Next.

The second guy wasn't terrible. Well, at least he looked normal. However he'd probably only fit the bill if you liked bald men who appeared to be in their mid-40s. Which would be fine... if I was close to my 40s as well. But I was 26. I deleted him as well.

Well, I was back to square one. I guess I couldn't be too upset, my profile had only been live for 12 hours.

I shut my laptop when I heard the front door open. I looked up in surprise to see Jessica walk in. She was dressed in a form-fitting pantsuit and carrying a large Jamba Juice cup. She looked at me in surprise as well.

"Jenn? What are you doing home so early?" She tossed her purse on the counter.

"Ann let me off a little early today, Carly's back so she's covering the counter." I eyed her smoothie with envy.

She noticed my look and offered the cup to me. "Ooo, how is the she-devil?"

Jessica was very familiar with my lack of love for Carly. In my defense though, Carly was the one that started it.

"Moody as ever, but now she has a nice tan to go with it." I took a swig of the drink and enjoyed the cool strawberry banana flavor as it hit my mouth.

"What are you doing home so early?" I asked around another mouthful of smoothie. I handed her back her cup and she took a drink herself.

Her shoulders shrugged. "Eh, I had a couple hours before I had to be up in LA, so I figured I'd come home and relax for a bit. Nothing pressing in the office." She slumped on the couch next to me and kicked off her suede heels.

After a slight pause, she asked, "Jenn, did you notice anything funny about Luke yesterday?"

I set up a little straighter, surprised by this turn in the conversation. "Funny? Like what?" I was very interested to see where this was going.

"I don't know, he seemed a little distant. Normally he's more touchy-feely with me. More affectionate. Most guys are. I'm like a magnet for hands. But yesterday I don't think he did more than give me a side hug."

She fiddled with the tassels on the pillow she was holding. "Just in general too. Lately he treats me almost like we're buddies now instead of boyfriend/girlfriend. I don't know if it's all in my head or if it's actually happening." She threw her hands in the air.

I didn't know what to say. There were two routes you could go in friendship dating advice. (At least in my professional opinion.)

Option one would be to reassure her that everything was fine, it was all in her head, the guy was so into her and she was just being insecure, etc...

Option two was more of the accusation approach. It was all the guy's fault—what was his problem, couldn't he see he was the luckiest man on earth, you were too good for him, he wasn't worth your time, etc...

I decided to feel out the situation a little more.

"So are you still hanging out the same amount or is he blowing you off more often?" I rested my elbows on my knees, in full inquisition mode now. "Like is it only noticeable when you're together, or can you tell he's not making as much of an effort to see you period?"

I felt the need to give Luke the benefit of the doubt. Something I didn't normally do for Jessica's boyfriends. I clearly had a soft spot for this guy.

"I guess we still hang out about the same amount. I haven't noticed any significant change." She was very hesitant in her response. "Although to be honest I've been busy at work lately, so we haven't had as much time together as I'd like."

"So basically you feel like he's not as touchy-feely anymore."

She blushed a little. "I guess so. That sounds kind of needy when you put it that way. But usually guys are really into me so it's surprising when one isn't."

I decided I didn't have enough information to use option two. So far all Jessica had told me was that Luke wasn't as affectionate as he'd been in the past. Not enough to write the guy off.

"Jessica, this sounds like it's more in your head. Like maybe you're reading too much into things." I leaned back into the couch, bringing Jessica's fruit smoothie with me. "Have you thought of talking to him about it?" I took a sip of the drink.

"Ugh, I know I should. I just hate bringing things up with relationships," she swiped the drink back from me. "Then it makes everything weird and awkward. Plus then he's going to think I'm a psycho-possessive girlfriend."

I nodded, there was truth in what she was saying. "But at least then you can stop stressing out about it right? Because if he really isn't into you—not that I think he isn't—but if he isn't it's better to know now right?"

She shrugged her shoulders. She knew I was right, but it was a hard pill to swallow. "Yeah, I guess so." All of a sudden her eyes brightened and she glanced up at me. "Maybe you could mention something to him."

"What?" Oh no, I did not want to go down this road. There were way too many conflicts of interest here. As much as I hated to admit it, there was a tiny, very minuscule, small part in the back of my mind still hoping they'd break up. Because then Luke would be free. Although I still could never date him because he'd be my roommate's ex-boyfriend which fell under best girlfriend code of never dating your roommate's ex-boyfriends.

"Yeah, I mean he's coming over tonight to finish the bread. Maybe you could slip it into the conversation somehow. Just ask how things are going with him and me." She waved her hands around innocently. "You know, make it sound casual."

"Don't you think he would assume I'd ask you that question and not him? You are my roommate." Please don't make me do this. Please don't make me do this. This mantra was racing through my head.

"Come on Jenn. I know you don't want to get involved but it would make it so much easier for me if you could get a feel for where he was." She looked at me with the saddest eyes she could muster. "I don't want to get my heart broken and my pride demolished all at once."

No, no no no. I tried to race through my possible excuses. "Jessica, this is your relationship. This is something you guys need to work out. You don't want a third person involved."

"You're not involved, you're just doing me a favor. She leaned forward and grabbed my hands. "Please, please pleeeeease?"

Erg, sometimes I hated having best friends. "Fine, fine, okay I'll ask him about it tonight." I held up my finger sternly. "But I'm just going to ask it lightly. If he tries to brush me off, I'm not going to keep digging for more."

"Yes, that's great thank you so much!" She jumped up and gave me a tight squeeze. As she stepped back she gave me an appraising look. "You always smell so good, like fresh bread. You should make it a perfume."

I rolled my eyes. Just what every girl wanted to smell like, bread. Here she was smelling like Chanel No 5 and looking like a sexy businesswoman, and here I was smelling like fresh baked cookies like the Pillsbury Doughboy.

"Yeah, whatever, you owe me one," I said to her and she retreated down the hall.

"I do, I'm going to get you the biggest Jamba Juice ever next time!"

Okay, that might be worth it.

*****

Jessica took off for her event about 30 minutes later and I finished typing up some notes for my cream puffs.

When that was done I checked on Luke and Jessica's bread in the fridge. It had risen perfectly. I pulled them out so they would be room temperature by the time Luke came over.

I didn't want to admit it, but I was a little nervous about being alone with Luke. Don't ask me why, I spent like three hours alone with him last Saturday. However there was something different about being in my apartment.

I probably spent an hour trying to decide what to wear. I obviously wanted to look good, but not so good that he knew I was trying. Because this wasn't a date. I just wanted to give off the "hey, I am so casual and yet so hot without trying" impression.

It was difficult to achieve.

After dumping half of my wardrobe on the floor, I settled for a slim fit skinny jean with a floral printed top. I even took the time to curl my hair in some light beachy waves. Although then I felt like I was trying too hard, so I pulled it back into a ponytail.

I was contemplating bagging the whole outfit and throwing on a pair of sweats when I heard a knock. I wiped my clammy hands on my pants as I walked to the front door.

There he was. Looking all gorgeous and casual without even trying. I guaranteed he didn't take an hour to get ready for this non-date.

"Jenn!" He exclaimed, stepping in the doorway.

He said it so excitedly I was a little concerned. Was he expecting somebody else?

"Hey Luke, you ready to finish off what we started yesterday?" Oh my gosh, did that sound like a pickup line?

I hoped I didn't spend the next hour questioning everything I said.

He rubbed his hands together with gusto. "You know it. Let's do this. Where is that bread?"

And with that, all my nervousness disappeared. I forgot how easy it was to be with Luke. Maybe that was why I was so attracted to him. Obviously he had the looks, but there was something about him that made me comfortable.

"All right Chef Boyardee. Your dough awaits you."

We walked into the kitchen where I had set up the two balls of dough and some bread loaf pans. "So I'm going to make you do all the work. I'll talk you through it, but this is your bread."

He nodded, all seriousness now. "Okay coach, tell me what to do."

He was such a dork. "First things first. You're going to want to preheat your oven. It takes a while for it to warm up so best to get it going now."

"Got it. Preheat the oven." He walked over to my oven and stared at all the buttons for a minute. "So, exactly how do you preheat an oven? Do I need to light a flame or something?"

"What?" I said incredulously. "Please tell me you've used an oven before. I thought you said you baked with your mom when you were growing up?"

"I did. But she took care of all the technical stuff like turning on the oven. My job was mostly to lick the spoon and bowl."

I tried to ignore how adorable I found this confession.

"So you've never baked anything in an oven before?" How had this man survived the last 30 plus years?

"Well, to be honest, if I'm cooking to impress somebody I almost always barbecue. It's the manliest cooking method," he said matter-of-factly. "Baking seems more of a woman's forte. When I'm cooking for myself, I stick to the microwave or take out." He stared into space for a moment, "I don't know if anyone's ever turned on the oven in my place before."

"Well, then today's your lucky day. I'm going to teach you how to use an oven." I walked over to stand next to him. I could smell the woodsy scent he always had and was momentarily distracted. Did he always wear the same cologne or was that just a natural body odor? I had to stop myself before I leaned in for another whiff of it.

"So is this a test or are you going to actually show me what to do?"

"Oh, yeah!" I sheepishly came back to the present moment. Focus Jenn, don't get distracted by a manly smell. Remember, you are his girlfriend's platonic roommate.

"Okay," I said, pointing to the buttons on the oven. "The button that says 'bake' is your on/off button. Push that first, then you adjust the temperature with these ones." I motioned to the two buttons that had the word 'Temp' listed above them. "Always check your recipe to see what temperature it calls for. Most recipes use 350°F, although some can be different so always check." Next I pointed to the start button. "After you hit bake and adjust the temperature, you have to push start so the oven starts warming up."

I turned to look at him. "Alright student, here's your test. Show me how to preheat the oven."

Luke took a deep breath and stretched his arms up over his head. "Luke, you can do this, you were born to do this.

A'int no oven going to get the best of you." I covered my eyes at his ridiculous pep talk.

He proceeded to correctly turn on the oven, adjust the temperature, and push start. He turned to look at me. "Did I pass?"

I smiled back, "Perfect, you got an A on that part. Let's move on." I showed him again how to dust the countertop with flour before we dumped the dough on it. "So we're going to knead this a little, but not nearly as much as we did the first time. This is more to redistribute the yeast for this last rise."

I grabbed Jessica's bowl of dough and showed him once again how to knead. It was a simple process of pressing the dough with the heels of your hands, folding it on top of itself, then pressing again. Luke did a pretty good job of it himself.

Next we greased the loaf pans and did a beautiful job of rolling the dough into a cylinder before placing it inside. Well, at least mine was beautiful. Luke's was a little lopsided but I gave him bonus points for trying.

I went to the sink and washed the remaining scraps of dough off my hands.

"We're going to give these guys another 20 minutes to rise and fill the pans." I picked up the loaf pans and placed them on top of the stove over the warm oven. "The heat from the oven will help them rise faster which is why I am putting them here." I indicated with my hands. "But now, it's just a waiting game."

"All right, I can do that." Luke washed his hands off in the sink as well and I tossed him a towel.

"You thirsty?" I opened the fridge and ducked down to look inside. "We have water, Diet Coke, and Jessica has a few protein drinks that I say try at your own risk." I glanced up at him with raised eyebrows.

"I'll take a Coke."

I bent down and reached into the fridge to grab one. When I stood up I was startled to find he had walked over next to me. I hadn't realized how tall Luke was. He was obviously over 6 foot but not in an ogrish way. More in a manly, I'm-ready-to-chop-some-firewood or save-a-baby-kitten-from-a tree, kind of way.

As I handed him his drink our hands brushed and I swear a jolt of electricity went through me. I quickly bent back down to grab a water for myself, hoping he didn't notice how unsettling his nearness was to me.

When I stood back up he had cracked open his can and was taking a long drink from it.

"Let's go hang out on the couch," I suggested. We needed to get out of this kitchen. Quarters were too tight in here.

In the living room he chose the loveseat and I relaxed on the larger couch.

"So," he asked, "how are things going with your bakery plans?"

"Bakery plans?"

"Yeah, remember how we talked about it? I thought I'd convinced you to go for it."

I was amazed at how matter-of-fact he was. In his mind he saw that opening a bakery was a goal of mine, so of course it was going to happen. I didn't think anybody had taken me or my dreams so seriously before.

"I-I, well I think you convinced *yourself* I should go for it. I'm still not sure if I'm on board." Even if he could take my dreams seriously I didn't know if I could.

"Why not?" He stared at me earnestly.

"Do you know how much work it would take? And what if it failed?" How could he not see that this was a huge risk? One I wasn't sure I was brave enough to take.

"Well, from what I've seen, hard work isn't something that scares you." He took another drink from his can. "And what if you failed? What's the worst that could happen? You'd have to close your bakery... but at least you tried." He raised his eyebrows at me. "What would be worse, trying and failing or never trying at all? You miss 100% of the shots you don't take."

"Don't give me any of your sports analogies," I retorted. I felt the challenge he offered me. As if he was testing to see what I would respond with. Well, if he wanted to know what I was made of, I'd show him.

"If you're really curious I have started some planning." I pointed my finger in warning, "Not that I'm saying I'll ever go through with it, I've just been thinking about it. I've set up a preliminary business plan. It would take quite a lot of arranging and there are several things that would have to occur first."

I lifted up my hand and began counting off on my fingers. "I'd have to prove the concept of my recipes first."

"Isn't that what your blog does?" he interrupted. "Doesn't everybody love the things you post? That should be proof enough that your recipes are good."

"Yes, but I still think there's a difference between offering somebody a free recipe compared to offering somebody a finished baked good that they're paying for."

He nodded his head in agreement.

I continued on. "Going to the farmers market actually gave me an idea. I was thinking about maybe renting a booth at one of those and selling my items. I could get some feedback from customers about which items they prefer and which items are most popular." I was gathering steam as I talked. "I'm planning on my bakery focusing on sweets. I want mine to be more of a novelty bakery in comparison to Bread & Butter which is more of a bread bakery."

Luke stared at me for a second. "Not to sound dumb, but what does that mean? What's the difference between those two?"

"So my store would sell things more like cookies, muffins, cupcakes, cakes, brownies, and bars, etc... basically everything bad for you," I finished with a laugh.

Luke leaned forward, resting on his knees. "Well if that's the case you definitely need to get this thing started. I find that there's a lack of fresh baked cookies and brownies in my life." He looked at me quizzically. "So you need proof of concept first. What else have you thought about?"

"Well, then there's all the boring stuff. Like the processes and procedures." I thought back to my college business classes and how proud my operations management professor would be of me right now. "Like if I had to hire an employee, I should be able to quickly train them on production procedures in place. I need step by step flow charts on how items are prepped, baked, packaged, and put on display." I leaned back and cracked open my water bottle.

Luke was staring at me in surprise. "Wow, you're legit. Do you have an MBA or something?"

I could tell he was messing with me but it still felt good. "This isn't my first rodeo wise guy. The good thing about working for Ann is I've been able to see how important processes are in a bakery." I capped my water bottle and put it back on the coffee table. "They really are essential for any successful business." I gave him a stern glance before adding, "And no I don't have an MBA. But I did take a handful of business classes in college."

He gave me his wide grin and sat up straighter. I loved how into this he was getting. "Well this is great; you're headed in the right direction. I can't believe you doubted yourself. So you need processes and procedures. Check. What's next?"

"I'll need to find a location. That's huge."

He was nodding his head. "You're right. That could make or break you." He drummed his fingers on the coffee table, rattling the empty Coke can set on it. "What about branding and everything? Do you have any marketing experience?"

I shrugged my shoulders. "I got my degree in communications, I had to take some marketing and sales classes but I wouldn't say I'm an expert. I'll need some outside help."

"That shouldn't be too difficult. Everyone's an expert on social media these days." He winked.

"Next is all the boring stuff. All the legal and financial side of things. I'll need to get a business license, all the health food licenses/certifications, and set up some sort of business LLC for tax purposes."

I stared at the ceiling, suddenly feeling overwhelmed. "I haven't even thought about all the distribution issues. I'm going to need to find suppliers for my ingredients and packaging materials. I'm going to need a supply of baking equipment, industrial mixers... holy cow I don't want to think about this." I laid back and threw my arms over my eyes.

Luke leaned forward. "Hey, it's okay. I know it seems overwhelming when you think of it all, but you just need to break it down piece by piece like you were doing." He rapped the coffee table, forcing me to lift my arms off my eyes. "Seriously Jenn, I'm shocked about how much you've thought through this already. You're going to do great. You need to trust yourself."

I peered at him with narrow eyes. "I think you're the first person that's ever truly believed I could do this. Why?"

He sat back, suddenly unable to meet my eyes. "Jenn, I can just tell you've got it. You got the drive. I think you need a few more people who believe in you." Just then there was a loud beep from the oven, signaling that it was fully preheated.

"All right, clearly we're getting too deep. Let's get back to the real business at hand." I was trying to bring some lightheartedness back to our conversation.

Luke caught on to my attitude and grinned at me. "Lead the way chef."

I had him put the bread in the oven and set the timer for 50 minutes. I couldn't believe what a baby he was about putting the bread into the hot oven. I'd never seen someone so afraid of getting burned before.

"It's a good thing you never became a firefighter," I told him, "there's no way you'd go into a burning building."

"Whatever, I just don't trust your hot pads to protect me from those scalding metal racks." He fidgeted with the oven mitts in question. "So, how's online dating going?"

Oh no, please don't ask me about that. It would be a lose-lose situation. Just the fact that he knew I was online dating made me feel pathetic. I didn't want to discuss that the only three men who had shown any interest were all flops.

"It's going fine. We'll see how things pan out." I tried to be as vague as possible. I suddenly remembered my promise to Jessica so I figured now was as good of a time as any to question him.

"Speaking of dating, how about you and Jessica?"

"Huh?" He asked, looking a little confused.

"I said how are things with you and Jessica? You guys getting serious yet?" I gave him my best wide eyed face.

I saw a look on Luke's I've never seen before. He was scared. Scared of what? Was he scared that I knew something about their relationship? Was he scared that maybe Jessica wasn't into him anymore? Or maybe was he scared because he wasn't into it, and he didn't want to discuss it with his girlfriend's roommate.

His hands were clenching the oven mitts until his knuckles turned white. "Things are great with me and Jess. I'm sure she's told you that." He didn't say this last part as a question, but he looked as if he was waiting for an answer.

"Yeah, she sounds like she's having fun. Jess has been busy with work lately so I haven't gotten to talk to her much." I decided to dig in once more. "I just wanted to hear your perspective. Sometimes girls and guys view the same thing completely different." I was challenging him. Daring him to tell me his feelings.

He didn't take the bait though.

"Yep, everything is great with me and her. No drama here." He tossed the hot pads back on the counter and glanced over at the oven. "So if this is going to take 50 minutes to bake, do I have time to go run a quick errand? Since I'll just be sitting here getting in your hair anyway."

Was he trying to escape this conversation? I never realized he was such a coward when it came to his emotions. The question was what did it mean?

"Well, a good baker never leaves their oven, you never know what might happen. But since I am here to keep an eye on it I guess you'd be fine." I cocked my head and looked at him again. "The question is what kind of errands do you need to run at 8 PM at night?"

He stumbled backward and shrugged his shoulders. "Oh you know, nothing important. My car is kinda running low on gas and I have to drive out to a client meeting tomorrow so..." he tried to avoid eye contact, "might as well fill it up tonight so I don't have to in the morning."

"Mmmm..." I wasn't letting him off the hook that easily. He was being ridiculous and I wanted him to know it. "You know, if you stay I promise not to ask you any more questions about Jessica."

"What? Oh—no that's not it, I just, you know... got to be prepared for tomorrow." Without another glance he walked to the front door. "I'll be back in about 20 minutes."

"See ya," I said quietly to the closing door.

Chapter 11

Just as he promised, Luke came back 20 minutes later. We made some awkward small talk until the oven timer finally went off.

I will say, the bread looked and smelled beautiful. Luke managed to pull both loaves out of the oven without burning himself which was quite the feat in his eyes.

We loosely wrapped up his loaf and sent him home with it. I promised to tell Jessica about his excellent baking skills.

Now I was in a bad situation because I was going to have to tell Jessica everything that happened. It wasn't going to be pretty. From everything I saw, there was something wrong between Luke and Jessica. And whether she was aware of it or not, he definitely was. The man literally chose to run away instead of talking to me about it.

I considered what my options were.

I could give her very limited details of what he said. Basically that he said everything was fine and there were no problems. Leaving out all the weirdness.

Or I could be honest and give her the full details.

I knew what I was going to do—I was going to tell her everything. Hopefully, I could convince her to have a talk with him.

I actually didn't have tons of time to brood over the subject the next day. It was a big day at work for me. I was going to make some test versions of my apple and pumpkin pies for Ann to analyze.

The crusts and fillings were all premade, I just needed to assemble and bake them this afternoon after the store closed. Ann said she had some bookkeeping work to do so she didn't mind staying late.

First I had to get through the normal day's work though.

Carly and I were packing rosemary bread for the sandwich shop we were partnered with. She was being quite pleasant surprisingly.

"So how much longer until graduation?" I asked, tightening the cellophane over the bread in my hands.

"Eh, I've got a solid two years left, maybe three. I just changed my major to English which puts me back another six months." Carly stacked two more loaves into the delivery box.

"Oh yeah? What do you want to do with that? Write?" I truly wasn't sure what one did with an english degree. However, considering I was doing nothing with my communications degree, I wasn't one to talk.

"I think I want to teach. Hopefully high school english if everything goes as planned."

"That's cool. I think you'll be perfect for that."

And I really did. English teachers always seemed to have that moody, dark attitude. Maybe it was what made them such deep thinkers when it came to literature. At any rate, I thought it would work well with Carly.

We finished packing away the rest of the bread and soon everything was done but clean up.

By noon I was able to start working on my pies. Carly already had plans that afternoon so she said to save her a piece for tomorrow. That was fine with me, Ann's opinion was the only one I really cared about.

I first worked on the pumpkin pie. I poured the filling into the graham flavored crust. I had used a heavy amount of molasses to give it a dark caramel color and add flavor depth.

Next, I gave my apple pie filling a quick stir before adding it to the herbed pie crust. It was a basic filling, par-cooked Granny Smith apples with butter and sugar. The only real difference was I used browned butter. We'll see if my extra efforts made any difference.

I put them in the still warm ovens, then sat down to wait.

Ann was in her office doing whatever paperwork she needed to work on, so I pulled up my dating profile to check out how things had gone in the last 24 hours.

I was beginning to realize I'd have better luck finding a guy I actually liked if I was the one weeding through profiles. If I just sat back and waited for Mr. Right to come, it might not ever happen.

A few more guys liked my profile over the last 12 hours. Only one of them interested me, the other two I automatically disregarded. The first guy said he was gluten intolerant (as a baker, I couldn't deal with that), the second guy said he had six cats. Anyone with six cats obviously had issues.

I checked out the third guy's profile. He looked fairly normal. He was an orthodontist who worked in LA, 32 years old, and his interests included hiking, tennis, and reading. As far as his picture went, I couldn't complain. He wasn't a model, but he had nice even features, light brown hair, and wore a pair of thick-rimmed glasses—which could totally be considered a hot nerdy look if you took it from the right perspective. I made a mental note to send him a message.

I spent the next 20 minutes scrolling through other men's profiles. I set up a location radius of about 30 miles. Next, I filtered out anyone who made less than me. I didn't want to seem shallow, but I also didn't want to be the main provider for my family. Considering I didn't make that much to begin with, I figured it wasn't asking for much.

Other than that I tried to be open-minded. As everyone said, looks fade but personality is forever. Actually, I don't think that was what people said but whatever.

I ended up with a list of about five guys I would consider. I was bookmarking their names when Ann came out of her office, stretching her arms high over her head.

"So, how is the pie baking going?"

"Oh they're in the oven," I looked over and checked the timer, "we got about 15 more minutes until they're done."

Ann nodded and did some more back stretches.

"Paperwork that bad?" Ann always resorted to stretching whenever she got stressed. I thought it was kind of funny but apparently it helped relax her.

She gave me a slight grin as she reached out to touch her toes. "Let's say I was not made for paperwork. My forte lies in mixing together flour and yeast." She looked thoughtful. "You know, I've been thinking about hiring an office assistant. Someone who could do all the paper and computer work every week." She had moved on to stretching her quads, standing on one leg and resting her hand on the counter to balance. "I'd probably only need about 5-10 hours out of them a week."

"How about Carly?" Carly actually did a pretty good job at the front counter but maybe she'd prefer office work.

"I ran it by her a week or so ago, but she didn't seem too interested. Plus then I'd have to replace her up front and I'd still need to hire someone." She stopped her stretching and sat down on a chair next to me.

"I bet you could hire a student pretty easily." There were about three community colleges around us that I'm sure had tons of students looking for work on the side. I remembered being in their position not too long ago. "I bet you could find a business student or someone decent with numbers."

Ann nodded her head as I talked. "You're right, it's not like it's that difficult of work, mostly keeping track of inventory and orders. I'm going to have to look into that." She looked over at the phone in my hands and noticed the dating website I had pulled up. "Scoping out the options? Anyone catch your eye?"

I considered brushing her off and saying I was still looking. But what the heck, maybe a second opinion would be helpful. "Here are a few guys I've been looking at." I handed her my phone with the five profiles I'd highlighted.

She took a minute to glance through each of them, starting with their pictures then scrolling through the personal information. She made a few hums and haws even laughed at one point. I wasn't sure if that was a good thing or a bad thing.

When she finally handed the phone back I leaned forward with anticipation.

"I liked the first guy; David I think was his name? He had a few quirky comments that shows he has a sense of humor." She looked at me seriously. "A sense of humor is a must in a marriage in my personal opinion. The second and third guy seemed stable and normal—which is kind of rare these days." She pointed to my screen. "The fourth guy I'm not so sure about. He said he still lives with his parents. Did you catch that?"

"He does?" I clicked on his profile again and scrolled through the information. "I didn't see that." But yep there it was. In his residency information he stated that he still lived in his parent's house. Oh sure, I should've given him the benefit of the doubt, maybe there were special circumstances. But any 32-year-old who still lived with his parents probably had issues I didn't want to deal with.

"Good catch. What about guy number five?"

"I thought he was by far the most attractive of the group. He's a lawyer too." She wiggled her eyebrows. "If you're lucky you'll never have to work again!"

I huffed loudly. "Are you trying to get rid of me?"

"No," she smiled, "you're the best employee I've ever had. I am going to be lost if you ever leave." She paused and looked back at me. This time when she spoke her tone was serious. "But don't let that ever hold you back Jenn. Never base your life or career choices on how it will affect me or anyone else. If you have an idea or a dream, I want you to promise me you'll go for it. I'll be sad to ever see you leave, but I'd feel worse if I thought you gave up something important for me."

I smiled at her. She was one of the best women I'd ever met and I thanked heavens for the day she hired me. "Thanks Ann, that means a lot. Both your belief in me and how much you value me here. Because you know I don't get paid enough to make it worth my while."

The oven beeped.

Ann looked over at it then back at me. "Well if these pies of yours sell like you think they will, maybe I'll increase your salary."

I stood and wrapped my knuckles on the countertop. "You just wait, these are going to be the best pies of your life,"

I pulled the pies out of the ovens and set them on the counter to cool. They actually looked really good.

The apple one still needed the crumb topping on top. I grabbed the bowl I'd set aside with the crumbled butter, brown sugar, and cinnamon. Quickly I sprinkled the mixture all over the simmering apples, the clumps of butter and sugar sinking slightly into the warm filling. Once it was all covered, it was popped back into the oven for another ten minutes.

I looked over my shoulder at Ann. "Do you want me to whip up some fresh cream to put on top or do you want to test the pie plain?"

"Well everything is better with whipped cream so let's make some obviously," she rubbed her hands together. "But I'll taste it first without. I don't want any distractions from your masterpiece."

I knew she was teasing me but it made me feel good that she had high expectations. I grabbed a carton of cream from the oversized fridge and poured about a cup into one of the mixers. After attaching the beater I turned the machine onto medium-high.

I returned back to our conversation about my dating prospects. "So what do you think I should do with these four guys?" Not that Ann was a dating expert, but I was a firm believer that there was wisdom with age. "Should I send them a message and ask if they want to meet me somewhere?"

"I don't think you should meet them yet. Why don't you first have a few email conversations back-and-forth? Just to get to know them. You might find out they hate ice cream or something and your relationship would be a total disaster." She said this last part with a straight face but I knew she was messing with me.

"Okay, so what do I say? Hi, my name is Jenn and I'm interested in you? Tell me about yourself?" Holy cow. It was no wonder I was still single. I laid my forehead on the table and groaned.

"Ha ha, Jenn, you're taking this all too seriously. You're not asking for these guys to marry you. Just imagine you were at a party and you walked up to somebody you wanted to get to know. What would you say?"

When I didn't respond she answered her own question. "First start by telling them a bit about yourself. Tell them your name, what you do, things you're into. Basically tell them all the stuff that's on your profile summarized into a sentence or two. Then ask them about themselves. Where do they work? What do they like to do? Where do they live? You don't have to get into the real deep stuff yet. You're just feeling each other out."

I turned my head but didn't lift it up from the table. "Can you write these messages for me?"

"Jenn, you need to put on your big girl pants. These guys don't want to date me, so there's no point in me sending them a message. It has to be from you."

She stood and walked over to the mixer that was still beating the cream. She turned it off and added a few spoonfuls of sugar, then set it going again.

"You just need to write one; then you can send a duplicate message to all the guys. When you get some responses it'll be a lot easier to compare." She waved her hand emphatically. "See which of them seems easy-going and which of them seems a little stiff. Some of them might reply quicker than others. Maybe there will be one that doesn't reply at all."

"Your confidence is overwhelming," I said in a muffled voice since my face was still pressed against the table. I had to give it to her though, she gave a good pep talk. I just needed to stop thinking about it and do it.

I sat up and looked back at my phone again. I clicked on the first guy's profile then hit the "send a message" option. A blank box popped up with a cursor blinking back-and-forth at me.

"Hey David, my name is Jenn. I came across your profile and was interested in learning more about you. I am 26 years old and have lived in Irvine, CA for the past four years where I work at a local bakery..." I continued to ask him a few questions about himself. I finished by signing off as "Sincerely, Jenn".

I reread it once to make sure there were no spelling errors then hit send before I could talk myself out of it.

I threw my shoulders back before announcing, "I did it. I sent a message to guy number one."

Ann looked up from the mixing bowl she'd just turned off. "There, that wasn't so bad was it?" she asked as she gave the cream a single stir.

I shrugged sheepishly. "No, I guess it wasn't that big of a deal."

I decided to send my generic intro message to the other three guys. Like Ann said, there was no reason to make it too personalized. As she had so delicately pointed out, who knew if they'd even respond?

Once I was done I stood and walked over to my cooling pumpkin pie. I touched the pan with my hand and was happy to see it was just slightly warm.

I looked over at the oven and saw the apple pie had about 30 seconds left. Perfect.

"So, first we'll try the pumpkin pie. That will give the apple pie a few minutes to cool. I think it would be best to try them today and then try them again tomorrow morning once they've fully chilled and set. Just in case somebody took the pie home to serve at a party the following day or something. I want to make sure the quality is still good." I looked up at Ann. "How does that sound to you?"

She gave me a smile. "Very professional and I fully agree with you."

I pulled out the apple pie when the timer beeped and set it on a cooling rack. Then I turned back to the pumpkin pie. I took a knife and made my first cut into the soft, spicy scented filling. After plating two decent sized pieces, I grab the bowl of cream. Without looking up I said, "I'll put a dollop of this to the side so we can add it as needed."

After adding a generous serving of whipped cream to each plate I handed Ann one. "So, do you want me to describe everything to you, or would you prefer to taste it first?"

"Why don't you describe it first." She was biting her cheek to hold back a smile.

I gave her the rundown of the molasses filling, but then spent most the time describing the graham flavored crust. She seemed intrigued and nodded at all the right places.

Once I was done with my spiel, she picked up a fork and dug in.

I got my plate and took a giant bite myself. Not because I wanted it, I was slightly nauseous because of nerves, but I needed something to do with my hands.

Ann was silent, no reaction whatsoever. I swear the woman could've been a poker player with that face. She took another bite, this one accompanied by a scoop of whipped cream. She eventually flipped the piece over, inspecting the crust and tapping it with her fork. The suspense was killing me.

Finally her face broke into a smile. "Jenn, this pie is perfect. It's so delicious. It reminds me of a pumpkin pie my grandma would make, but there is something else to it, something that makes me keep coming back for more. You nailed it."

I gave a little squeal and jumped up and down. I didn't know why Ann's praise meant so much to me but it did. I think it was because she had always been my baking mentor; her good opinion was more valuable to me than anyone else's.

"I am so relieved!" I said with a giant sigh.

Ann glanced at me in surprise. "I didn't realize you were so stressed about this Jenn. I only did this taste testing as a formality. I was going to let you sell whatever you wanted, I trust your palette. I just wanted to get a couple free pies out of you." She winked.

"Really?" I knew Ann trusted me with the shop. I stood in for her whenever she went on vacation or out of town. However I didn't realize she had so much faith in my ability to create recipes or come up with new ideas. Once again a feeling of gratitude washed over me. "Ann you have no idea how much that means, thank you. Thank you for giving me the chance to do this."

She smiled and patted me on the back softly. "You need to believe in yourself a bit more Jenn. There are plenty of us that already do."

She took the last bite of her pumpkin pie and set her fork down. With questioning eyes she asked, "So how about that apple pie?"

Pumpkin Pie Recipe

· 1 (15 ounce) can pumpkin
· 1 (14 ounce) can Sweetened Condensed Milk
· 2 large eggs
· 1 Tbsp molasses
· 2 teaspoons ground cinnamon
· 1/2 teaspoon ground ginger
· 3/4 teaspoon ground nutmeg
· 1/2 teaspoon salt
· 1 (9 inch) unbaked pie crust

1.) Preheat oven to 425 degrees F. In a medium pan over low heat, heat up the canned pumpkin puree, molasses spices, and salt. Stir together until well combined, then set aside and allow to cool. (Heating it up like this takes out the canned pumpkin taste)

2.) Whisk cooked pumpkin mixture, sweetened condensed milk, and eggs in medium bowl until smooth. Pour into crust.

3.) Bake 15 minutes.

4.) Reduce oven temperature to 350 degrees F and continue baking 35 to 40 minutes or until knife inserted comes out clean.

Chapter 12

The apple pie was a success like the pumpkin. Ann said we could start selling both of them the following week. We just had to make sure our ingredient stock was in place.

On the way home from work I stopped off at my local gym. I know, I haven't mentioned I'm a member of a gym. I like to think of my monthly payment as more of a charitable contribution. I'm just helping out the gym employees, making sure they can put food on their tables.

But really, every time I paid my credit card, I looked at that gym membership line item amount and cringed. Then I usually re-committed myself to going more often (or at all) the following month. It rarely happened.

But since I was planning on meeting my future prince charming via Match.com soon, it was time to get that beach body I always talked about.

When it came to exercise I had a few issues: I hated running, I hated the elliptical, I basically hated any extended period of cardio. I was also not confident enough to go lift free weights with the rest of the bodybuilders. So my only other option was the gym classes.

I'd spent a solid hour scrolling through the class options last night and settled on something called Power Plus. Supposedly it was a mix of Pilates, yoga, and weightlifting. I was sure I'd regret it tomorrow, but they had a 3 PM class today which fit perfectly in my schedule. So that was where I was headed.

As I walked through the gym doors I handed the front desk girl my card, (which took me a solid 20 minutes to find since I couldn't remember the last time I'd used it). While waiting for her to scan it my phone buzzed with a text message.

I looked at the words on my screen. It was from Jessica. *Hey, how was last night? Did Luke tell you anything?*

Dang.

It was possible that the second reason I was going to the gym this afternoon was to avoid meeting Jessica at home. I wasn't ready to have that conversation with her.

"Excuse me, miss?"

I realized the girl at the desk had been holding my card out to me for about 30 seconds now. Her hair was pulled up in a tight ponytail and she was wearing a black spandex tank top that showed exactly how fit she was. I swear her arms would rival Arnold Schwarzenegger.

"Oh sorry, thank you!" I self-consciously took my card from her, very aware that my baggy T-shirt did nothing whatsoever for my figure. (Note to self: invest in a new workout wardrobe)

I started walking towards the locker room and quickly typed a message back to Jessica.

Tell you about it when I get home.

Yes, I was being a chicken.

I spent most of my time in the locker room trying to avoid all the naked women who had clearly lost all sense of modesty. Why were there always people like that in public gyms?

I found an open locker and stowed my bag and keys inside. I hung my lock on it and gave myself a mental pep talk. Okay, I had this, I was a healthy, young woman and I could tackle any fitness class here. I looked at the wall where the class schedules were listed and found the room number Power Plus was in.

I stopped at the drinking fountain on my way and used the time to spy on those entering the Power Plus classroom. The first two women looked to be in their mid-40s, nothing too threatening. I started feeling confident. That confidence dissipated when the next five women who entered looked like they could've been in a fitness magazine. Seriously, how did one even get quads that big?

I almost turned around but then I thought about the women in the locker room and how I didn't want to see them again. Beach body, here I came.

*****

An hour later I realized starting my new fit life with a Power Plus class wasn't my best idea. I probably should've started out with an hour walking on the treadmill.

The instructor could see me waning about 15 minutes into the class, so she tactfully informed everyone that the moves could be performed without free weights. Although when I say she "informed the class", what I really meant was she announced it over her microphone while staring directly at me.

I was grateful all the same. I didn't think I would've survived the rest of the class still holding those 8-pound dumbbells.

I bypassed the locker room showers, figuring I could shower at home. Public showers and restrooms always gave me the heebie-jeebies.

As I bent over to retrieve my bag from my locker my legs buckled. Tomorrow was going to be painful. If I was already sore now, things were going to be really bad in a few hours.

I made my way towards the gym front doors, hoping nobody noticed my stumbling walk. The girl at the desk was still there. She gave me a light wave and said, "See you soon!"

I smiled but what I really wanted to say was I wasn't sure if I would be walking tomorrow, let alone exercising.

I checked my phone one more time as I got in my car. Jessica had responded to my text.

Okay, see you around 6.

So that meant I had about an hour and a half to shower and decide what I was going to say to her. Scratch the shower, I was taking a long soak in the tub.

I never realized how many steps there were leading up to our second-floor apartment. There were exactly 18. It felt like 100.

I dropped my bag in the entrance of my room, stripped my clothes, and began running a bath almost hot enough to burn. I personally thought there was only one proper bath water temperature: scalding.

I decided to go extra fancy and threw in a bath bomb I'd picked up at Target last week. That dang dollar section aisle. It got me every time.

Our small bathroom was flooded with the scent of Jasmine as the bath bomb fizzled. When the tub was full I turned off the water and gingerly stepped in. My muscles ached and the water burned my skin but in a good way. I leaned back and rested my head on the edge of the tub. This was heaven. Well, actually our tub needed some jets, and then it would be heaven. But this was pretty close.

I soaked until my muscles felt like jelly and my skin was properly wrinkled. I stepped out and wrapped up in my sky blue robe.

There was nothing in life quite like a good robe. I wasn't one to pamper myself, but one of the best purchases I'd ever made was this organic, cotton terry robe I'd bought as a graduation present from Nordstrom. I didn't know if the organic part made any difference, but it sure sounded fancier.

I went to the kitchen and grabbed a water bottle, realizing I hadn't drunk anything since my class and was probably dehydrated. I even grabbed an apple and patted myself on the back for my serious commitment to becoming healthy.

Once I was back to my bedroom I eased on my bed, enveloping myself with pillows. After taking a long drink from my water I started considering how to break the news to Jessica. I should come straight out with the story. No trying to soften the blow or anything. That way she could draw her own conclusions and I wouldn't feel like I was influencing her one way or another.

With that decided I flipped open my laptop to check on my blog. My cream puff recipe had been a hit, but I'd seen several questions about the directions that needed to be addressed.

I was midway through explaining to someone that a half a cup of butter was the same thing as eight tablespoons of butter when Jessica got home.

She walked into my room and raised her eyebrows in surprise. I probably did look pretty funny, bundled up in a bathrobe, hair still semi-wet, propped up by pillows.

"You look cozy, what's the occasion?" She asked, sitting on the corner of my bed. She was dressed in one of her classic pants suits. It was a light gray color with a fuchsia pink blouse peeking through the top. Her hair was pinned up in a sophisticated bun as well.

"I went to the gym," I said simply.

Jessica, ever the exercise lover, was way too excited by this announcement. "You did? Yay, I'm so happy for you! Did you love it?"

She would ask if I loved the gym. "Well, I'm not sure if I'll be able to stand tomorrow, but hopefully I at least worked off the Snickers I ate for lunch."

Jessica looked at me sternly. "Jenn, you can't just work out and expect to get results. You have to fuel your body properly too. I'm not saying you have to cut out all sweets." Oh no, she was warming up to one of her favorite topics, "But you need to make sure you're eating plenty of lean proteins and complex carbs. They'll really help get you through your workouts and build muscle mass."

Before she could give me a full health spiel I cut her off. "I know, I know. Look," I said lifting up the apple I had taken a single bite out of, "I'm already changing my ways. Next thing you know I'll be drinking a kale smoothie."

Jessica rolled her eyes but it seemed to settle her down. "Fine, enough about your new love for fitness. Tell me about last night."

I took a deep breath and slowly closed my laptop. "So, first off I'd like to say that your bread turned out very well." I was hoping this would get a smile out of her, but she just narrowed her eyes. "Anyway," I rushed on, "so when I asked Luke how things were between you two he told me they were fine." I lingered here for a moment, seeing if she had any reaction to this.

"So? That was it? That's all you both said?"

I looked away and fiddled with the ties on my robe. "No, I probed him a little more, seeing if he'd give me any information or thoughts." I glanced up quickly then back down. "I don't know Jess, the second he could tell I wanted information he clammed up. He even left the apartment for a little bit."

"He left?" Her eyes were wide, obviously not expecting this answer.

"Yeah well, the bread was in the oven so we were just sitting around waiting for it. He said he had an errand to run so he left. When he got back we didn't say much. I could tell he didn't want to talk about you guys so I didn't bring it up again. He basically waited for the bread and then left once it was done." I chewed on my bottom lip and waited for her reaction.

"Was he normal before that?" Poor Jessica looked so confused. "Like was he weird all evening or was it just after you asked him about me?"

"It was after I started asking him." Despite my resolve not to influence her, I had to do something. She looked so sad. "But you never know Jess, maybe he just doesn't like to talk about his feelings. Maybe the thought of his girlfriend's roommate questioning him made him nervous."

Jessica made a face. "Not Luke. You know that's not his personality. And when has he ever been nervous to talk to you? He tells me all the time how awesome he thinks you are, he would've had no problem spilling everything to you."

I really wanted to pursue her comment about Luke thinking I was awesome but I refrained. This wasn't about me. Focus Jenn. "It was a little bizarre."

"I knew it," Jessica's eyes were beginning to well up with tears. "I knew something was up. I kept trying to tell myself it was all in my head but it clearly wasn't." Jessica kicked her heels off on the floor and curled her legs up under her on the bed. "I just don't understand, why he wouldn't say something to me! If he's over it, why doesn't he tell me instead of acting all weird?"

"It's a pretty stupid move." I tossed her a pillow and she flopped back on it.

"Right?" Jessica was warming up to her subject. "It's not like I'm some crazy girlfriend. I'm not going to stalk him and beg him to come back. Ugh! Men are so dumb sometimes!"

"They really are." I knew my role here. Be the sympathetic friend who offered soothing yet pointless commentary while she let loose all her feelings.

"I should call him up right now and tell him that I'm done with us. I don't have time for ridiculous games. I can't believe I'm even sitting here wasting time thinking about him." Jessica went on like this for another five minutes or so. I let her go until she ran out of steam.

When she had nothing left to say I intervened.

"Come on," I said as I chucked my apple into the trash. I hopped over to my closet, looking for some clothes. "We need to go pick up some real reinforcements."

"Reinforcements?" Jessica asked.

"Yes, I'm sitting here eating an apple during a boyfriend bashing session. It goes against all of nature's laws."

Jessica caught on to my meaning. "But you just started your healthy eating!"

"Psssh, healthy eating is for the birds. This is an emergency." I threw on a T-shirt and jeans. "And good news," I added with a grin, "I have it on firsthand account that Oreos are on sale at Target this week."

*****

We did what two girls who were ticked at a guy did best: stocked up on all the junk food available.

We looked like quite the pair, Jessica, still dressed in her business suit and rocking some high heels compared to me who appeared to have just rolled out of bed (which I guess I literally did).

But considering we had a cart full of Oreos, salt and vinegar chips, red vines, Ben & Jerry's, a 1/2 lb chocolate bar, and finally a tub of hummus and carrots (Jessica threw that in at the last moment out of guilt)... I didn't think too many people were focused on what we were wearing.

They were probably more concerned about our cholesterol levels.

We brought the goods home and settled on the couch to eat ourselves into a coma. We continued bashing Luke, getting ourselves into fits of giggles at the ridiculousness of our accusations.

But by the end of the night though Jessica had turned somber again.

"So, honestly what do you think I should do?" She was scooping out the last bites of the ice cream carton.

I stopped chewing my red vine and considered for a moment. "I still think the same thing I thought before. You should ask him where he's at. Just clear up the matter once and for all. Despite his communication issues, Luke is a pretty awesome guy." I didn't say that these were actually my personal feelings towards him. "I think if there's any chance that this was a fluke, he had a bad week at work or something, you should give him the opportunity to explain himself."

"Fine," she said with a sigh. "I guess you're right."

"Of course I am," I said with confidence. "Now onto more important things. Do you want to split the chocolate bar with me?"

Jessica just laughed.

*****

We finally went to bed around 11 PM, which I know isn't a big deal for most people but that was super late for me. Four in the morning came very early. The worst part was once I got into bed I couldn't even fall asleep. My head was full of all the things that happened that day.

First I continued thinking about Jessica and Luke. I was so bugged by Luke. Did he have any idea the turmoil he was causing over here? He needed to just talk to Jessica if he was feeling uncertain about them.

Next, I start thinking about my online dating. I'd usually sat back and let things happen when it came to my love life.

Which, to be clear, nothing had ever really happened with my love life.

So I was proud of myself for sticking my neck out there with online dating. It wasn't something I normally would've even considered. Who knew, maybe it would pay off.

I also thought about my gym regime. Even though today was completely wasted after our late junk food binge, it was a start. I needed to go through the classes again and choose one I was more suited to. Power Plus was too over my head at this point.

Finally, I started running over the pie taste testing with Ann. While I was excited she wanted to include my pies in the menu, the real thrill I got was thinking about how this could be the start of my own bakery. It would be great to see what the demand was for pie in the area, was it as high as I thought it would be?

At the same time, I realized how nuts it was that I was even contemplating opening my own store. Who did I think I was? I didn't have any business experience. I didn't know how to finance, market, or run a company.

If someone would have asked me six months ago if I would ever open my own bakery, I would've laughed. I would've said it was a great dream but not a reality. And here I was writing out business plans and contemplating how I could get there. I tried to think of what the turning point was for me. What was it that had made me start believing I could really do this?

I realized there was one influencing person: Luke. From the beginning, Luke had been supportive about everything I'd mentioned.

The first time I suggested the idea of my own bakery he'd been all for it. Every time I threw out any shred of doubt he combated it with confidence. I didn't think anyone had believed in me as much as he had.

It was an ironic twist that now he and Jessica were probably over, my main cheerleader was disappearing.

And as sad as I was for Jessica, I felt a sudden sense of loss for myself.

Chapter 13

Friday morning everyone agreed my pies still tasted amazing. Even Carly said the apple pie was one of the best she'd ever had.

As such, orders were put in for the additional ingredients we needed to start selling them.

Ann also started looking into hiring a student part-time to help with the bookkeeping. I didn't want to say it, but I was happy Ann was branching out and hiring new employees. Not that my plan to open a bakery was even slightly settled, but it made me feel better knowing I wouldn't leave Ann high and dry if I did.

I plowed into the weekend happy and hopeful. Well at least about everything besides Jessica and Luke. By Saturday evening Jessica still hadn't resolved anything with him since our powwow.

When I asked her about it she made non-committal excuses. Luke was busy at a work event, she had some unexpected errands to run, etc.

But on Sunday night when she asked me if I wanted to stay in and watch old Friends reruns with her (not that I was busy, my current Sunday night plans were to fold the mountain of laundry on my bed) I had to push her.

"Jessica, I thought you were going to figure this out with Luke. What's going on?"

She looked away from me and shrugged. "I am going to; we just haven't been able to get together yet. He's on a work trip until next Tuesday." She lifted her hands in mock resignation. "So there's nothing I can do until then."

I rolled my eyes at her. "Jess, you are two adults. You both have phones. Pick up your phone and call him."

"I've texted him a couple times asking how he is. I don't want to bother him at his conference though. She turned and walked over to the couch. As she slumped down she simultaneously grabbed the remote off the coffee table. "Besides," she said, talking over her shoulder, "that is a conversation I should have face-to-face. No one wants to break up over the phone."

I guess she was right. I scooped up my laundry and carried it to the living room. If I was going to fold laundry I might as well be watching TV. "All right, what season are we on?"

Jessica smiled at me. "Let's start at the beginning."

*****

I spent Monday afternoon finishing two new posts for my blog. I was aware that my interest in blogging had been waning. I used to put out at least three posts a week, however the last month I was averaging only one or two. Luckily I had a library of recipes already on my site so I didn't have any lack of traffic.

That was the good thing about blogging, especially food blogging. Half the battle was building up your repertoire of content so when people landed on your website, they stuck around for a while.

But mainly I was realizing that I didn't want to spend the rest of my life as a food blogger. It had been a fun side hustle for a while, but I wasn't super passionate about it long term.

I needed something bigger and more challenging. I think this was why I was spending so much time thinking about my own bakery. I don't think I'd ever be satisfied until I did it.

I was pondering all this as I walked into the gym Tuesday afternoon.

Yes, I had re-committed myself to stay in shape after Thursday night's binge. It might've had something to do with the fact that two of the men I messaged on Match.com had responded.

One of them that replied was David, the first guy. He was actually pretty cute and funny in his reply. I'd already answered him and hoped it went somewhere.

The second guy was named Ron. He seemed pretty nice but very reserved and formal. I figured that wasn't something I should hold against him so I also replied to him. I had to keep my options open after all.

A third had also replied, but he mentioned that he was in the middle of a move to New York City, so he'd be unavailable. I still hadn't heard back from the fourth.

So here I was, getting my fitness on. There was a different girl working the front desk, but she looked as ripped as the first had. I wondered if I'd look like her one day. Probably not, I loved my sugar too much.

I was nervous as I entered. At least I had done my research this time. Considering I spent two days after that Power Plus class walking around like a corpse, I decided I wasn't ready for it yet.

Instead, I was trying out a class called Beginner Pilates today. Anything with the word beginner in it was right up my alley.

As I walked past a mirror (why were all gyms covered in mirrors?) I remembered my other motivation to work out today. I'd gotten some new workout clothes. I had done some online shopping over the weekend and bought myself a new pair of cropped leggings that felt like butter they were so soft. I'd also purchased a purple tank top with a cute keyhole cutout in the back. I knew it sounded vain, but I was way more motivated to exercise while wearing an attractive outfit.

Once I reached the locker room I threw my hair up in a tight ponytail and stowed my bag in a locker. There was the same horde of women throwing modesty to the wind in the locker room.

It took me a minute to find the classroom. As I scanned the area a second a guy walked by me and caught my eye. He was probably in his early 30s, attractive, and extremely in shape. When he smiled and gave me a small wink I almost felt like turning around to make sure he was looking at me.

It was amazing what a confidence booster that was. Maybe I did need to put myself out there more often, stop staying in my safe shell of work/home life all the time.

I felt like the last month and a half I had mentally been doing a 180 in terms of what I wanted in life. Not only was I taking command of my career goals, I was taking command of my social and love life. I was being assertive and taking chances that I never would've before.

I liked it. I liked the new me. I liked the confidence and the determination I was allowing myself.

I strutted off to my classroom with a new pep in my step. Watch out Beginner Pilates, here I came.

*****

Pilates kicked my butt pretty hard, but the new me took it as a challenge to get better.

I smiled and waved at the desk girl as I left, informing her that I would see her soon before she could say it to me.

As I stepped outside the gym doors, the bright sunlight pierced my eyes. I felt my phone vibrate in my bag, with a text message. My hand fumbled around for a minute, trying to locate where it was.

It was a message from Jessica. It read:

We're done. Luke broke up with me this afternoon. I'm heartbroken.

TWO YEARS LATER

Chapter 14

Beep... Beep... Beep...

I could hear the sound of Mitch's delivery truck backing up in front of the shop.

"Hey Olivia! Mitch is here for pick up. Can you help me take some of these out to him?" The blonde girl I was speaking to popped her head up from under the counter.

"Sure Jenn, let me just finish putting these bowls down here."

I loaded myself up with two trays of pies and headed out towards the front of my shop.

Yep, you heard that right, my shop. Well, technically it was just a kitchen, no actual storefront. But it was mine. Home of Jenn's Sweets.

I know, the name was totally boring and unoriginal. It didn't start out that way. Actually, none of it started out the way it was now. It was a long story.

Out front was a white delivery truck with its back open and a man standing next to it. He was wearing cargo shorts a decade out of fashion, a loose grey T-shirt, and a Dodgers baseball cap. At a heavy 6' 3" and with a scruffy beard to match, he looked like he belonged in the middle of a forest hunting bears, not in the heart of Orange County delivering baked goods.

But Mitch was the best delivery man south of LA and I'd worked hard to gain his services.

"Morning Jenn, how's the day going?"

"Oh good," I replied, "the same old same old."

He took the tray of pies from me and motioned to the clipboard he'd set on the hood. As he settled the pies into the truck I flipped through the clipboard's pages. It was a list of the scheduled drop-offs for the day. I scrolled through and double checked that everything was correct. I signed my name at the bottom.

"Yep, everything looks good, as usual." I set the clipboard back on the truck and turned around as Olivia came out with an additional load of pies. I headed back in to grab the last load of pies and cookies.

So what is this Jenn's Sweets?

It took me about nine months of prep work before I finally was able to open my own store. Months of business planning, getting permits, real estate hunting, getting bank loans—basically one headache after another. There were several times I wanted to throw in the towel, but I kept going.

Eventually I did it. A little under a year and a half ago I opened The Rolling Pin.

That name was so much cuter than Jenn's Sweets.

I started out with a bang, so gung-ho and excited to be selling my wares. I was hawking pies, cookies, brownies, cupcakes—basically any bakery item you could think of was coming out of my shop in the beginning.

And guess what? It totally bombed. I mean I was in *serious* financial trouble after about two months of opening. It's not that people didn't love my stuff. Because they did. I think my biggest failure was my lack of marketing. Well, at least effective marketing. I just didn't realize the volume of customers it took to keep a bakery running. Baked goods aren't known for their high profit margins.

To be honest, my life in general had gone downhill. I had no energy for dating, no time for exercise, my blog was like the forgotten middle child, and all because my great big business gamble was turning out to be a flop.

I spent my days working like a maniac and my nights stress eating all my feelings on my couch. (And I couldn't even afford to binge eat Ben and Jerry's at that point—I had to stick to the cheap store brand ice cream)

Let's just say those were some dark weeks, I didn't like to think about them anymore. However, like most things in life, another door opened.

One day a man came in my shop. He wasn't one of my regular customers, he was dressed in a sharp business suit and had a corporate air about him.

He spent a couple seconds scanning the items I had out on display before turning to me.

"Can I help you find something today?" I was a one woman show in those days. I did all the baking and front cashier work.

He shoved his hands in his pockets and fidgeted a minute, "Do you happen to do catering?"

I didn't, but at that point I was willing to take anything. "Of course we do! Do you have an event you need help with?" I like to think of it more as flexing the truth then straight up lying.

"I'm kind of in a tight spot. My daughter's eighth birthday party is this weekend and my wife and I agreed that she would take care of all the party planning if I'd take care of ordering all the food and stuff." He stared at the display case instead of me. "I, uh, unfortunately forgot about it until yesterday when she asked if I had everything in place."

I bit my cheek to stop my laugh.

"Well, that does sound like quite a tight spot. May I ask how many are coming to this party?" I was surprised he was so worried. It couldn't be that hard to find some treats for a little girl's birthday party could it?

"Probably close to 100."

Oh. Well that was a different story. How many friends could one eight year old have?

He must have noticed my reaction because he began explaining. "My wife and I are both fairly prominent in our careers, so we have a lot of family and work friends coming to the event. I'm actually not sure how the guest list got so big. My wife was in charge of that."

I quickly calculated how possible this job would be. I could probably do it. I probably wouldn't sleep the next few nights but I could do it.

"Looks like I'm your girl." I finally answered.

Like I imagined it was a hectic next couple of days. But I pulled it off beautifully and the guy was extremely appreciative. Turned out he was the CEO of a small manufacturing company. He ended up using me for several work events and passed my name along to other work contacts.

It was a snowball effect from there, but about four months later I was almost exclusively doing corporate catering. Not only was it more lucrative but I was much better at managing that style of the business.

I realized I needed a brand pivot. I officially branded myself as a corporate catering company and changed the name to Jenn's Sweets. Branding for the corporate world was very different than for a retail location. I wanted companies to recognize what I offered immediately from my name. Even though The Rolling Pin was a whole lot more fun, Jenn's Sweets got a whole lot more clientele.

It took another year before I became financially stable. But I did it.

And slowly we'd grown. I currently had two part-time assistants. Olivia was a college senior getting a degree in food science. She worked with me on Mondays and Wednesdays. My other assistant was Becca. She had plans to become a professional cake decorator and she worked with me on Tuesdays and Thursdays.

Jenn's Sweets was only open Monday through Thursday. Fridays I officially set aside for working on my blog. My blog had taken a backseat the first year Jenn's Sweets opened, but now that things were steadier I was able to give it more time. I enjoyed it more too.

The menu of Jenn's Sweets had transformed over the years as well. Instead of focusing on all the possibilities, I was much more targeted.

Jenn's Sweets only offered three major options.

First, we had our oversized cookies that were individually wrapped in kraft paper sleeves.

Second, we offered a collection of mini, individual pies. Essentially I took all my normal pie recipes and sized them down into 2-inch mini pie pans—the perfect single portion. These were by far my most popular item for catering events. There was something about getting your own pie that people loved.

Finally, we offered a selection of bars and brownies. These were offered party platter/tray style and were great for really large events. I didn't want to brag, but I probably made the best brownie west of the Mississippi.

And this was what my dream had become. The goal, the one I never thought in a million years I'd actually go for, had happened.

Olivia helped me bring the last of the items out of the truck and Mitch looked over the clipboard one more time before nodding at me. "All right boss, I'll have this delivered for you. Anything else I should know for the day?"

Running my fingers through my hair I looked up thoughtfully. "Nope. Let me know if you have any issues."

He gave me the thumbs up and looked over at Olivia. "How's school going missy?"

That was the best part about Mitch. He treated everybody as if they were his kid sister.

She grinned. "It's killing me, but I only have three more semesters so I think I'll survive."

He smiled back at her. "What's Jenn going to do when you're gone?"

I threw my hands up in mock exasperation. "We're going to have to close that's what. No Olivia, no Jenn's Sweets!"

Olivia laughed and Mitch smiled as he hopped into the truck. He left with a light beep of his horn and Olivia and I went back inside the building.

I went to the oversized calendar on the desk in the corner. I double checked today's events to make sure we'd covered them all. It was Thursday, so we had nothing to worry about for tomorrow. I scanned ahead to Monday. Nothing too big then either. We had two luncheons, one for an engineering firm and one for a dentist office. Then a real estate company had a series of open houses they wanted pies delivered to. Everything else looked good.

I turned to Olivia who was putting away the pans we'd used that morning. "Well looks like we're all finished for the day." I raised my eyebrows. "Any weekend plans?"

She shrugged her shoulders. "Nothing big. I'm sure there will be a party somewhere. Nothing crazy though." She walked over to the desk and grabbed her shoulder bag. "How about you? Any plans?"

"You know me, I'm a party animal. Always something going on."

She lifted her hands as if to raise the roof, bringing a grin out of me.

"Actually, I do have a baby shower, but other than that the only thing I have scheduled is a cycling class this afternoon." I shook my head. "Don't get old Olivia, all that happens is you become boring."

"Well if you're already considered old, I don't have too many years left."

We made our way towards the front door. Olivia got in her little Mini Cooper and I walked down the block to my Honda Accord.

Oh, I didn't mention I got a car upgrade. I am officially driving a vehicle from this decade. It's the little things in life.

From work I drove directly to the gym where my cycling class was waiting for me. After I made it through Jenn's Sweets rough beginning I re-dedicated myself to exercising regularly. I wasn't saying I was a workout warrior, but I was a regular at my gym about three times a week. Anymore was too much commitment, any less and my curves got a little too curvy.

Lately I'd really gotten into cycling classes. There was something about being in a dark room with music blaring that pumped me up.

I waved at the front desk girl as I passed through the entrance. I didn't actually know her name, but we had one of those relationships where we were like: "hey, we're kind of friends, neither of us knows each other's names but we always give a friendly wave".

I was running a little behind so I quickly stowed my stuff in my locker. The last year and a half I'd claimed locker 24C as my own. Don't ask me why, but I always used the same one. It gave me a sense of belonging, probably like how an NBA basketball player feels when they walked up to their locker. Maybe we weren't quite in the same classification but still.

I laced up my shoes and I hustled off to class.

The best thing about working out at two in the afternoon was there weren't many other people at the gym. The class usually only had about 7 to 8 other cyclists, which was perfect in my mind.

"Alright folks, let's get started!" the instructor was getting into her pre workout pep talk. "I want you to forget about that brownie sundae you ate last night and think about how many miles you're going to kill on your bike today!"

A brownie sundae actually did sound pretty good right now...

Fifty minutes later I finished my cycling class dripping with sweat. There was something about having sweat actually falling off your face that made you feel like you'd been working extra hard. It helped that they kept the room uncomfortably warm.

I toweled off as best as I could, then headed out to my car. As I walked I thought about what I was going to do next.

The baby shower I told Olivia about was for Bree's baby. Yep, a year of marriage had pulled out all her domestic instincts and she was now seven months pregnant with a baby girl.

And as strange as it seemed, she was really excited about it. Bree attacked the idea of motherhood with a bizarrely organized and structured viewpoint. Basically how you'd assume a lawyer would do it. I was pretty sure she'd read every baby book available and had a spreadsheet of every baby item she needed.

At any rate, her baby shower was this weekend and I still had to pick up a present. Something I wanted to get done this afternoon since I was planning on spending tomorrow baking and photographing some new recipes.

I decided the people of Target could deal with my slightly sweaty appearance and I would stop on my way home.

On my drive over I texted Paul asking how his day was. I haven't mentioned Paul have I? Paul was my boyfriend. Yep. That's right. I had an official boyfriend.

About three months ago I met Paul online. I'm an online dating success story. Well at least I hope I will be.

Similar to my baking business, it took awhile for the online dating to get off the ground. I don't think I had my first date until four months after I posted my profile. But once things got rolling I met a good amount of potential men. Most of them lost their potential after the first date, but still.

The first year was a lot of fun. I never met anyone I was really excited about, but it was still new. Then I met Paul.

Initially, I wasn't super interested in him. He was your average, boy-next-door kind of guy who worked as a pharmaceutical sales rep in LA.

Our first date was dinner and a movie. It was so cliché I almost said no. I had a surprisingly good time though so I ended up going out with him a second time. Next thing I knew we had been steadily dating for three weeks and Jessica was asking if we were official.

That was about three months ago, we'd been going steady ever since.

I still wasn't sure about my feelings. I liked him. He was a great guy. One of those guys who would make a great husband, a great father, a great provider... he basically checked all the boxes.

It was just... he was a little boring sometimes. But maybe it was me. Something I needed to get over.

At any rate, we were still together and I could truly say I was happy. Just maybe not excited. It was a topic for another day.

His response to my text was quick.

Good, work is pretty boring—we were at a health seminar all morning. How about you?

It was good, nothing crazy happened. I'm headed to Target to get a present for Bree's baby shower tomorrow.

Cool. You doing anything tonight?

No, probably do some financial stuff for the bakery—
you have your work dinner right?
Yeah, I'd rather be hanging out with you though.
I sent him a little emoji heart as a goodbye. I probably
should feel more remorse that we couldn't hang out tonight
but I wasn't really bummed. I was probably a terrible
girlfriend.

Pushing the thought from my mind I headed inside for
the baby section of Target.

If there was anything that could make a woman baby
hungry, it was shopping for them. Thank heavens for
registries because I'd have bought the entire baby section
otherwise.

I pulled up Bree's registry on my phone and scrolled
through it. I saw a set of bottles she'd saved. It wasn't the
most exciting present, but it was definitely something Bree
would appreciate.

I couldn't resist throwing in an adorable set of pajamas
with pink elephants on them as well. It was amazing what
babies could get away with wearing. I picked up a few
random necessities while I was in there too. Shampoo, new
razor blades, replacement light bulbs, a pair of high heels...
like I said, necessities.

By the time I checked out I made my usual vow to not
shop at Target ever again. A vow I was never able to keep
longer than about two weeks. But at least the shoes were
cute.

*****

By the time I made it home it was about 5:30 PM.
Jessica was home, doing what I would consider her new

favorite hobby: looking through wedding magazines on our couch.

Because Jessica was basically engaged.

Every time I said that she got all huffy and said she wasn't actually engaged yet. Considering she and her boyfriend Jake had gone ring shopping together, picked out a wedding venue, and scheduled flights for their honeymoon, I would call it pretty official.

But that was just me.

Jessica protested it wasn't official until Jake got down on one knee and she had the ring on her finger. It had to be coming sometime in the next month. Knowing Jake, he was probably coming up with some elaborate proposal scheme that Jessica would love. That was why they were perfect for each other.

Ironically enough, Jessica and Jake met online. After Luke broke up with her, Jessica had a rough couple of months. I didn't realize how invested she had been in that relationship. She'd gone through lots of guys over the years, but Luke had really gotten a hold of her heart.

When she finally came out of her post breakup shell she decided to try online dating. She'd seen the fun I'd been having and was in desperate need of some herself.

Turned out Jake was the first guy who messaged her. Let's just say she shut down her account after their first date. The rest was history.

She looked up at me when I walked in the door. "Jenn, perfect, I need an opinion. Which of these dress styles do you prefer?" She held up two magazines and I could see that both were thoroughly bookmarked with sticky notes.

I set my bag down and walked over, taking the magazines from her hands. I looked at the two pictures; the dresses were very similar. One had a strapless, sweetheart neckline, while the other had an asymmetrical, one-shoulder neckline. Other than that they could've been the same dress. Both were fitted through the hips then flared out in a full skirt. There were delicate beading patterns on the bodice of both. The one-shoulder dress appeared to have a long train as well.

"Well, obviously you would look beautiful in both of these," I began diplomatically. "The sweetheart neckline would show off your shoulders, but the one shoulder is a little more unique. Plus I looove that long train."

I know some people were all about simplicity when it came to their wedding, but in my mind you only got married once (hopefully) so you might as well go all out. Long trains, floor-length veils, I loved it all.

Jessica was nodding her head. "I know, those are kind of my thoughts too. That long train is dreamy isn't it?" She ripped the two pictures out of the magazines and set them on a large stack on the table.

I eyed the pile questioningly. "Well, it doesn't look like those are your only two options anyway."

She let out a long sigh. "Yes, this whole wedding planning is way more stressful than I thought."

"And think, you're not even engaged yet. How's it going to be when you actually have a fiancé?" I said with a straight face.

She chucked a pillow at me. "You can mock me Jenn, but when you get married you're going to realize what I mean."

I smiled brightly, but inside I felt that same twinge of sadness. What if it never happened to me? What if I never found *the one*?

All my other friends had tied the knot and were living out their lives. Sometimes I felt like I was in the same spot as I was ten years ago. Not in my career. I'd made more leaps and bounds in that than I ever thought possible. But emotionally I felt stuck. Which was ridiculous considering I had a boyfriend.

Paul was great. He really was.

Sometimes I felt like this was my mantra that I had to continually repeat to myself. Yes, that should have been a red flag. But the fact that I was finally in a committed relationship, even if I was only halfway committed, was a big step for me and one I wasn't ready to let go of.

Jessica didn't seem to notice my melancholy thoughts as she looked at my Target bag. "Target huh? I thought you'd banned yourself from that store?"

"I had to get a baby present for Bree. So I made an exception to my rule. But I'm going back to banning the store after this trip," I said like the sacrificial lamb I was.

"What did you get her? I could barely stop myself from buying all the baby shoes last week." Jessica hopped up and rummaged through my bag. Of course she first admired the high heels. They were a pair of nude slingbacks that I didn't need. It was a pity Jessica and I had different sized feet. With our powers combined, we would've had a shoe collection to rival Macy's.

Next, she pulled out the pajamas I bought and appropriately squealed in delight. "Oh my gosh, these are so cute! I want a baby just so I have a reason to buy their clothes!" She folded the jammies up and placed them back in the bag.

"The boring side of my gift is some bottles." I shrugged my shoulders helplessly. "Somebody had to buy them for her so I took the fall."

Jessica grinned at me. "You always were the martyr of our group. Thanks for letting me buy the cute stuff."

I picked up my gym bag and started heading towards my room. "You have any plans for tonight?"

"I'm going over to Jake's in a bit. We'll probably watch a movie or something. You?" She started stacking her bridal magazines in a nice pile.

"Nothing exciting. I need to work on some financial reports for the bakery so I'll most likely get that done before the weekend." I hadn't quite gotten to the point where I could hire outside help for my bookkeeping. Maybe another year or so, but for now that was part of my job description.

Jessica smiled at me, "Don't have too much fun with that."

"Oh, you know me, nothing riles me up quite like an Excel spreadsheet."

Chapter 15

I ended up going to bed fairly early that night, I knew I had a full day of baking tomorrow and I wanted to get an early start. It was strange, but by spending less time on my blog these days, I was more purposeful in the direction I wanted it to go. It was like taking a step back and looking at the big picture made me see where I really needed to spend my time.

I was now only posting one new recipe a week which allowed my blog to live off the horde of recipes I'd already published. Plus it gave me more time to actually interact with my readers.

But today was a day for some new stuff. I had this idea for a s'mores trifle. I was going to make a layer of toasted marshmallow whipped cream, a layer of graham cracker crumbs, then a layer of crumbled fudge brownies. It was going to be good.

The second recipe I was going to try out was a peanut butter version of chocolate lava cakes. Anything that combined peanut butter and chocolate was a definite winner in my book.

I spent most of the morning working on the trifle. While it was a straightforward dessert, it took a fair amount of time since it had so many parts.

It was around noon when Paul called to see what I was up to. I was waiting for the brownies to cool so I could assemble the trifle and start taking pictures.

"Hey babe," he said when I answered. He always called me babe, which I know was a totally cliché pet name, but I loved it just the same. "What are you up to today?"

"Oh you know, the usual. Finding all the ways I can combine butter and sugar together." This was our running joke.

"Typical." I knew he was smiling into his phone. "I was wondering if you want to go out to dinner with me tonight. Or do you have another date scheduled?"

"Hmmm," I said noncommittally. "I'll have to check my schedule. I'm a hot item these days."

"What if I told you we'd get Italian? Does that change your mind?" Italian food. It was the perfect combination of carbs and more carbs. My heart's true love.

"Done," I responded immediately. What could I say, I was an easy target.

We chatted for a few more minutes. He told me about his work dinner last night. I told him what I was making this morning for my blog. He made me promise to save him some.

After I hung up I tested my brownies, they were the perfect room temperature. Time to start layering.

The bottom of the trifle was a thick layer of crumbled brownies. On top of that, I scooped out dollops of my marshmallow whipped cream. On top of that, I sprinkled crushed graham crackers and drizzled it with fudge sauce.

Rinse and repeat. By the time I was done it looked like a culinary masterpiece. I set it in the fridge to chill until it was time to photograph.

Now time for the peanut butter chocolate lava cakes.

*****

Paul picked me up around 6:30 PM.

I figured Italian was somewhere in between formal and casual, so I wore a pair of dark wash jeans and a black tank top topped with a slim cut blazer.

I just finished putting on a dash of lip gloss when I heard the doorbell ring.

When I opened the door Paul was standing there. He was dressed in dark jeans himself and a forest green polo. He was actually a pretty good looking guy. He had more of the 'hot nerdy guy' vibe than the 'hot athletic guy', but I wasn't going to complain. His dark hair was set off by green eyes, which were always framed by a pair of thick-rimmed glasses. He even managed to pull off the fair, freckled skin he was stuck with remarkably well.

When he saw me he responded with his usual "Hey babe!" and gave me a quick peck.

I always wondered at those pecks. It was our usual greeting and I often speculated if it was a sign. Shouldn't I want to have a serious make-out session, if not at least a legit kiss with my boyfriend every time I saw him?

Because I didn't. I was totally satisfied with that quick peck. I probably could've even done without it if I needed to. I moved on from this line of thinking and focused on what he was saying to me.

"So, how was the photography session?"

Sometimes I hated how nice he was. He was always asking about me and my life, wanting to know everything. It was a hard act to keep up with.

"Great! All my desserts were on their best behavior." I gave him a little wink. "And I even saved you some."

He smiled and grabbed my hand. "Sounds awesome, you'll have to show me the photos later. Are you ready? I'm starving."

I grabbed my purse on the counter and nodded. "You know I'm always ready for Italian."

*****

Our date went well, we chatted about the usual stuff, his work, my work, he asked if Jessica was officially engaged yet... we somehow managed to fill a full two hours of dinner, but looking back I couldn't tell you if we discussed anything meaningful.

Our conversations were kind of like our relationship, surface level.

As silly as it sounded, I wasn't sure if that was normal. I hadn't had too many serious relationships in my life. Maybe this was just the natural progression. But I didn't think so.

Jessica was my biggest confidant. I didn't tell her all my worries, but enough to make her question why Paul and I were still together. That was not to say she didn't like Paul. When we began dating she was actually super excited for me—he seemed like my perfect match on paper. However the longer we dated (and the less enthused I was about it), the more she thought I should end things with him.

I had to say I agreed with her most of the time. One of my biggest hang ups was the actual breaking up part. I didn't know how to do it. It seemed like way too awkward of a conversation to have.

The other reason I kept holding off was because there was nothing seriously wrong with us. He was fun to hang out with and it wasn't like I had anyone better on the horizon. Why mess up a good thing?

Saturday morning started with my usual routine. I went to another cycling class, then came home and did the housework/laundry I'd put off all week.

Bree's baby shower was at 1 PM, but it was up in LA, so Jessica and I were planning on leaving around noon to make it in time. Good old LA traffic was always something you had to account for.

I wrapped my present in the oversized gift bag I picked up at Target. Wrapping up baby clothes was almost as much fun as buying them. I think I probably killed at least three trees with the amount of pink tissue paper I stuffed inside.

When I was done getting ready I knocked on Jessica's door. "You ready to go?" There was a muffled reply so I opened it. Jessica was walking out of her closet with a pair of shoes in hand and a gift bag in the other.

"You know it, let's do this." She held up her light pink gift bag in mock victory. "I even managed to wrap my present. That's a feat for me."

I smiled and held up my bag as well. "We are on our A-game today."

We drove Jessica's car. She was more familiar with the route since she drove to LA almost on a daily basis these days. We chatted about all the important topics. Aka: her wedding and my relationship with Paul.

"It's so hard to narrow it down! I mean I love the rustic vibe with its rich colors and textures, but then I love the light and airiness of a neutral theme too." Jessica smacked the steering wheel.

We'd spent the last 20 minutes discussing her wedding colors and theme and had so far gotten nowhere.

"There's got to be some sort of middle ground. Maybe do the rustic theme with neutral colors? The best of both worlds?" Considering the frown on her face she wasn't buying into my theory.

"But the dark colors are what I love about the rustic theme!"

I blame Pinterest for her indecisiveness. These days a girl couldn't choose a theme and stick with it for longer than about two weeks before another one caught her eye on there. We needed to go back to the good all days were all you had was the wedding magazines to get inspiration from.

We eventually moved on to Paul. It was the same conversation we'd had before. Was the spark really there? But he was such a good guy! Was I was even into him? But what else was I looking for? It was like a seesaw back-and-forth, back-and-forth.

"I don't know Jenn. I don't want to tell you what to do, but I'm not sure if this thing between you guys is going anywhere. Could you ever see yourself marrying Paul?"

"I don't know... probably not. But maybe? He'd be a great dad you know."

"Yes, he would. And I hope whoever you marry will be a great dad. But I don't think that should be the deciding factor on your future spouse." Jessica was back to smacking her steering wheel for emphasis.

Luckily for me I was saved from having to answer by arriving at the address listed on the shower invite. We both fell silent as we looked up at the house. It was one of those mini-mansions that randomly dotted the normal neighborhoods of LA. It was so out of place compared to the rest of the homes on the block that I assumed it must have been a total rebuild. The owner was a woman Bree had done some work for. Obviously she had money.

Jessica and I walked up the front steps and rang the doorbell. Even the doorbell was impressive. Instead of a normal chime, it played some classical piece probably from Beethoven or something.

A man in a black suit opened the door and suddenly I felt very conscious about what I was wearing. Was this a black tie event? I thought it was a baby shower? It turned out he was the butler of the house. I didn't know people still had butlers these days. Wasn't that a lost art or something?

He led us through an oversized entryway, passing a library full of plush leather chairs and old books into what must've been the living room of the house.

It could have been on the cover of an Architectural Digest. You could tell every inch of it had been planned out. From the perfectly placed books on the coffee table to the eclectic artwork lining the walls. Even the pillows were strategically placed on the white leather couches.

To the left was a dining area. There was a long table flawlessly settled in front of a bay window. That was the most striking thing about the room—the large windows that flooded in the area with natural light. Over by the table stood Bree chatting with two other women. When Bree saw us she grinned and came over for a hug.

I hoped I looked as cute as her when I was pregnant. She was wearing linen pants and a flowy maternity blouse that highlighted her little belly. Apparently this was what the "pregnancy glow" looked like.

"Bree you look so great!" Jessica squealed as she gave her a tight hug.

"Seriously," I added, "you do! What is in those prenatal vitamins you're taking?"

She laughed and slapped my arm. "Come over here guys, let me introduce you to Mariam, this is her house."

I spotted Mariam before Bree even introduced us.

She was one of those people that radiated success. I swear she smelled like wealth. Or maybe it was just her designer perfume. At the very least, I guaranteed her outfit cost more than my entire wardrobe. She was dressed simply, some black slacks and a white blouse and her hair was tied up in a loose chignon. She had accessorized her outfit with matching silver earrings and a chunky silver bracelet. Simple sophistication.

Overall Mariam was pleasant looking, but I wouldn't say she was a knockout. Her confident air overrode any of that though.

"Hello ladies," she said, the air of a perfect hostess about her, "so glad you could make it today. Bree has told me all about you."

We found out later that out Bree had helped Mariam out on a legal issue with one of her clients. Mariam was a book agent, and apparently a very good one at that. I didn't quite hear which type of publishing she was in though. At any rate, she and Bree had hit it off quite well and were now close friends.

A few more people trickled into the party. I recognized one or two of them, but most were strangers. A lot of them were friends from Bree's work or her husband's. Most of Bree's family lived on the east coast so only her mom had flown in for the shower.

After a few more minutes of mingling, Mariam gathered everyone's attention and welcomed us. We then followed her out to the oversized patio where caterers had set up a beautiful buffet styled luncheon.

There were croissant sandwiches set on giant white platters at either end of the table. Next to them were cheese and veggie platters, artfully surrounded by various dips and spreads. There was a large bowl of a spinach salad dotted with berries and some sort of chilled pasta dish as well. The centerpiece of the table was a giant fruit bowl with beautifully sliced berries and melons arranged in ascending colors.

The whole setting, similar to the inside of her house, was the perfect appearance of sophistication.

I chatted mostly with Bree and Jessica while we ate, making light conversation with a few other women.

Afterward, Mariam had a few games ready for us to play. My favorite was seeing who could change a diaper on a doll the fastest. To no one's surprise, Christie was the winner of this round. Twins had made her the master of diaper changes.

"If there's one good thing that came out of twins, it was my diaper changing skills," she joked to me as we squished together on the couches. Bree was about to start opening presents and we wanted a comfy seat.

I had to use the restroom about halfway through the gift opening. As expected, Mariam's guest bathroom was as gorgeous as the rest of the house. It was also about the size of my bedroom.

When I came back, my seat had been taken by another woman so I stood watching the rest of the unwrapping from the back of the room.

After a minute I heard a voice from behind say, "I'm so excited for Bree, she's going to make a great mom isn't she?"

I turned to see Mariam herself speaking to me. I was surprised she had singled me out. I assumed she was just being the polite hostess.

"Yes! Though it is a little hard for me to imagine Bree with kids. I have a hard time imagining her in anything other than a courtroom."

"She is an excellent lawyer. She did wonders for my client a couple of years ago." Miriam lifted her shoulders, "Although I will say, these last few months she's changed a little. I think the idea of being a mother has made her softer. There's a little less of the cutthroat lawyer in her these days."

"Ha ha, let's hope so."

Mariam's next question surprised me a little. "So, Bree tells me you own a bakery. How did you get started in that?"

I was surprised she and Bree had discussed me. I wasn't sure why my name had ever come up in conversation. Regardless, I spent the next few minutes telling her about my catering business.

At some point I also mentioned that I had a baking blog. This seemed to interest her too.

Our conversation got interrupted though when Bree started unwrapping my gift.

"Yes!" she exclaimed as she held up the baby bottles. I knew she'd be excited about those. "I'm so excited to have these Jenn! They're the perfect ones!"

Again, thank you baby registry.

She oohed and ahhed when she pulled out the pajamas as well.

I turned back to Mariam when Bree moved on to the next present. "I'm sorry, what were we talking about?"

Mariam waved her hand and just said, "Oh nothing, I was bugging you about your baking." She smiled then glanced around us. "I better get back to my hostess duties. Don't want anyone's drinks to get warm."

I smiled and simply said, "Well you throw a great party, this was beautiful."

She patted my arm and walked away to chat with others. I rehearsed our conversation in my head and still couldn't figure out why she initiated it. I shrugged it off.

I found Jessica leaning against the counter checking out Mariam's collection of travel books.

After giving her a nudge I asked, "How much longer do you want to stay?" It wasn't that I wanted to leave, I just knew LA traffic was going to pick up the longer we waited. The nightlife in the city was definitely hopping.

She glanced at her watch and nodded at me. "I'm ready to go whenever you are."

"I think Bree is about finished opening presents. Let's say our goodbyes and head out."

We elbowed our way through the crowd of women to Bree.

I caught her eye and she waddled her way to us. "Girls, thank you so much for coming and for your gifts! You guys are the best!" She gave us a double hug, managing to belly bounce us both.

We laughed and squeezed her back. "I'm so happy for you Bree, you're certainly going to be the best mom ever. This little girl doesn't know how lucky she is."

"And I know you haven't picked out a name yet," Jessica added, "but Jessica I'm assuming is still the front-runner."

Bree laughed and shook her head. "I don't know if this girl is ever going to get a name with our indecisiveness. We might just end up calling her baby girl."

We next found Christie and said goodbye to her. Then we were headed home. Fingers crossed we didn't hit too much traffic.

S'mores Trifle Recipe

· 1 box brownie mix (or your favorite from scratch recipe)
· 2 sleeves of graham crackers, crushed into bite sized pieces (about 15 crackers)
· 1 1/2 cups whipping cream
· 1 small jar of Marshmallow Creme
· 2 cups mini marshmallows
· Jar of hot fudge sauce

PREP:

1.) Start by baking a 9-13 pan of brownies according to the package directions. Once done, allow to cool and cut up into 1 inch cubes.
2.) Next begin whipping the cream in a clean bowl at medium high speed. When stiff peaks begin to form, slowly add in marshmallow cream in 3 stages, beating between additions.
3.) Finally spread mini marshmallows evenly onto a baking sheet and broil for about 30-45 seconds or until nicely toasted.

ASSEMBLY:

1.) In a trifle dish add an even layer of brownie pieces. Drizzle that with about 1/3 of the hot fudge sauce. Top that with 1/3 of the crushed graham crackers. Top that with 1/3 of the whipping cream mixture, spreading to smooth. Finally add a 1/3 of the toasted marshmallows. (They are sticky so spray a spatula with nonstick spray to transfer them)

2.) Repeat layers 3 times.

3.) Chill in fridge for at least an hour before serving.

Chapter 16

We ended up getting home around 6:30 PM, a lot earlier than I thought we would. Everyone must have been heading into LA, not leaving it on a Saturday night.

Jessica dropped me off at our apartment. She called Jake on the drive home and was meeting him at some Mexican hole in the wall place he wanted to try out. That was Jake for you. He loved finding hidden diners and dives that he insisted Jessica try out with him.

I knew it was true love because Jessica was always happy to go, despite the fact that she was normally a germaphobe. She insisted being with Jake made her happy, no matter where they were. Let's just say my best friend had turned into a sappy lovesick girl.

I kicked my shoes off as I entered our apartment and stretched out on our couch. I reached for my phone and sent Paul a text saying I was home. To be honest, I actually just wanted to curl up with a book or show that night, but I felt obligated to see what he was up to.

That was the problem with having a boyfriend or girlfriend. You had this moral obligation to spend time with the other person whenever you were free. You could no longer hang out by yourself every night.

Yes, I knew I should be dying to spend time with him, not avoiding it. Not all of us could be like lovesick Jessica and Jake.

Paul quickly replied.

I'm doing nothing. Want me to come over?

I halfheartedly replied.

Yeah, come on over.

About 20 minutes later he showed up on my doorstep with a carton of ice cream. That was when I remembered why I was still with him. He even brought a jar of hot fudge. He truly knew the way to my heart.

We snuggled down on the couch, forgetting bowls and just eating straight out of the carton. I warmed up the hot fudge and poured a generous amount on top.

"So how was the baby shower?" Paul asked, a spoonful of cookie dough ice cream halfway to his mouth.

"It was fun; you should've seen this house though. It was straight out of Crate and Barrel or something. I have no idea how much this woman makes, but she's loaded." I was emphasizing all this with my spoon.

He grinned and pretended to duck my flying utensil. "Oh yeah? What does she do? Is it her money her or husband's?"

I shook my head, "I don't think she's married, at least I didn't see a ring. So it must all be hers. She is a book agent." I sat there for a minute. "I didn't ask what type of books she works with. Must be something fairly lucrative though."

Paul rested his spoon on the coffee table and leaned back, apparently done with the ice cream. What a lightweight. "Huh, that'd be interesting to know. What'd you say her name was?"

I nestled the carton of ice cream in my lap, if he wasn't having any more I'd better finish it off before it melted. "Her first name is Mariam. I don't think I caught her last name."

Paul rested his arm along the back of the couch and began to play with my hair. He pulled out his phone with his other and typed something in. "Well, let's see what Google has to say about a successful literary agent named Mariam."

We were silent for a few minutes, Paul clicking away on different search results, me scooping out the last remains of the cookie dough.

"Hmm," he finally said, sitting up suddenly. "You might find this interesting." He looked over at me, his eyes raised in question. "Did you talk to her personally? Does she know what you do?"

"We did talk for a few minutes. She was pretty interested in my blog and my bakery, but I thought she was just making conversation." I pointed at his phone with my spoon. "Why? What'd you find out?"

He cleared his throat. "Mariam Wells is the well renowned literary agent to culinary non-fiction titles, specifically cookbooks and nutrition-related health and wellness narratives. She's been known to represent some of the biggest chefs and cooks in their debuts to the publishing realm..." he paused for a moment and looked up at me. "Want me to continue?"

I grabbed his phone and scanned her bio page. Yep, it was her. There was a picture at the top of the same stylish woman I'd spoken to this afternoon. It listed some of her top publications, many of which I'd purchased myself.

"Oh my gosh! I can't believe I was talking to her!" I flipped through her bio. "I totally own some of these cookbooks she's published. They are some of my favorites! Why in the world didn't I ask more questions?"

I had two secret desires in my life. One was to open my own bakery. Something that if you'd asked me years ago, I would've said was not even a possibility. But here I was, running my own bakery.

My second desire was to publish my own cookbook. Which was ridiculous, because you either had to be a chef with actual credentials—culinary school and big restaurant experience. Or you at least had to have a serious following if you were the self-made chef.

Since I was neither, I kept that dream on the back shelf. I think the only person I'd ever mentioned it to was my mom. I'm pretty sure she had smiled and said something to the effect of, "That's a great dream honey. Maybe one day." She'd probably patted my hand or something else humiliating as well.

I glanced up at Paul and said half-jokingly, half-seriously, "You think I should ask her to get me a book deal?"

His immediate laughter made me regret my question. Even though I had had a teasing note to my voice, I'd secretly hoped he'd take it sincerely.

"Sure Jenn," He gave me a hug which was definitely not returned. "Your book could be right up there with Rachel Ray and all those other guys!" His sarcasm wasn't doing anything to lighten my mood.

I was too embarrassed to let him know he'd hurt my feelings though, so I picked up the remote and turned on the TV.

"So," I said as I flipped through the channels. "What do you want to watch tonight?"

We ended up watching a chick flick. That, combined with the foot rub Paul gave me placated my grumpy mood. But to be honest, I'm pretty sure Paul had no idea he'd upset me with his joke. He clearly couldn't see me as an actual author.

The worst part was I didn't know if I could even see myself as one.

*****

Monday morning came way too early for me. Didn't it always work like that? I swear Monday through Friday took an eternity, and then you blinked and Saturday and Sunday were gone.

Little did I know how this Monday was going to shake my world.

We started our days at 4 AM at Jenn's Sweets. There were a few things I had carried over from Bread & Butter, one of them being an early morning start time.

The good thing about not dealing with yeast bread was you didn't need to wait for the proofing time. Pie crusts and cookie dough could be made ahead of time and frozen, so most of the early morning work was baking and packaging.

Becca, my Monday and Wednesday assistant, was a whiz when it came to packaging. My assembly line process was a chaotic mess before she came along. She came in and put together a systematic approach for me.

Our kitchen was smaller than the one I worked in with Ann, however with Becca's system it was almost to our advantage. She had set up a map and flowchart of how things would move through our kitchen efficiently. It was silly how simple the process was, yet it saved us countless hours. I should give Becca a raise.

Anyway, Monday morning we were filling the ovens full of frozen cookie dough, soon to be followed by a few batches of mini pies. Our most common pie flavors were chocolate chess, apple crumb, and lemon tart. We offered a few other variations, but these were the standards.

At about 7 AM I got a text message from Mitch.

Sorry Jenn, I think I got the stomach flu last night. I don't think I'm gonna be able to do deliveries today. Let me know if you need to use my truck to make your rounds.

Ugh, that stunk. I didn't have any hard feelings towards Mitch about it. He was much worse off than I was right now. It did put me in a bind though.

I had to think. Today's orders were pretty small. If Becca and I split them up, we could probably deliver them in our cars. That way we wouldn't have to drive over to Mitch's to borrow his truck.

"Hey Becca, how are your delivery skills?"

*****

We decided Becca would deliver the pies to the real estate office. They said their agents would take care of taking the pies to each specific open house. I gave them a 10% discount for the inconvenience.

Meanwhile I was going to take care of the two cookie deliveries. I was grateful I decided to wear my black pants that day. Not that they looked super professional, but they were better than the ripped jeans I normally wore.

The first delivery was for a dentist office only about 10 minutes away. I decided to take care of them first.

It was your standard office building, they were in a suite on the second floor. A perky little receptionist took the cookies from me with a smile and I was on my way.

One more stop and I was done. Unfortunately, the engineering firm wasn't so close. They were in Anaheim, another 20 minutes away. At least it wasn't rush hour traffic. I made it to the office around 11:30 which was good since our contract guaranteed delivery before noon.

The office was a standalone building. They obviously didn't get much foot traffic since the place appeared to be more of a warehouse. I did a full circle of the building before I found the front doors.

I opened one of the dark double doors and felt a rush of cool air conditioning. The place was quite nice inside, a receptionist desk was centered in the entryway and there were two plush armchairs on either side of the room. A large palm plant rested next to one of them and the other was flanked by a water cooler.

As I said, a pleasant enough office, there was only one problem: no one was in sight.

I set my load of cookies on the counter and peered behind it. There was a blank pad of paper and a computer that wasn't turned on. I guessed I'd have to do a little snooping until I found someone.

A hallway went past the desk to the rest of the building. I followed it a few yards until it opened up to a larger space full of about six cubicles. The computers on these desks were at least turned on. Still no one was around. They must have been in a meeting or something.

I continued down the hallway which led me past a small kitchen space and bathrooms. A little ways further there were a couple more office doors, all closed. However, there was a considerable amount of noise coming from one of them.

I put my ear to the door and listened. There was a single person talking, but every so often I could hear comments from various others. It was probably a company meeting.

Interrupting their meeting simply to say some cookies had been delivered seemed silly to me. Instead I decided to put the cookies on one of the cubicle desks. I'd leave a note explaining I didn't want to interrupt the meeting and that these had been ordered for their luncheon.

Easy peasy.

I turned back to where I had come from. I was just passing the kitchen/bathroom area when I heard a doorknob rattling and came face to face with a swinging bathroom door.

The next thing I knew I was laying flat on the ground staring at a face hovering above me. The man's face was shadowed by the overhead lights but I'd recognize it anywhere.

Luke Bradley.

And that was when I blacked out.

Chapter 17

"Jenn... Jenn?"

The voice sounded far away. As if I was in a subway tunnel and someone was calling me from the next stop.

I cracked one eye open then immediately shut it. Luke Bradley was crouched over me. At least I think he was. Was I dreaming? The last thing I remembered was getting hit in the head by the door. Maybe I was in a dream.

"Jenn... can you hear me?"

Well unless that dream came with a Luke voice impersonator, I probably wasn't dreaming. I opened both eyes this time.

"Oh good, you're alive!"

I wasn't sure if he was happy to see me or just relieved not to have a murder charge against him?

"Can... can you sit up? Wait—no. Don't sit up. You might have a concussion. Or wait, I think you're supposed to stay awake if you have one of those so maybe do sit up..."

I slowly began to rise amidst his bumbling. My head spun a little but other than that there was no real damage.

Well, besides my pride obviously. This man had a knack for finding me in embarrassing situations.

"Uh, Luke, hey.... long time no see."

Yes, this was a ridiculous statement since I hadn't seen him for precisely two years. The last time we'd hung out we had been baking bread together. Next thing I knew he had broken up with my roommate and I hadn't seen him since. But someone had to fill the silence because he certainly wasn't.

He cringed. Apparently he remembered the last time we had seen each other too. His arm went around my back to help me sit up. "I am so sorry about that, I didn't see you there... obviously."

I waved aside his apologies and closed my eyes, trying to get the pounding out of my head. "It's fine, total accident." I tried to not enjoy the feeling of his arm around me and had to stop myself from leaning into it.

He stared at me for a second, as if analyzing how bad the damage was. I tried to give him a winning smile to prove I was all right. Fingers crossed it didn't look like a grimace.

"Can I get you a chair to sit in?" He finally asked.

I nodded and he dragged a chair over, the legs scraping across the laminate floor. I slowly started standing (again with the assistance of his arm) and made my way to the metal chair.

"I really am fine; I'll probably just have a headache." I raised a hand to my head. "You guys don't happen to have any aspirin do you?"

"Uh, let me check the kitchen." He disappeared for a moment.

I leaned back in the chair and let out the breath of air I didn't realize I was holding.

Luke. Of course of all people to get knocked out in front of it was Luke. Why couldn't I ever run into him when I was looking super hot and fabulous and out on a date with Brad Pitt or something? This was not the way I wanted to reunite with him after two years.

I shook my head noting that we were not "reuniting". We had (literally) just run into each other. Plus, I had a boyfriend. Luke likely had a girlfriend or was maybe even married by now—I hadn't had the conscious skills to do a ring check.

I was going to treat this as a simple, accidental meeting of friends. I squared my shoulders, wincing as the movement shot pain through my right temple.

Alright Jenn, I mentally told myself, pull yourself together girl. You are a professional. You are simply delivering some items to a party. When Luke gets back, you are going to get off this chair and leave with your head held high.

"I am a professional. I am a professional." I repeated under my breath as Luke entered the room. He had a cup of water in one hand and two white pills in the other.

"We had some Tylenol, does that work?" He offered the pills to me.

"Yeah that's great." I took the pills and cup from him.

There was a moment of silence after I swallowed the pain medicine. I couldn't deal with awkward silences. I stood up to leave a little too quickly and I began to sway.

Luke reached out and grabbed my arm. "Whoa, are you okay? Maybe you should sit down for a bit longer."

He was right, but I wanted to seem tough. "Oh, I'm fine. No worries." I pulled my arm from his grasp and waved my hands around. "See? Good as new."

Luke didn't look convinced but I could tell he didn't know what to do.

I turned on my heel, ready to head out of there when I remembered the cookies. Dang, I probably needed to explain why I was even here.

I spun back around and faced him. "I'm actually delivering some cookies for a luncheon somewhere?" I asked, hoping he knew what I was talking about.

"Oh yeah, we're doing a team building day, the cookies are for the group lunch."

"I left them on the front desk in the entryway." I motioned awkwardly with my hands towards the front of the office. "I'll go get them."

"No, no I'll grab them. You relax for another minute." Before I could stop him he was marching past me.

Okay, I told myself. He's going to come back and this time I am going to say a pleasant goodbye and be on my way. (I was getting good at these self-pep talks).

He came back, his arms full of cookie boxes. "These are a lot heavier than they look!" He set them on the kitchen counter.

"We only make the best!" I said a little too brightly. "Anyway, thanks for grabbing those. I really need to be on my way now though, I have some... stuff to do. Important stuff." Well that sure sounded legitimate Jenn.

"Oh, are you sure? Because..." He seemed to be fumbling to say something. Suddenly he pulled out his phone. "Here, at least give me your phone number, I'll feel terrible if I don't check up on you to make sure you're all right in a few hours."

It was totally unnecessary but I didn't know how to tactfully refuse him. I rattled off my number.

I began walking towards the front door, hoping to leave him in the dust. Unfortunately, he was pretty quick on his feet and dashed forward to open the door for me. "Thank you for the cookies!" he said genuinely.

"Well, you guys did pay me for them so I felt obligated to bring them," I said.

His face broke out in that grin I was so familiar with and I almost melted right on the spot.

"See you later!" I said quickly and was out of there.

*****

I stared at the text message.

Hey Jenn, how's your head feeling? Everything end up okay? I'm sorry again about nailing you with the door.

Luke had sent it to me 15 minutes ago and I still hadn't replied yet. I was being ridiculous, I knew that. But what was more ridiculous were the nonstop butterflies I had in my stomach since I first laid eyes on Luke three hours earlier.

After our unexpected encounter, I had driven directly home and did what I did best when stressed: I started baking.

I was midway through frosting a batch of chocolate cupcakes when I got his text asking how I was. Those dang butterflies.

The worst part was I had been dating Paul for approximately three months now and I was pretty sure he had never once given me butterflies. Or anything remotely close. I had just assumed I wasn't the type of girl to get those feelings. I wasn't into all that sappy love stuff anyway, I'd told myself.

Yet after a three-minute conversation with Luke, who I hadn't seen in over two years, I was nervous as a teenager going on her first date.

I needed to pull myself together. The man deserved a response.

Hey Luke... (delete delete). *Hi Luke...* (delete delete). *Good afternoon Luke...* (delete delete delete).

This was getting absurd. I hit the voice record button on my phone and began dictating my response to him.

Hi Luke, yes I'm doing much better, no concussion. Thanks for checking up on me!

I hit send before I could overanalyze it again. I set my phone down and picked up my piping bag. Back to more important things.

I was shocked when less than 30 seconds later my phone beeped with a reply.

Oh good, I was worried. Hey, so I noticed those cookies had your name on it. Looks like you ended up opening that bakery after all?

What the... What was he doing? Why was he trying to continue our conversation? I gave him the perfect closing text. All he had to do was say "I'm glad, hope everything goes well" or something non-committal like that.

I didn't want to take another 15 minutes to reply. Then he'd think I was spending a lot of time on my response. Texting was so ridiculous sometimes.

Yes I did. All your good advice paid off. I am now the proud owner of my very own bakery: Jenn's Sweets.

I sent it and then felt a little dumb because obviously he knew it was called Jenn's Sweets. It was plastered all over my boxes the cookies were delivered in. So I added:

But you probably knew that from my cookies.

His reply came just as quick as the first had.

Yeah, I noticed your name. So when did you open? I am going to need to come by and pick up some more cookies. They were some of the best I've ever had.

The little punk. He would try to win me over with flattery. Unfortunately, it worked. Anybody who complimented my bakery had me as putty in their hands.

Thank you! I am proud of it! But you'll have to order some ahead of time, we're a catering company only. No storefront. Although I could make an exception for you. Tell me when you want to stop by and I'll make sure to have a few extra on hand.

Holy cow why did I send that? Why why why? He was just being complimentary. He didn't really want to stop by my bakery. I didn't even want him to come by. He was the enemy. I shunned him from my life two years ago when he broke Jessica's heart. Come on Jenn!

Perfect! When can I stop by?

This guy was the fastest texter I'd ever met.

I sat there staring at the blinking cursor for a minute. What had I gotten myself into?

How about Wednesday at noon?

I was actually free tomorrow too. But I needed a day to process this and also to clean up my kitchen. Not that I cared what he thought, I just wanted to put my best foot forward and all that. Purely from a professional standpoint. As I told myself before, this was a strictly non-romantic friendship we had.

Perfect, what's the address?
Strictly friendship I told the butterflies.

*****

Every Tuesday I had a standing lunch date with Ann. Yes, she still talked to me even after I left Bread & Butter. She was sad to see me go, but she was actually one of my biggest cheerleaders when I started Jenn's Sweets.

Ann helped get me through those first dark months when everything seemed to be spiraling out of control. When I began focusing on catering, she was the one who gave me tips on establishing myself. She also was the one who introduced me to Mitch, the best delivery guy around—except when he had the flu.

Our favorite lunch spot was a little diner that made some of the best turkey sandwiches in Ann's opinion. They also made some of the best hot fudge sundaes in my opinion. It was a matter of taste.

Ann arrived first today, she'd already gotten a lemon water and was sipping away at it contentedly when I walked up.

"How's it goin' boss?" It was our running joke even though I hadn't worked for her for over a year now.

"Doing good," she said in between sips. "How about yourself?"

"Ah, things are fine..." I contemplated if I should bring up meeting Luke yesterday then decided against it. Ann only knew Luke as Jessica's ex-boyfriend that dumped her unceremoniously. Not the best reference.

Jessica had gotten home late last night so I hadn't told her about my experience with him either. I wasn't sure how she'd react anyways. I wasn't sure how I was reacting myself.

So basically, I hadn't told anybody. And it was bottled up inside me ready to burst.

As I settled in the waiter came by and asked if we were ready to order. We both got the same thing every time. Ann ordered her signature turkey sandwich with a side of chopped fruit. I got their turkey burger with a side of ice cream.

After the waiter left we chatted about work for a minute. Bread & Butter had been nominated in the OC Register as one of the best bakeries in Orange County this last week. It was a huge honor for Ann, one she deserved. I told her how proud I was of her.

"Seriously Ann, that is huge. Is business booming since the nomination?" The list of nominations had been printed in the last edition of the paper.

"Nothing too crazy, but we are definitely hitting our capacity. We have been sold out by 10 AM every day." She stared down into her drink, suddenly thoughtful. "I don't know Jenn, with things picking up I am realizing how old I am really getting. "I used to love the busyness, the early mornings, the hours of nonstop baking. But now my bones are getting achy. The idea of waking up early is no longer exciting; it's more of a chore." She lifted her hands and looked at them.

I didn't know what to say. I knew Ann wouldn't run her bakery forever, but thinking of her quitting shocked me.

"I need to plan what I want to do with Bread & Butter long term." She gave me a wink. "Once upon a time I had this amazing assistant who I would've left it to, but she left me for bigger and better things."

I smiled at her. "She obviously didn't know what she was doing. Why would she leave such an incredible place?"

Ann laughed. "Yes well, at this point I think my best bet would be to sell it. I've had a few people show interest over the years, I just need to go back and see if it's still on their radar."

I had to agree with her. It would be the smartest thing to do. That way the business could continue on—it would be terrible to close and lose everything she had built over the years. Plus she'd get a little cash out of it for retirement.

The waiter brought our food out. We spent the next few minutes eating in a comfortable silence.

"I have a question for you, have you ever heard of a Mariam Wells?" I asked suddenly.

She looked at me thoughtfully, thinking as she finished her bite. "No, I can't say I have. Who is she?"

"She's a very successful literary agent for cookbook authors. I'm talking big-name cookbooks." I proceeded to tell her about meeting Mariam at Bree's baby shower. I told her about how she inquired after my bakery and blog.

"What do you make of it?" I finally asked.

Ann seemed to be thinking. "Well, you should be very flattered that she was interested in what you do. Has writing a cookbook ever interested you?"

I shrugged noncommittally. I always felt a little dumb saying I wanted to write a cookbook. "I don't know, I just thought it was interesting talking to her. I wish I had known who she was when I was at her house."

"That's true; it would've been fun to pick her brain about things." Ann speared a cantaloupe with her fork. "Writing a cookbook would be pretty awesome, probably something you could do given all the writing you've done with your blog. However, if Mariam Wells is as successful as you say, it seems like a long shot to get her as an agent."

I nodded, a light flush running up my neck. Of course it was a long shot, I didn't know why I kept thinking about it.

I changed the subject and asked her about how Carly had been doing lately. Carly worked at Bread & Butter about another six months after I quit, then she went back east. She had decided to transfer schools for one reason or another. Ann updated me about what she was up to.

We spent a few more minutes lightly chatting until the waiter brought us our bill. We said our goodbyes and promised to meet up again next week. The usual.

I still had Luke on my mind when I left. Ann would've been a great person to talk to about him. She could have come from a more objective perspective than Jessica.

But I couldn't bring myself to talk about it yet. There was nothing to talk about after all. He was just an old friend from my past that I ran into again. That was all.

I just wish I could get him out of my mind.

*****

That night I was supposed to go over to Paul's house to hang out. I canceled.

I canceled for absolutely no other reason than that I was going to see Luke the next day. I couldn't deal with talking to Paul while the image of Luke was constantly running through my brain.

Instead, I spent a solid hour picking out what I was going to wear tomorrow.

It wasn't like it should have been a difficult decision. I had a standard uniform while working: black on black. So my choices ranged between my ripped black jeans or my black slacks topped with either a black T-shirt or a black v-neck.

I went with the black slacks and the v-neck. It seemed the best choice. Not too casual and not too fancy—I didn't want him to know that I spent an hour picking out this outfit.

The next morning I went through work robotically, half aware of what I was doing, half thinking about Luke. Becca had to tell me twice that I was packaging the wrong items in the delivery boxes.

"You okay?" She asked me. "You seem out of sorts today."

"Oh yeah, I'm just... tired," I finished, trying to come up with a justifiable explanation. "Stayed up way too late—watching TV and stuff." That was partially true. I did stay up late last night, but mostly because I couldn't sleep.

After loading up the last of the orders in Mitch's truck I checked the clock for the 624th time that morning. It was 11:15, another 45 minutes until Luke was stopping by.

I told Becca she was welcome to go home, I was going to stay and finish up the cookie dough for tomorrow's orders.

"I can stay and do that," she said. "Especially since you're so tired today."

Becca was seriously a sweetheart. But I didn't want her there when Luke came by. I didn't want to have to explain my awkwardness that was bound to happen.

"No, you go on home. You've done plenty today." I waved her on and she finally agreed.

Once the door shut I figured I'd better make the dough I said I would and got out some butter. I was making a batch of my famous double chocolate cookies. I didn't want to brag, but these were probably the best chocolate cookies in the world.

Contrary to most cookie recipes, this one started with cold butter. The key was to chop it up into small chunks so it could still be whipped together with the sugar. I used a fair amount of brown sugar as well; it kept the cookies nice and chewy. The third element was using some cake flour. It kept the dough magically light, despite the significant amount of butter in them.

I sat back and let my industrial sized mixer do its magic. This machine was my baby. It was one of the most expensive things in my kitchen, but also the most used. My goal was to get enough regular orders to justify a second one. Currently we were subsidizing with two smaller mixers. They worked fine, but they couldn't produce the same large batches this one could.

After the dough was mixed I laid out parchment lined cookie sheets and began scooping out the dough, the systematic task soothing my nerves. There was nothing more comforting than being in my kitchen. I knew some people thought I was nuts, but baking was like therapy to me.

After the dough was all scooped out, the sheets would sit in the fridge overnight. This made the process streamlined in the morning, but it also allowed the dough's gluten to rest and the flavors to combine. I would compare to letting meat marinate before cooking it. Something about giving the flavors time to meld together made them so much richer.

I was finishing the last pan when I heard a deep voice call out, "Hello? Jenn?"

Luke was here.

I instinctively started running my fingers through my hair, checking to make sure everything was in place. I had spent the time last night to actually curl it, so today it fell in casual loose waves. I didn't have time to check my makeup so I just had to trust that my mascara was still in place.

"Hey!" I called out, "Come on back!"

A few seconds later Luke walked through the doorway, a hesitant smile in his eyes. "Oh good, I was hoping I had the right spot."

Just seeing him sent an explosion of nerves through me.

He was coming from work, dressed in grey suit pants and a blue collared shirt. He'd loosened his tie giving him this slightly rumpled business look. There was something about a man in a suit. Or maybe it was just Luke in a suit.

I smiled back at him. "I know, I should do better advertising. I had a great sign made when I first opened and we had walk in customers." I shrugged. "But since I rebranded to Jenn's Sweets, I've never gotten around to ordering a new one."

He nodded as he scanned the kitchen, taking it all in. I was surprised by how vulnerable I felt. This kitchen was my baby, something I created. I really wanted Luke to like it. Even though he didn't know it, he'd been the catalyst to get me started with it all.

"Wow, I can't believe you did all this!" He waved his hand at everything. "I mean, I didn't doubt that you could, but you did it." His admiration sent warmth running through me and I could feel a flush heat my cheeks.

"Uh, yeah thanks. I mean it's not that special or anything... I'm just baking cookies and stuff..." I was rambling. He was standing too close and it was making me nervous.

"So," I said, grabbing one of the trays I'd filled with cookie dough, "want a formal tour?"

"Yes ma'am."

"First I'll have to go get you a hair net, sanitary reasons you know..."

His eyebrows lifted in a questioning look and I couldn't keep a straight face.

"Just kidding, although you probably could pull it off." I gave him a mock assessment. "Let's start at the fridge since I have to get these in there."

He looked down at the other trays and shrugged out of his suit coat. After laying it on the counter he picked one up.

"Lead the way chef."

I loved the ease with which he entered my world. "These beauties are my fridge and freezer combo," I began, resting a loving arm on my restaurant sized fridge/freezer.

"I can see what you mean," Luke agreed, a glint in his eyes, "I don't think I've ever seen such beautiful stainless steel."

I laughed and opened the doors. "You can put that tray here. I have custom shelving inside that allows me to store twice as many baking sheets." We placed the rest of the cookies in then continued on our tour.

"So back here is the prep counter and the ovens." I felt like Vanna White waving my arms around. "These ovens bake some of the finest pies, cookies, and bars you'll ever taste."

"I believe it," he said solemnly. "They have a special aura about them."

I rolled my eyes and moved on. "This center island is mostly for packaging up finished items. You wouldn't know it, but at least a third of our time is spent boxing up all the goods to be delivered." I next showed him the mixers, my impressive collection of baking sheets, pans, and mixing bowls. He ooh and ahhed in all the right places, keeping up a witty, borderline flirting banter with me.

"And that's it," I summed up. "That's where all the magic happens."

He began a slow clap, then looked around him as if offended no one else was joining in. I slugged him on the shoulder. "You're such a dork," I said.

He laughed and stopped his ridiculous clapping. "I was joking with the clapping but I am actually impressed. I can't believe what you've made here. I hope you're proud of yourself."

I smiled. "I am." And I really was. Sometimes I got down on myself that business wasn't booming enough, or that things weren't happening as smoothly as I'd envisioned. But I'd come far and was proud of myself.

"So how did you turn into a catering company?" He leaned against the wall with one shoulder.

I swear the man looked like a male model, perfectly posed for a shot. I stared at his mouth as he talked and wondered what it'd be like to kiss him. "I... uh..." I missed his question because I was too busy ogling him. "What'd you just ask?"

He smiled with uncertainty. "I asked how you went from a baking storefront to delivering stuff."

"Oh, right," I tried to hide the flush filling my cheeks. I gave him the short version of switching over to event catering. He'd already heard enough about my business for one day, he didn't need another monologue about the woes of Jenn's Sweets.

"It's good that you didn't start off as a total success. Sometimes failing a little helps you get stronger." He lifted his hands emphatically. "I bet you wouldn't have considered catering if business had boomed from the beginning. Think of what you would've missed out on!"

"Endless work parties and luncheons?"

"Well that... and most importantly you would've missed getting smacked in the head by me." He peered at me from the corner of his eye.

"Yeah, I'm still thinking about suing you for that. I may have long-term neck damage." I began rubbing my neck and grimacing.

"Ha ha, you wouldn't do that to an old friend!"

"I don't know, I've never had a friend knock me out before," I replied. In my head though I was repeating his comment. Friend? Were we friends? I probably would've described us as acquaintances, maybe that we'd crossed paths several times in the past. Friends indicated something closer though. I couldn't figure Luke out.

We spent a few more minutes chatting. He gave me an update on his work; yes still the same company, a higher position and longer hours. He hadn't moved either, still in the same townhome in Irvine.

The whole time he talked he was fiddling absentmindedly with a cookie scoop that'd been lying on the counter. I'd forgotten about his little habit of always moving his hands. It was slightly endearing to see and remember.

I was waiting for him to ask me about Jessica, wondering if he'd bring her up. After all, she was the reason for our past. And the reason we hadn't talked in two years. But he seemed to be purposefully avoiding the topic, never once inquiring about where I lived or if Jessica was still around. I let it go.

"Well," he said, obviously wrapping up our visit. "I hate to go but I've gotta get back to work." He took a deep breath, "I don't want to brag, but I'm kind of an important person back there."

I scoffed loudly and he laughed.

"Okay, well let me get you the cookies I promised. I'd hate for you to come all this way and not get what you came for."

He looked at me strangely then said, "Oh I don't know if I'd say that..."

I wasn't sure how to respond to his strange answer so I just shrugged and went over to the box I'd set aside for him. "I gave you the full selection. There are a few mini pies, a double serving of all our cookies, and a brownie or two thrown in for good measure." I handed him the hefty box.

"Wow! Thanks, I'm going to probably gain 10lbs tonight." He peeked inside the box. "But it looks like it'll be worth it."

I smiled in response. "It will be."

We said our goodbyes, but no commitments were made to meet again. As I shut the door after him I let out a long breath.

And made a firm resolve to stop thinking about what it would be like to kiss Luke.

Chapter 18

It was that evening around six I got another text from him.

Thanks for the tour and all the cookies today. I'm going to need a Jenn's Sweets delivery weekly now because I'm hooked.

I didn't have much time to process the deeper meanings of this note because there was another one about three seconds later.

Also, I think I left my suit coat in your kitchen this afternoon. I can come by and pick it up tomorrow? Or maybe I could treat you to lunch on Friday and you could bring it then?

Treat me to lunch. So was that like a date? I mean, obviously I couldn't go on a date with him, I had a boyfriend. It was a wonderful relationship. Well, sort of. I mean Paul was loyal and reliable, steady and nice... Love took time... right?

I'd analyze my relationship with Paul later. I had to figure out this date/non-date offer from Luke.

He'd called us friends today—clearly this was just a friendship thing. I mean, there was no way a guy like Luke would go after me. He dated girls that looked like Jessica. Perfectly blonde, size 2 bombshells.

I shook my head, I was reading way too much into this. The guy left his jacket at my work and needed it back. He was simply being gentlemanly and offering to buy me lunch as a thank you.

I picked up my phone and responded that lunch would be great.

*****

While I had convinced myself I wasn't doing anything wrong last night, my gut was telling me something different this morning.

Paul had actually called after Luke's text and I had screened his call.

I think this was a turning point for Paul and me. If it was coming to the point that I didn't even want to chat with Paul, let alone hang out with him, that probably was a sign things needed to end.

And while Luke was somewhat of a catalyst to this decision, I knew he wasn't the real reason. Even if nothing happened between Luke and me, nothing was *ever* going to happen between me and Paul. It wasn't fair to keep stringing him along.

I pondered these deep thoughts as I rolled out pie crusts on Wednesday morning. Pie crust making was always a great time for introspection.

I needed a second opinion on a decision this big. I should've asked Jessica, but that meant I'd have to bring up Luke and I wasn't ready to do that.

Becca," I asked, "have you ever been in a serious relationship?"

She was next to me, cutting circles out of the rolled out crusts for the mini pies. She looked up with lifted brows. "Yeah, one or two. Why? Trouble in paradise with you and Paul?"

I looked away. "It's not that there's trouble, I'm just not sure if I'm into him anymore." I set my rolling pin down. "I mean Paul is great, he really is. I think that's part of the problem. I don't have a good reason to want to move on. Am I being silly? What else am I looking for?"

Even as I asked this Luke's image flashed through my mind.

"Hmm," Becca tossed her pie cutter from hand to hand. "I mean, I'm no love expert, but I don't think you should stay with someone because they're a nice person. That's not fair to you or him."

"Yeah, I'm not sure if I just see him as a safety net or what." I rubbed my temple with one hand. "I haven't had many relationships. I'm afraid if I let Paul go, I won't find anyone else."

"Oh Jenn, that's ridiculous. Just because you haven't had many relationships doesn't mean you're not a catch." Becca went back to cutting pie crusts. "Plus I don't think Paul wants to be with you as a safety net."

"Yeah, I'm leading him on at this point. I don't want to be that kind of girl." I drummed my fingers on the counter, rattling the rolling pin I'd set down. "I don't know what to do now. This sounds silly, but how do I break things off with him? Like nicely?"

Paul was a great guy. I didn't want this to end in an ugly way or anything.

"Well, you should do it face to face. Nothing is worse than a breakup over the phone or worse a text. I think it's best to do it in a neutral location too, not your house or his or anyplace sentimental to you guys. Go for a walk in a park or something."

This was good advice; I needed to be writing this down.

"Don't use the 'it's not you it's me' line, but also don't pin blame on him unnecessarily. Just let him know it's more about you changing and understanding what you're looking for in a relationship." She gave me a grin. "All guys have an ego—even the nice ones like Paul. Make him feel like it is a consensual breakup, one that's best for the both of you."

Becca began placing her round little pie crusts into their tins. I went back to work rolling.

"So exactly how do I do that?"

She smiled wistfully. "No one really knows."

*****

I texted Paul while I headed to my cycling class after work. I figured if I was going to do this I'd better get it over with. The longer I thought about it the more painful it would be.

Hey, you want to go on a walk this evening? We can grab some frozen yogurt on the beach.

I went with Becca's idea of a walk and I figured frozen yogurt made everything better.

He agreed to meet me at 6.

This was the first time I'd had butterflies about hanging out with Paul. I wished it was under better circumstances.

At 5:45 I was on the boardwalk, waiting for Paul to show up. There was a frozen yogurt place right next to the pier, only about a quarter mile from where I was parked. I planned it that way because I didn't know how long I could fake small talk.

Paul showed up at exactly six because punctuality was another one of his great traits. Why was I breaking up with him again?

He was wearing his work attire, slacks and a button-down shirt, which looked fine. But I couldn't help comparing it to the picture Luke made in his work clothes. Somehow Luke made everything look good.

We hugged and he gave me our customary peck, a kiss that would've been equally appropriate for his grandma.

"Hey babe, how's it going?" He put his arm around me with a grin.

"Oh... f-f-fine," I lied. I was not meant for breakups. I couldn't deal with uncomfortable situations. The only thing that made this more awkward was the fact that Paul didn't even realize it was awkward. It was all in my own mind.

"Let's go get yogurt," I said, I'm starving. "Which of course was a lie. My stomach was in knots. But I had to get this show on the road.

We walked hand in hand down the boardwalk. At least until I pretended to fix my flip-flop and shook my hand free from his. I was sure he'd notice their clamminess if I didn't pull away.

Generally I took my frozen yogurt seriously. I was all about the taster cups, getting the perfect combination of sweet and tart flavors, and the right amount of crunch from the toppings. Today? I didn't even glance at which flavors I put in my cup. I just walked to the first handle and pulled. It wasn't until we were paying that I realized I had a mixture of gummy bears and brownies as my toppings.

Paul looked over at my creation and raised one eyebrow. "Well that's an interesting mix."

I tried to play it off. "Oh, you know, just trying new flavor combinations... for my pies."

He didn't look convinced but he also didn't question me further.

We took our yogurt outside, the sun, while low in the sky, was still giving off enough heat to begin melting them. I checked out the options, looking for what could be considered a good breakup spot. There was the sand, but it seemed like sitting on the sand overlooking a sunset should be reserved for romantic things. Not breakups.

There was a grassy patch to the side of the yogurt place, but there were a bunch of high school kids hanging out on it. I definitely didn't need an audience for this talk.

Then there was a solitary bench sitting right off the boardwalk, on the sandy side of the trail. There was even a trash can next to it so I could discreetly toss my gross brownie/gummy bear concoction. Perfect.

I made my way over there and Paul followed unquestioningly. We sat for a couple minutes eating in silence. Well, Paul was eating, I was mindlessly stirring my yogurt in circles.

Okay, I told myself, this is it, you can do this. Just tell him how you feel and he'll understand. It was Paul after all; he was probably the nicest, most understanding guy out there. Just do it.

I took a deep breath.

"So Paul," I began, having absolutely no idea where I was going with this, "we've been dating for a while, and I think you're a great guy."

He grabbed my hand and looked at me warmly. "And I think you're a great girl too Jenn.

No, wait, this wasn't the direction I was going for. I quickly pulled my hand from his grasp. "Yes, er, well, the thing is, we've kind of been at this same point in our relationship for a bit and I'm just not sure—that is—"

"You know, I've been thinking about us a lot too," Paul said, interrupting my stuttering. "And I agree things have been moving a bit slow." He slid closer to me on the bench and put his arm around me.

Wait wait wait, this was not going well.

"Yes, um," I stood under the pretense of throwing my yogurt away. "You see Paul, what I'm trying to say is I'm just not sure if it's working between us."

He stared at me blankly.

"You know, I'm just not sure if we're perfect for each other."

His mouth opened in silent confusion.

"But it's not you, it's me." Crud I wasn't supposed to use that line.

He raised one eyebrow, clearly not impressed by the cliché comment.

I tried again. "You're such a great guy Paul and I think that you deserve someone who's totally into you." Okay, that came out a little harsher than I planned. Why was there not a manual on proper breakup etiquette?

"Wait, are you breaking up with me?" Paul finally asked, his voice laced with confusion.

"Um, yes?" For some reason I didn't think I should've phrased that as a question. "Yes." There, that sounded a little more confident. "I really like you as a friend Paul. You are one of the nicest guys I know and you have some awesome qualities. I'm just not sure if the spark is there for me anymore." (I wasn't sure if the spark was actually ever there but no reason to bring it up now)

"This is so out of the blue. How long have you been feeling like this?" Surprise. That was the expression on his face. Total surprise. Had he seriously not felt even a tinge of doubt about us lately?

"Oh, for a bit." I didn't know what to say. I didn't want to say I'd been feeling this way for a month, that would sound bad. However I also didn't want to say I'd just decided this today. That might give him hope I wasn't serious.

"What did I do wrong?" His frozen yogurt had melted into a puddle by now, totally forgotten.

"Nothing! You didn't do anything wrong, I'm telling you it's me not you." There was that line again. "I'm the one who's changed. There's nothing you've done Paul."

He shook his head clearly not grasping what was happening.

"Look, I've done a terrible job with this. Breakups are not my thing. I just don't want to waste your time because you are an awesome guy and there's going to be a perfect girl out there for you." I waved my hands around dramatically.

His face flushed. "That girl is just not you."

"Um, no, I don't think so." I shook my head. I felt helpless at this point. I mean what else should I say?

Paul stood suddenly, his yogurt falling off his lap to the ground. I scooped it up.

"I... I think I've got to go. I got to think about this Jenn." He took a few steps then stopped. Turning back to me he ran his fingers through his hair, disheveling it. "I'll—I'll call you later I guess." Then he was gone.

And I was left holding an empty yogurt cup, somehow feeling lighter than I had in a long time.

*****

When I got home that night Jessica was on the couch watching TV. She still had her work clothes on, so she hadn't been home long. She smiled when I walked in. When she saw the look on my face though, she grabbed the remote and hit mute.

"What's wrong?" She leaned forward, her brow furrowing.

"Ugh, do we have any ice cream? Or Oreos? Or both?" I asked as I flopped down on the couch.

"Wait here." She stood and stepped over my legs resting on the coffee table. She came back from the kitchen two minutes later holding a white bakery box.

"One of my clients brought in cupcakes as a thank you this afternoon. I brought the leftovers home." She opened the box under my nose. "There's a cookies n' cream and a peanut butter one left."

"You are literally my most favorite human being ever," I half moaned as I grabbed the one with an Oreo cookie on top of a mountain of frosting.

She set the box on the coffee table and grabbed the other one. We ate our sugar bombs in silence, Jessica glancing at me every few minutes to see if I was ready to talk.

I finally chucked my empty cupcake liner into the box and stated, "I broke up with Paul."

Jessica coughed on the bite she had in her mouth as she sat up suddenly. "You what?"

"I broke up with Paul."

"But—why? What happened?"

I gave her the rundown. How I realized how distant our relationship had become. I strategically left out any parts about Luke and how he had expedited my desire to end things with Paul.

Jessica listened in silence, letting me gab until I'd spilled everything.

When at last I'd stopped for breath she reached over and gave me a hug, ignoring the Oreo crumbs I got all over her. "Oh Jenn, I'm so sorry, I wish I had known!" She released me from her squeeze. "I've been a terrible friend, I've been so MIA lately with Jake and work—I'm sorry!"

I reassured her there was nothing anyone could've done.

"So how did Paul take it? Is he okay?" She was unconsciously fussing with her engagement ring, something I'd noticed her doing when she became agitated lately. I appreciate how much she cared.

"Ugh, Jess... that was one thing I should've gotten your help with. I totally botched the breakup." I leaned back and covered my eyes with my hands. "How in the world do you tactically tell someone you don't like them anymore?"

"There is no good way to do it Jenn, there really isn't."

I gave her the long version of my experience, sparing no details.

Jessica was trying hard to bite back a grin by the time I was done. By the time I got to me saying it was "me not him" for the second time, she couldn't hold back her laughter.

"It's not funny!" I said, laughing myself as I threw a pillow at her.

"I'm sorry—it's just—I wish I could've been there," she said gasping between her words.

Her laughter at least brought some lightness to my mood.

"So," She asked once she'd finally got control of herself, "the question is are you happy now? Like do you feel relieved to be broken up or are you sad?"

I thought for a split second before responding. "Relieved. Definitely relieved."

"Well, then as painful as it might have been, you did the right thing."

I nodded. "Yeah, that was what I figured. I just wish it could've been a smoother process. For Paul's sake and my own."

"Well, on the bright side," she said with a half smile, "now you can set your dating profile live again."

My mind immediately went to Luke. And I couldn't help thinking I might not set that profile live just yet.

Chapter 19

Friday's lunch date was something I was equally excited for and dreading. Not that it was a date. Friday's "old friends, get together" lunch. There, that was a more appropriate title.

Whatever it was, it was on my mind all morning.

The worst part about it was I wasn't coming from work, meaning I couldn't just default to my black on black attire. I knew I was being ridiculous. Friends didn't care what other friends were wearing.

But possible future love interests did.

The only one around to give me their opinion was good old Athena. Yes she was still with me, kicking it in her original glass bowl. I had never gotten her the upgrade I'd promised. (Note to self: get Athena a bigger, newer fishbowl). Unfortunately she wasn't known for her great fashion advice—she tended to keep her opinions to herself.

I tried to spend the morning working on my blog, I had about three different recipes I needed to edit pictures and write posts for. I think I spent the majority of my time imagining all the ways Luke and my acquaintanceship could end up.

The ideal scenario of course was him and I getting married, having 4 beautiful children, and living in a house by the beach. I was midway through imagining an alternate scenario where we had a destination wedding in Maui when I decided to close my computer.

Obviously work wasn't distracting me so I decided to go on a run. Luckily, the physical effort kept me occupied enough to get through the rest of the morning.

By the time I showered and was ready it was about 11:35. We were supposed to meet at noon at a little burger place about 20 minutes away. Perfect.

I got there with five minutes to spare, just enough time to air out my sweaty armpits with my car's AC vents. What was it about this guy? I never sweated unless I was super nervous. Why did I turn to jelly when I was around him?

I parked on the street about a block from the restaurant. I wanted to give myself a moment to compose myself (and air out my armpits), plus then I could see if Luke walked in before me.

I didn't see him, and as much as I wanted to be the fashionably late person, my punctual self couldn't do it. I walked through the doors at exactly twelve o'clock, his suit jacket in hand, and requested a table for two.

The hostess seated me, saying she'd direct my date to my table once he arrived. I liked how she assumed he'd be my date. I almost clarified that he was just my non-date friend, but she'd already left me alone with the menus.

It was a cute little restaurant, a beach themed place with a casual vibe. I'd never been there but Luke said it was one of his favorites.

Luke walked in about five minutes late, dressed in jeans and a button-up shirt. I didn't know how to greet him. With a hug? A handshake?

I decided on awkwardly standing halfway and tossing him his jacket. Perfect.

He took it with a smile. "Thanks, sorry for making you meet me for this."

I shrugged. "It was no problem."

He sat across from me and added, "The good thing is it gave me an excuse to see you again."

I didn't know how to respond so I said the first thing that came to my mind. "How come you're dressed so casually? Didn't you have work today?" I almost smacked myself.

He looked down at himself with raised eyebrows. "I'll have you know this is a very high quality shirt that I probably paid way too much for."

"Oh, I mean, I didn't mean it looks bad, I just thought your work was more formal..." I was fumbling for words.

He fiddled with his collar, a sly grin on his face. "I'm messing with you Jenn. We do casual Fridays at my office. No suit and tie necessary."

I should've known not to take him seriously.

Just then the waiter came back with my water and to get Luke's drink order. He said he'd give us a few more minutes to peruse the menu.

"So," I asked, scanning the menu, "what's good here?"

Luke didn't even pick up his menu. "Honestly, every burger here is good. I've never had any of the chicken sandwiches because I don't believe in white meat."

"You're such a dork." I loved how easy it was to talk to him. How he never took himself or anyone else too seriously.

"I personally always get the bacon ranch burger with extra bacon."

"Well that sounds healthy." That one actually did look pretty good. "Have you tried the blue cheese one?" I found blue cheese to be a very polarizing ingredient. You either loved it or you hated it. I loved it.

"Mmm, yes I have and I can vouch for it. Although it'd probably be better if you asked them to put bacon on it."

I laughed against my will, why did all men love bacon? We spent the next few minutes analyzing milkshake flavors. We settled on him getting the peanut butter Oreo and me getting the mint chocolate chip.

They were surprisingly prompt with their service, our burgers coming out less than ten minutes after we ordered. Luke was in the middle of telling me about a work project when they arrived. Most of it was going over my head, a lot of engineering terminology that I didn't register, but it was clear that Luke was very passionate about what he did.

Our shakes arrived about two minutes later, each topped with a generous dollop of whipped cream. I instantly dove into mine, the cool mint the perfect contrast to the chocolate chips.

"Mmm...," I moaned, "this is so good."

I was surprised when he swiped my glass out from under my nose and took a big swig. Well, apparently we were close enough to share milkshakes.

"Excuse me," I said haughtily, "did you ask for a taste?" At the same time, I stole his peanut butter Oreo one and took a sip.

He slid my glass back over to my side. "You're right, the mint is good. But my peanut butter one is better." With that, he snuck his back.

"You wish." It was time for my burger anyway. I took a big bite and the flavors melted in my mouth. The warm meat combined with the juicy tomato, the crunchy lettuce, and of course the tang from the blue cheese. It was heaven. Luke watched me chew. "So? How is it?"

"Mmmm," I shook my finger at him, not willing to let him interrupt my happy moment.

He looked pleased. "I told you this place was good." He picked up his burger and took a big bite. We spend the next few minutes making small talk as we ate. The waiter came by to check that everything was okay.

"Ugh," I leaned backed once I finished my burger. "That was so good, but I'm stuffed."

Luke eyed my leftover steak fries. "You too stuffed to finish those?"

I pushed my plate over to him. "They're all yours." I reached over for my shake. "I am not, however, too full to finish this."

"Nothing like a girl with a good appetite."

"You know," I said, leaning into the table. "That's got to be the biggest lie all men say. They want a girl with an appetite, but they also want a girl that looks like a size 0 supermodel."

Luke looked at me blankly. "I don't."

"You don't what?"

"Want my girlfriend to be a size 0 supermodel. They always look so hungry. Like they need a good meal or something." He smiled at me. "Not that I'm saying I don't admire fitness and health, I just don't believe skinniness is as attractive as some girls think."

I may have fallen in love with him at that moment. "So what do you do to keep in shape?" I asked, hoping to steer my thoughts in another direction.

He shrugged. "Nothing big. I lift, run occasionally. I work out regularly, but nothing hardcore." He smiled at me. "I just do it enough so I can eat giant burgers and shakes like this without feeling guilty."

I nodded and lifted my glass in agreement.

"How about you? You clearly stay in shape. What's your workout of choice?"

He thought I was in shape? Had he been checking me out? "I'm into spin classes lately," I answered, my thoughts still racing.

"Oh yeah? I've always wanted to try one of those," he said.

"You should come with me sometime." Why did I say that?

"Really? When and where do you go?"

Uh oh, I'd gotten myself into this. "I go to 24-Hour Fitness. I usually go after work, but they have a Saturday morning class I go to too."

"I can make that work. Tomorrow then?" He looked at me questioningly.

"I, uh, yeah tomorrow at 9 AM." What the heck was I doing? I was supposed to be keeping this a distant friendship. Returning his jacket today and telling him to have a nice life. Not inviting him to work out with me. Not sharing my milkshake and fries with him.

"Perfect." He pulled out his phone and typed something into his calendar. Just then it beeped and he appeared to be reading a text.

"Oh dang, I got to get back to work. My boss wants to discuss that project I was telling you about." He pocketed his phone and flagged the waiter down for the check.

When it came I told him I could pay for my meal. He rolled his eyes. "I'm paying for your meal Jenn. Think of it as payment for returning my jacket."

"Well, you pay pretty well. Let me know if there are any other services you need me for." I almost ducked my head under the table. I couldn't believe I said that. What would he think I was insinuating? I tried to pretend my face hadn't just flushed a bright red.

He looked at me oddly for a second, and then was gentleman enough not to notice my embarrassment.

"I'll try and think of something," was all he said.

We said our goodbyes with the awkwardness of two people who didn't know what to do. Did we hug? Shake hands? Simply wave?

I was already so embarrassed by my last comment I didn't care. I just did my best to get back in my car as quickly as possible where I could question what the heck I was doing with Luke Bradley.

*****

My mom called me that night. It was a truth universally acknowledged that an unmarried girl, in the midst of boy trouble, will get a call from her mother.

Moms had a sixth sense about these kinds of things.

My mom called at 7 PM on a Friday night. If she thought I'd be available to chat then she knew there was something going wrong with my love/social life.

I considered ignoring her call. I was halfway through a Bachelor rerun, the ring ceremony was up next and I didn't want to miss it, but I answered anyway.

"Hi Mom," I said, trying to sound chipper.

"Hey honey... how are you?"

She knew. I didn't know how she knew, but she did. "Oh fine, just you know, hanging out." I still held on to a shred of hope that she'd think everything was normal for me.

"By yourself?"

Dang it. "Um, yeah."

"But, where's Paul? It's Friday night, why aren't you hanging out with him?" I could hear a knowing sympathy creep into my mom's voice.

"Um... well, Paul and I aren't together anymore. I broke it off with him." I spent the next 30 minutes giving my mom details about everything going on. Everything.

That was the good thing about living two states away from your parents. There was no way she could get involved so I was free to tell her everything. When I finally finished and took a deep breath there was silence on the other end.

I couldn't deal with silence.

"So?" I prompted, "what do you think I should do?"

"Well, probably exactly what you are doing," she responded.

"What do you mean? Continue sporadically hanging out with Luke? With no idea what it's leading do? Even though he's my roommate's ex-boyfriend who broke her heart!" Wow, I sounded dramatic even to myself.

"Jenn, how do you think any relationship starts? No one decides after one date that they're going to have a serious relationship," she said matter-of-factly. "Those things take time to develop."

She was right. I couldn't expect Luke to declare his intentions after inviting me to one lunch. This wasn't a 19th century Jane Austen story.

"And as for Jessica, you should bring this all up with her. She's bound to find out sometime, and she'll be hurt you didn't tell her if you wait much longer."

Ugh, sometimes I hated it when moms were right.

"Plus honey, I think you're making this into a bigger deal than it has to be. Yes, Luke and Jessica did date, but that was over two years ago." Mom was in full reasoning mode now. "Think if the roles were reversed, how would you feel?"

I thought about that for a second. If I found out two years from now Jessica started dating Paul how would I feel? It was a little different since Paul hadn't broken my heart, but what would I think?

If I was being honest with myself, at first I would be a little bugged. I might feel a little betrayed. But I didn't think I'd care that much. If Jessica truly did like him and he liked her, I'd be happy for them both.

Would Jessica feel the same way if I dated Luke?

"You still there?" My mom's question interrupted my thoughts.

"Huh? Oh yeah, just thinking." Something I'd been doing way too much of lately. "You're right, I should talk to Jessica about this." I let out a sigh. "I just don't want to."

"I think you'll be happier if you do," my mom said bluntly.

And she was right. Like moms usually were.

*****

I resolved to talk to Jessica after my cycling class with Luke. I figured that would give me one more opportunity to gauge his feelings. Because to be honest, sometimes I thought I must be making all this romance up in my head.

I put on my cutest workout outfit—black slim leggings with a neon pink stripe running down the side, and a form-fitting pink tank top.

I tied my hair up in a high ponytail, and I may or may not have used my curling iron to add some totally natural, I-woke-up-this-way beach waves. After a layer of waterproof mascara, I was ready to go.

Luke also had a 24-Hour gym membership so we agreed he'd just meet me there.

When I arrived ten minutes early, I was the second person in the class, the first was the actual instructor.

He was a substitute instructor; the regular gal was out sick or something. I'd taken a few classes from him before and knew he was pretty hardcore. I didn't know if that was good or bad. I mean, I liked to get a good workout, however I wanted to impress Luke with my athleticism. Passing out wouldn't help my cause.

I took a bike closer to the back for this reason. I made sure to save the one next to me for Luke by slinging my spare towel over it.

He and the rest of the class meandered in about ten minutes later. The instructor had the music pumping so we couldn't talk much. We waved at each other over the noise and I gestured towards the bike next to mine. He gave me the thumbs up as he walked towards it.

I had already adjusted my bike, shortening the pedal and seat heights so they fit me. Luke took a minute to do the same. Clearly this wasn't his first time riding a bike. Or at least a stationary gym bike.

The instructor got us warming up and my blood and my breathing began to pump.

Every so often throughout the class Luke would glance over at me and smile or we'd share looks of exhaustion during peak moments. It hit me during the last 15 minutes that this was what I wanted. Someone I could go through life sharing experiences with. Sharing in the good times, the hard times, someone who would laugh with me and motivate me. I didn't want just a nice guy who checked the boxes. I wanted someone who I could relate with and ultimately fall in love with.

I wanted Luke.

And for goodness sake, I was going to go for it. I was sick of being scared to do things. Everything good in my life came from taking a leap. From starting my blog to opening my own bakery. From online dating to maybe starting something with Luke. Being scared got you nowhere.

By the time class was over we were both soaked in sweat and exhausted. A good exhaustion though. I didn't even care how I looked. Even if my hair was sweaty and matted to my head, or if I smelled like a stinky gym, I was just happy being with Luke.

We headed to the gym's juice bar afterward and got large fruit smoothies. The smoothies probably undid all the calories we'd burned, but they were worth it. We chatted about the workout. Luke said he was converted to spin classes now.

"They are a pretty legit workout," I agreed. "I swear my abs are stronger than they've ever been before."

"Is this class every Saturday?" Luke asked.

"Yep, there's always a 9 AM and 10 AM spin class," I answered.

"Well, I might have to make this a Saturday morning tradition then." He said before taking a long drink from his smoothie.

My heart stopped a little and I wanted to ask him to clarify what he meant. Did he mean taking the class with me every Saturday? Or just the spin class in general? Did he have to be so vague about these things?

"So," he interrupted my thoughts, "how are things at the bakery?"

The change in subject drew my mind from its deep thoughts. "Good, nothing too new, just pushing out orders."

"Are you still doing the blog as well?"

I forgot how much he knew about my life. "It's going well. I've slowed things down on it lately. I'm more focused on making use of the content I've already created than churning out new recipes every day."

I described my work schedule, my Monday through Thursday bakery hours and then Friday's blogging focus. He was thoroughly interested in the whole thing, asking questions and making comments throughout.

"So what's next?" He asked when I was through.

"Next?" I responded.

He tapped his cup on the table. "Yeah, I mean, you're clearly not the type to be settled with where you're at. There's got to be something else on your horizon."

I thought about Mariam and my dream to write a cookbook. Don't ask me why, since everyone else had shot me down, but I decided to tell him about it.

"Well, I know it's a little far fetched," I began, "but I've always wanted to write a cookbook." And to my astonishment, Luke was all in.

"Of course!" he said. "That'd be perfect—you already have a solid fan base from your blog. I bet all your readers would buy a cookbook from you." He stared off, obviously thinking. "Writing it shouldn't be too hard since that's what you do on your blog right? Write new recipes?" He looked at me with wide eyes.

His energy was addicting. "Yeah, that's kind of what I've been thinking. I actually have a repertoire of recipe ideas I've been collecting over the years, some of my favorites. I keep telling myself I'm just scheduling them out to post on my blog later, but honestly, they're ones I want to save for a cookbook."

"So what do you need to do to get it going?"

We spent the next bit discussing the need for a book contract from one of the bigger publishers. How I'd need a literary agent to represent me. I loved Luke's energy and total belief in my abilities. It was refreshing to talk to someone who didn't think my dreams were over the top.

Luke finally leaned back with a smile. "Well, I definitely think you should go for it. You do have a good amount on your plate right now... but I think you could do it." He looked down at his watch then back up at me. "This was fun, we'll have to continue making this book publishing plan later. When are you free this week?"

I loved how confident he was about us. Like of course we were going to hang out again. Of course we were going to continue working on my life dream of publishing a cookbook.

I grinned. "Let's do lunch on Tuesday, I'll take you to my favorite lunch spot this time."

"Perfect, I'll plan on it."

He stood and helped me out of my chair. There was a split second when we were standing inches apart, face to face, all it would've taken was for one of us to lean forward slightly and our lips would have met. I was rooted to the floor though.

Luke seemed frozen for a second too. His eyes roved my face. Finally he pulled me into a quick hug.

When we drew apart there still seemed to be some longing in his eyes, and I was sure there was plenty in mine.

He smirked. "Sorry about the smell, I'm telling you, that cycling class whipped me."

I laughed. "Don't worry, I don't smell any better."

With that, he grabbed his bag and turned to go. "See you on Tuesday."

And this may have been the first time in a while I was looking forward to the week starting.

Chapter 20

The next week went by quickly. Like we planned, Luke and I met for lunch on Tuesday. I took him to Gijorno's. Yes, the famous girl's night spot. I hadn't been there in quite a while. What with all the babies being born and weddings to plan, we had had fewer and fewer girls nights together.

Luke thoroughly enjoyed it. I felt like it took a special person to appreciate that much grease but he performed admirably. He was even down to finish off an entire order of cannoli with me.

From Thursday to Sunday Luke was going to be out of town, he had some big engineering conference in Chicago. He was going to miss Saturday's spin class so he insisted on coming with me on Wednesday afternoon. I wasn't complaining.

Like every other time we were together, it was easy and comfortable. I never had a problem talking with Luke, there were never painful silences or stalls in our conversations. It was refreshing after the endless awkward dates I'd had over the years.

I still wasn't sure what we were yet. We had to be more than friends right? I mean, why else would he repeatedly want to hang out with me?

As much as I wanted answers, there was no way I was going to bring it up. Relationship conversations were definitely not my strong suit. Plus, if I was being honest with myself, there was a small part of me that was scared.

I was scared that if I brought it up, it might ruin whatever we did have. What if Luke didn't want to make us serious or official and I scared him off?

No, I wasn't ready to take the next step with him, but one thing I did need to do was talk to Jessica.

*****

I brought home some leftover chocolate cookies with me from work that evening. Sugar always made uncomfortable conversations better.

Jessica got home around 5:30 and she seemed in a fairly good mood. She and Jake were finally "officially" engaged as of last week. He'd taken her out to dinner at a fancy restaurant in Laguna and then proposed on a cliff overlooking the sunset. A classic scenario but Jess loved it and she finally had the proof on her finger.

Now that they were official she was free to begin serious wedding planning.

"Hey," I said as she walked in the door. "How's the day been?"

"Oh good," she said as she finished a text on her phone. When she was done she tossed it into her purse and sat next to me on the couch. When she spotted the bakery box she squealed excitedly. "Ooo, are these for us?"

Before I'd even answered she'd opened it and peered inside.

"Yep, we had some leftover double chocolate cookies today. I brought them home because I know they're your favorite." It was only a half lie, we did have extras, but it may have been because I purposely made too many.

"Mmmm..." she sunk deep into the cushions, a giant cookie in hand.

We spent the next few minutes discussing her work. I was really only half invested in the conversation. My mind was occupied on how I was going to bring up Luke to her. Finally, after a lull, I decided to be blunt.

"Jess, there's something I have to talk to you about... and I'm not sure how you're going to feel." I played absentmindedly with a strand of hair. I didn't know why I was so nervous.

She turned to me with an open face. "What's up?" When I hesitated she added, "You know you can tell me anything Jenn."

So I began. I told her about Luke. How we met by chance at his work and then had continued meeting on and off since. I talked fast, wanting to get it all out before she could interrupt me.

When I was done she sat silently for a minute.

"I know Luke was a turd the way he broke up with you and we swore him off," I said, wanting her to know that I was torn, "so if you're not okay with me seeing him I totally understand."

Jessica looked at me studiously. "My question is how do you feel about him? Do you truly like him?" She played with the cookie wrapper in her hands. "I'm not going to lie; this does kind of come as a shock. I still kind of think of him as a jerk, and it wouldn't take much to convince me to egg his house." She stopped messing with the wrapper and looked at me. "But if you like him, I can be fine with it."

There was a glimmer of hope that hit me. "I... I think I do like him. I'm not sure, I think I haven't given myself permission to fall for him because I'm not sure how you feel." I didn't mention that I wasn't really sure how he felt either.

She pulled me in for a hug. "Oh Jenn, you know I would never come in the way of something or someone that made you happy. Luke might have broken my heart a few years ago, but that was in the past. I've got Jake now." She gave me a half smile. "I can give Luke a second chance for your sake, even though he was a punk."

I laughed a little. "He did handle that situation pretty badly." I sobered up. "Seriously though, if you're not comfortable with it, I don't have to continue seeing him. I don't even know what his feelings are."

"Well first off, of course he's falling for you or else he's nuts." She held up a finger when I tried to interrupt her. "However we also know he is a little romantically unstable due to past experiences, so you'd better clear the air with him soon. You need to straight up ask him what things are between you two."

I nodded, Jessica was right. I didn't want to be blindsided by him like she had been. "I know I just hate awkward conversations." I covered my face with my hands. "Last time I talked about my feelings with a guy things ended up badly." I was thinking about Paul.

"No one likes them," Jessica patted me on the back. "They are the worst." After a pause she added, "What ever happened with Paul? Did you hear back from him after your breakup?"

I nodded. "He texted me once or twice. He kept asking if I still meant what I said and if we could meet and talk it over more."

"You told him no right?"

"Yeah, I can't deal with more feelings conversations. And it's not like I'm going to change my mind anyways."

"Good. I think it's better to just make a clean break from it all."

I agreed.

"Well," she pointed her finger at me, "I appreciate that you told me about Luke. Even if you went a little behind my back at first."

She leaned forward and grabbed another cookie out of the box. "However, if it makes you feel obligated to bring me cookies, you're welcome to go behind my back anytime you want."

*****

Monday was busy. We had six events we were catering that afternoon so our ovens were going full speed. Olivia was my assistant that morning and our hands were packing and assembling boxes nonstop.

It wasn't until almost noon that we were able to slow down. Mitch came and picked up our orders, commenting about the recent increase in the deliveries. I had to agree with him. If this kept up I'd have to contract out another delivery man and possibly an additional assistant baker.

Olivia was putting away pans and I was turning on the dishwashers when Paul showed up.

Yes, Paul.

He held a bouquet of red roses as he walked into the kitchen.

"Paul?" I wasn't really sure if I was actually seeing him. "Wh—what are you doing here?"

"I needed to talk to you and you wouldn't meet me so I had to come to you." He said it so bluntly, like obviously what else was he to do?

"Paul, that's because I don't have anything else to say to you." I tried not to sound patronizing but I didn't think he noticed anyway.

"Look Jenn, I just think you're making a mistake. You and I are perfect for each other." He spent the next five minutes giving me a laundry list of why we were a perfect match. They included things like we both liked Italian food, we were both early risers, we both liked watching comedies... I didn't have the heart to tell him that those probably weren't enough to build a long-term relationship on.

"Paul," I began when he finished his monologue, "you're right, we do have a lot of similarities. However the main part of a relationship, the spark and love, isn't there for me. I don't want to steal your potential for a happy future by lying about the way I feel. It's not going to work out for us."

He looked at me blankly.

I sighed deeply. "I'm glad for the time we had together, it was fun, but it's over between us." I took him by the arm and slowly started walking towards the door. "You're going to find a great girl one day who loves you for everything you are. Trust me."

We reached outside and I saw his car parked in front on the curb.

Paul turned to me and offered me the flowers with a sigh. "Well, it was worth a shot at least. Here, you can keep these; I think I'm allergic to roses anyway." He itched his nose.

I took the flowers from him and smiled. "Thanks Paul, I really do think you're a great guy, I'm not just trying to make you feel good."

I leaned forward to kiss him on the cheek. At the last second he turned his head so I was kissing him on the lips. I jerked back .

He gave me a wink and said, "Well, figured I'd better get at least one last kiss from you."

I rolled my eyes at him but grinned anyway.

He turned to the curb. "Goodbye Jenn, and good luck."

"Same to you Paul." I watched him get in his car. Realistically I wasn't going to miss Paul too much. We'd had fun but like I said, we were done.

It was just then something caught my eye from the side. I turned and saw Luke standing there looking at me wide eyed. "Luke!" I said in shock. "What are you—how long—," I was fumbling for words. Had he seen me kiss Paul?

After a second's pause, he stepped forward, handing me a gift wrapped bag. "I uh, I wanted to give you this, just something I picked up for you in Chicago." He was mumbling. "Anyway I can see you're busy," he looked pointedly at the roses in my hand, "so I'll get going."

He turned on his heel without another word and started towards his car.

"Wait—Luke!" I called out but either he didn't hear me, or more likely, he ignored me. He got in his car and quickly took off.

And there I stood. Once again alone.

*****

I went back into my kitchen and immediately tried texting Luke. I wasn't sure what to say. Should I explain the kiss I gave Paul? But what would I say? "Hey, yeah I was just kissing my ex-boyfriend in the parking lot, but seriously, it was no big deal." I didn't think I could make it sound any worse.

The situation needed to be addressed though. It took me about 15 minutes to draft a text I was willing to send.

Hey Luke, we need to chat. I promise what you saw in the parking lot was not what you think.

I wasn't exactly sure what he thought it was, but I assumed it wasn't anything good.

I also wanted to thank him for the gift he gave me. They were a set of measuring cups designed to look like mini deep dish pizzas. Very appropriate coming from Chicago. I loved his thoughtfulness and humor in the gift. I couldn't think of anybody else who would pick them out for me.

Also, thank you for the measuring cups. I was dying when I opened them, they're perfect!

I contemplated adding a little emoji happy face but I wasn't sure if he was in the mood.

I sat on my desk and waited for a solid 15 minutes with no response. If I was going to hang out in my kitchen all afternoon I'd better do something worthwhile.

So I started prepping some cookie dough. We didn't have any orders for it tomorrow, but I typically liked to keep a few batches frozen for emergencies. I was adding eggs to the mixer when my phone buzzed. I ran to check it.

Glad you liked them, it was no big deal. And you don't have to explain anything to me. We're good.

That was it.

What did he mean by "we're good"? Did he mean everything's fine and normal? Like, see you on Saturday for our regular spin class kind of normal? Or did he mean "we're good" as in now he sees the real me? Like I'm clearly not into a serious relationship right now since I'm off kissing other guys?

Sometimes I hated texting.

I wanted to respond again, but I wasn't sure what to say. I decided to wait until I got home and call in the big guns for help: Jessica.

*****

Jessica's advice was to just straight up call Luke.

"Text messages are too easy to misinterpret," she insisted.

She was right but I didn't have the guts to call him yet. So I formulated another text response. It only took approximately 30 minutes. My masterpiece said:

You want to go to lunch tomorrow?

I know, I should be an author with those writing skills.

I ate my way through two bowls of Lucky Charms while waiting for Luke's response. When it came I was sorely disappointed.

Busy at work. Sorry, can't make it.

Not even a "let's reschedule" or anything. He was definitely mad at me. I decided to make one more attempt.

Okay, see you at spin class this Saturday?

I didn't want to wait until Saturday to see him again but it was my best chance at a positive response.

Two hours later I still had no reply. Jessica had offered to stay home with me for moral support. She was supposed to hang out with Jake tonight so I had insisted she go.

I was starting to regret it. I needed someone there who could tell me what to do. Here I was, finally determined to put my whole heart in and really go for the guy I wanted. And it had to get screwed up from a simple misunderstanding. Were things ever going to work out for my love life?

While I was lying in bed, half awake and half asleep, I made an ultimatum to myself.

It didn't matter that things had gotten mixed up. It didn't matter that Luke was not speaking to me. I was still going to put my whole heart in and go for the guy I wanted. Even if he rejected me, at least I wouldn't have any regrets.

*****

I decided there was only one way to confront him, with cookies.

Luckily most of the orders we were filling on Tuesday included cookie trays so I had plenty leftover.

His home was likely the best place to corner him. I considered tracking him down at work, but I didn't want to have an awkward conversation in front of all his coworkers. Luke probably wouldn't appreciate it either.

I didn't actually have his address, but he'd said he hadn't moved in the last two years. So Jessica came to my rescue. She still had his address saved on her phone and was able to send it to me.

Good luck! She'd said in her text.

She was right; I was going to need all the luck I could get.

It was Tuesday, so I had my standing lunch date with Ann. We met at our usual place but I couldn't quite stomach my usual burger and shake. I ended up ordering a chicken salad. Ann knew something was up.

"Okay spill it," she said. "You'd only get a salad if something was seriously wrong."

I smiled faintly. "You know me too well." I pushed the lettuce around on my plate. "It's a guy problem."

Ann set her chicken sandwich down and leaned forward on her elbows. "I'm all ears. Shoot."

I gave her the quick version of breaking up with Paul and my latest interactions with Luke. I was getting pretty good at telling people this story. When I got to the part about Luke seeing me kiss Paul she cringed.

"Well, that's an unfortunate chance of luck. You're sure he saw you kissing?" She'd gone back to eating her sandwich.

"Yeah he saw it; he was basically standing right in front of us. Plus he's not answering me now so something must be bugging him." I took a sip of water, trying to wash down the crouton stuck in my throat.

"Well on the bright side, at least you know he's jealous. And if he's jealous that means he must like you." She tapped her finger on her chin thoughtfully. "So your plan is to woo him with cookies?"

"I know I'm being ridiculous or probably naive. I just don't know what else to do." I rested my face in my hands.

"No, it's not a bad idea. I've successfully appeased many men in my life with butter and sugar. I'm just curious what you're going to say to him." She looked at me pointedly. "Are you going to tell him how you feel?"

I pinched the bridge of my nose. "Maybe? I don't want to, that'd make me so vulnerable. But I probably should."

She was nodding. "All I know is you can't expect him to open up to you about his feelings if you won't do the same with yours. Not that you actually did anything bad, but in his eyes, you're in the wrong right now. So you're going to have to be the first to be honest about how you feel."

I sank lower in my seat but knew she was right. "Yeah, I guess I'll have to."

She looked down at my half eaten salad. "You better eat something girl, you're going to need all the strength you can get."

Chapter 21

I got to Luke's place around seven that night. I wanted to
be sure he was home from work or any other errands he had
to run. I may or may not have also been looking for any
excuse to put off this confrontation.

As per Jessica's directions, he lived in a townhome
complex in the heart of Irvine. I was quite impressed with
the neighborhood. It looked like a quiet, but very
sophisticated area. The number of BMWs and Mercedes
parked in the neighborhood may have added to the vibe
too.

Luke's place was an end unit in the back of the complex.
It appeared to be a two-story townhome, attached on one
side to his neighbors. The front yard, if you could call it
that, was a small patch of green grass that ended at a quaint
little porch. Nothing fancy, but it looked clean and well
kept.

The blinds were closed on all his windows, but I could
see light filtering through the downstairs one. The upstairs
looked dark. While this made me feel slightly stalkerish, I
took it as a good note. He was most likely awake and
hanging out downstairs. Hopefully alone.

I parked my car and tucked the box of cookies under one arm.

I took my time getting up his front door, taking deep slow breaths to calm my nerves. If I thought breaking up with Paul was nerve-racking, that was nothing compared to this. I wiped my sweaty palms on my jeans before knocking lightly.

Obviously too lightly.

After two minutes of no response, I considered giving up and heading home. But, I knew that wouldn't solve my problem, so I rang the doorbell. I could hear the loud chime echoing inside.

After about ten seconds I heard feet shuffling and the porch light flipped on. Next thing I knew the door was swinging open. Luke stood in front of me. He was dressed in navy jogging shorts and a t-shirt that fit perfectly to his athletic frame. He would make a T-shirt and shorts look good.

"Jenn?" He said, leaning forward slightly. "What, what are you doing here? How did you know where I live?"

So not the response I was hoping for. In my ideal situation, he opened the door, cried out my name in joy, and hugged me tightly. Then we would share our first magical kiss and all would be forgotten.

Well, you get what you get, I told myself.

"I came here to talk to you," I began, hoping he didn't hear the quiver in my voice. "You didn't answer my text so I figured I'd come to you." I shrugged my shoulders, "And Jessica gave me your address. I promise I'm not a stalker."

I could see him fighting back a smile. "Okay, what did you want to talk about?"

Again, in an ideal situation he would've at least invited me inside; clearly this wasn't going to be as easy as I hoped. "Um, well I wanted to explain what you probably saw yesterday."

He folded his arms stiffly. "What I probably saw? I think what you mean is what I did see. I am pretty sure, unless my eyes have failed me, I saw you kissing a guy outside your work yesterday." Then he demonstrated holding something under his arm. "And I'm also pretty sure you had a bunch of flowers. A gift perhaps from your *friend*?"

I held up one hand in defense. "I know, I know what it must have looked like. It wasn't what you think though. That guy was Paul, my ex-boyfriend."

Luke lifted his hand over his chest in mock relief. "Oh, your ex-boyfriend! Well that's good to know, I feel much better now."

I glowered at him. "Stop being such a twit. Let me finish. He is my ex-boyfriend. I broke up with him about a week ago. He came to my work, uninvited," I raised my finger to emphasize that point, "to try and talk me back into a relationship. But that was it. That kiss you saw, first off wasn't supposed to be a mouth to mouth kiss—I was going for a goodbye kiss on the cheek when he turned at the last second. But," my hand was flailing through the air dramatically now, "that was a goodbye kiss. As in 'it was good knowing you, we had some fun times, but it's over now' kind of a kiss." I looked at Luke, trying to gauge his reaction.

He leaned against the door frame and twisted his mouth. "So you're expecting me to believe that this guy means nothing to you? You broke up with him what, last week and now you're over him? Why?"

"First off, I may have only broken up with him last week but our relationship has been done for a while now. And what do you mean why?" He of all people had no right to be giving me a hard time about breaking up with someone. Hadn't he done the same thing, totally out of the blue, to Jessica two years ago?

"I was wondering why you broke up with him? Why did you decide to sever a relationship that apparently he was still into?"

Oh crud, here's the part I was dreading. The part where I had to tell him how I felt. I was really hoping that ideal scenario where he hugged me and everything was good was going to happen. Then I could avoid all this awkward "talk about our feelings" stuff.

I fiddled with the box in my hands, at that moment not sure if he deserved the cookies I brought.

"Because of you," I said quietly.

"What do you mean because of me?" He sounded surprised.

"I broke up with him because of you. Because I knew if I wanted any chance with you I needed to end things with Paul." I realized that sounded bad so I had it explain further. "Not that I'm saying you're the only reason. Paul's and my relationship has been dying a slow death this whole last month. I'm not even sure if I was ever really into him." I shrugged my shoulders. "But I couldn't bring myself to break up with him. I think I was secretly hoping things would just fizzle out. It wasn't happening though."

Luke was staring at me intently. I hurried on, I couldn't deal with this vulnerability stuff much longer.

"What I'm trying to say is I like you." I looked him straight in the eyes, "I've liked you for a long time. Probably too long. I think I was mostly just afraid of that. Afraid you would have no interest in me and it was all on my side." I looked down at my feet. "When you didn't respond to me yesterday, it actually gave me a shred of hope. I figured you must have feelings for me in some way, or you wouldn't have been so mad about that kiss between Paul and me." I quickly looked up at him and then back down.

"Anyway, my whole life I've always been afraid to go for what I wanted. I've always been afraid to ruffle feathers or do things that might make me or anyone else uncomfortable. But I'm learning being comfortable isn't how you make progress. So, as uncomfortable as this is making me, I came here to tell you all this. To explain things to you and to tell you how I feel." I let out a slow breath of air. Mentally and physically exhausted from the speech I'd just made.

I waited, looking into his face for some shred of an answer.

He stared back at me, his face half hidden by shadows. Then he slowly looked down, stopping at the box in my arms.

"Are those cookies?" he asked and he stepped back to open the door wide for me.

*****

The punk. Here I was spilling my whole heart out to him and all he cared about was the chocolate chip cookies I held under my arm.

I stalked past him into his living room, my frustration evident in every stomp of my feet.

I plopped the box down on his black ottoman and turned to see him closing the door, not taking his eyes off me.

I was a bit unnerved by that stare, it was what I imagined a lion looked like before he pounced on his prey. I wasn't going to let him see my uncertainty though so I crossed my arms and stuck my chin out. "There are chocolate chip and double chocolate cookies in there. I hope that meets your desires."

I meant to disarm him with my comment but he just broke out into a sly smile as he walked towards me. "Well, as long as you come with the package I think my desires will be met perfectly."

When he reached me he grabbed my hands and untwined my folded arms. We were standing inches apart at this point, our faces about as close as they could be without touching.

I couldn't deal with the tension in the air. "So—so you like chocolate chip cookies?" I asked breathlessly.

He let out a little chuckle. "Almost as much as I like you." And then he was kissing me. A slow, deliberate kiss that was ten times better than any one I'd imagined.

When I couldn't breathe anymore we stepped back, our hands still entwined.

"Holy Cow," I said. Way to kill the moment Jenn. I never could deal with romantic moments in movies. They always made me squirm. Clearly I felt the same way about real life moments too.

"I hope that was a good 'holy cow'," Luke said as he led me to the couch.

For the first time, I looked around and noticed the room I was in. It was simple but nicely decorated. A manly touch to it all, but in a classy way.

"So," Luke's voice rumbled close to my ear, "about this Paul fellow, do I need to go beat him up for messing with my girl? Or are things fine between you two?"

"Your girl?" I asked, not even hearing the rest of his question.

"Yes, because that's what you are now. I'm making it official." He said this with a smile but I could tell there was some seriousness behind his words. He pulled me over to the couch and sat me down next to him. Our hips were snug next to each other and his arm wrapped comfortably behind me.

"I think I owe you a confession as well," he said getting somber all of a sudden. "I actually like you too. I have a lot longer than I want to admit."

"Really?" I asked. I mean I had suspected he was developing feelings for me, but I never thought he had from the beginning.

He nodded, never taking his eyes from my face.

"I think I started falling for you the first time I saw you baking in your apartment two years ago."

I'd like to pretend I had forgotten that incident. That utterly lackluster first impression I left on him. Or so I thought.

"You're kidding right?" I asked.

"No, I'm not. Do you remember the time I'm talking about?" He cocked his head at me in question.

"Yes."

"I just remember you looked like this Amazon woman in the kitchen. Like the kitchen was your total domain. I was so intrigued, you had such confidence."

"I'm pretty sure I looked like a hot mess version of Betty Crocker."

"No, you didn't. Trust me I remember."

I may have questioned his sanity at that moment, but he was in full explanation mode.

"I wouldn't have admitted it at the time, but I did all I could to hang out with you back then. Remember when we were at the farmers market that Saturday?" He asked. "I ended up staying an extra three hours over what I had planned simply because you were there."

I didn't mention that he was the only reason I stayed myself.

"I started feeling a little ashamed of myself. Instead of wanting to hang out with Jessica, all I wanted was to find ways to be around you. I made myself pretty sick over it."

Luke suddenly reached out and touched my knee with his hand, concern lacing his face. "Not that you were the reason I broke up with Jessica, because you weren't. She was a great girl, but my feelings for her had been decreasing for a while before I ended things." He ran his other hand through his hair, giving it the disheveled look I found endearing. "I should've done it sooner, or at least been more open with her, but I just hate breakups. They never go well for me."

I thought about Paul and our awkward breakup scene. Luke had something there.

"The problem was I put myself in a bad spot. Even after I broke up with Jessica, I knew there was no way you would have considered dating me. I'm a guy, but even I know that girls don't date their friend's exes." He gave me with a sheepish grin. "I made up my mind to forget about you. I chalked you up to as a fling that never happened."

"Excuse me—," but he waved me off and kept going.

"It worked, for a few months. I kept myself extra busy with work and other things, but eventually it wasn't enough. I kept coming back to you and thinking about you. Wondering what you were up to, wondering what creep from your dating website you were going out with."

I laughed. "Well you were right; there were a bunch of creeps on there. But I was able to filter most of them out before we ever went on a date."

He stood abruptly and began pacing the room. It was strange to see him so flustered like this. He was always so cool and collected when we were together. I liked seeing this new side of him, it made him more real.

"I finally decided I just wanted to check up on you and see how things were going. I actually started stalking your blog. I tried to read into all your posts to see what you were doing or if there was anyone new in your life. You're pretty cryptic on that thing. You don't get into too many personal details."

"Well sounds like it's a good thing I don't. With creepers like you hanging out on the Internet who knows what could happen to me?" I pointed my finger at him sternly.

He laughed. "Good point. After a few months of that not working out, I decided to be more daring. I knew I couldn't show up at your apartment, l assumed Jessica was still your roommate and that would be extremely awkward. So I decided to show up at Bread & Butter in hopes of catching you there." He tapped his foot on the floor. "I figured my best bet of starting a relationship with you was to begin one as a friendship. If I could pretend like we had an accidental meeting, then develop that into something more serious, I thought you'd reconsider me. I knew I needed to overcome your prejudices against me for breaking up with Jessica first."

He was probably right. If he had point-blank asked me on a date, I would've said no out of loyalty to Jessica.

Luke continued talking. "Unfortunately I didn't realize you had moved on and opened your own place. I tried to ask the girl at Bread & Butter about you, but she didn't seem to know much. All she knew was that the old assistant baker—you—had left and opened her own place a few months earlier. So I did what any lovesick guy would do," he said with an embarrassed grin, "I started researching all the bakeries in Irvine. What I didn't realize was that you weren't an actual bakery, you were a catering company by then."

"Ah, and the plot thickens!" I announced. I was pretty dumbstruck actually. I had no idea that Luke had any remote interest in me before this. And the lengths he had gone to find me were astonishing. I'm not going to lie it made me feel pretty good about myself.

He let out a long sigh. "You're telling me. At this point, I was beginning to lose all hope of coming in contact with you. It was pure luck that you catered our office party. Our office assistant was supposed to schedule the catering for the meeting, but she put in her two weeks notice about a month before it and everyone else forgot about scheduling the food. Somehow I got put in charge of it."

I mentally recorded that tidbit. I could see many future jokes about his apparent party planning talents.

"Luckily a buddy of mine said a place called Jenn's Sweets had catered his daughter's graduation party and was awesome. You can imagine my curiosity at a place called Jenn's Sweets." He wiggled his eyebrows.

I laughed out loud. The story was almost too good to be true. "And the rest is history?"

"Well, I didn't plan on knocking you out with the bathroom door. That was just luck."

I slapped his arm.

"Ha ha, I really was sorry about that. You said you forgave me."

"Well that was before I knew all this scheming you had done. Was everything between us pre-planned? Anything else you need to confess?" I put my hands on my hips.

"Well..." he seemed a little embarrassed about something. " I may or may not have purposely left my jacket at your work that one day too. I needed a good excuse to see you again."

"Holy cow, I feel like I've been living a lie!" I wasn't sure if I was supposed to be angry at how much he'd gone behind my back, but I wasn't. I was elated. Luke liked me. Like he really liked me. "Well, since we're sharing all our dirty secrets, I should probably tell you that I've liked you for a while too." He looked at me with raised eyebrows. "I may have been a tiny bit jealous of Jessica while you two were dating."

"A tiny bit?" He was totally egging me on.

"Maybe a smidgen more than a tiny bit. But I'll have you know it made me feel like the worst friend ever. You know what it says in the Bible, "thou shalt not covet"? I'm pretty sure that includes your roommate's boyfriend." I covered my eyes with my hands. "I can't believe I'm saying this, but

I was the tiniest bit glad when you two broke up. Not that I thought I would ever date you, but I don't think I could've handled it if you two had gotten married and lived happily ever after."

"That sounds like more than a tiny bit of jealousy to me."

I threw a pillow at him.

He laughed and reached down to grab my hand. He pulled me up so I was standing face-to-face with him.

"Jenn Harvey, I have been searching high and low for you for the last two years."

I coughed mockingly.

"Okay, maybe only the last nine months or so. But in my heart, I've been searching my whole life for you." He continued on past my giggling. "And now that I have you before me, complete with a box of my favorite chocolate cookies..." he reached down and picked up the box I brought.

"I'm actually regretting bringing these for you..." I reached to take the box out of his hands but he set it back down on the ottoman.

"Okay Jenn, enough messing around." He pulled me close again. "I've wasted the last two years of my life either denying or trying to hide my feelings for you. I'm done with that." He let out a small breath of air. "I am terrible at talking about feelings. As a matter of fact, relationship conversations are one of my worst nightmares. But I want you to know that I care for you. There's something different about you that I've never found in anyone else. I love being with you, I love talking with you, everything feels more alive and vibrant when I'm around you. I don't know if you feel the same way, or anything even remotely close, but I hope you'll give me a chance. Because I promise I'll prove to you I'm right."

I smiled up at him, still not quite believing everything he was saying. I hesitated for a split second before leaning close and saying softly, "I hate relationship conversations too."

Then I was kissing him. Slow and deliberate as if I had all the time in the world. And he was giving it right back to me.

After a few moments we broke apart and I leaned my head against his chest.

"So I'm assuming that's a yes?" He said softly into the top of my head.

I leaned my head back and peered into his eyes. "That's a definite yes," I replied with a smile.

"Well in that case," he said, reaching for the white box on the ottoman, "I think it's time for a celebratory cookie."

The Best Double Chocolate Cookies Recipe

· 1 cup cold butter, cut into small cubes
· 1 cup brown sugar
· ½ cup sugar
· 2 eggs
· ½ cup cocoa powder
· 1 cup cake flour
· 1 ½ cup all purpose flour
· 1 teaspoon cornstarch
· ¾ teaspoon baking soda
· ½ teaspoon salt
· 1 cup chocolate chips

1.) In a large bowl, beat cold butter and sugars until fluffy, about 3-5 minutes. Add eggs and mix well.

2.) Add cocoa, cake flour, all-purpose flour, cornstarch, baking soda, and salt and mix until combined. Stir in semisweet chocolate chips by hand.

3.) Scoop out heaping tablespoonfuls of dough on greased cookie sheet. Let chill in fridge for 15 minutes.

4.) Bake at 375 degrees for 9-11 minutes or until golden brown on the top. Let them rest for at least 15 minutes to set.

Epilogue

"Seriously? Seriously Luke? We are going to be late because you wanted to watch the end of a football game!"

"Jenn, it was the national championship! It was a big deal—they were tied with two minutes to go in the fourth quarter. You think I am going to drop out in the last two minutes?"

"Yes." I turned and looked at him sternly. "This is a big deal. It's my best friend's wedding. I expect you to stop watching a football game so we can make it to my best friend's wedding on time."

We were driving in his car, on our way to Jessica and Jake's wedding. Which, unfortunately, was happening in Newport Beach, in the middle of a Saturday. Everybody and their dog was on the freeway headed towards the beach. And we were stuck in bumper-to-bumper traffic.

Luke had arrived to pick me up almost 20 minutes late because he was watching a football game, hence our current argument.

"Look buddy, you knew when you started dating me punctuality was important to me. If you make me late to my best friend's wedding I will never live this down." I folded my arms with a huff.

He reached over and grabbed one of my hands, bringing it to his lips to kiss. "Have I ever told you how much I love you Jenn? Even though you are overly anal about getting to things two hours early. You do realize that the wedding still doesn't start for another hour right?"

It was possible that I may have given us a large time buffer in my planning... just in case something happened. What can I say? It was clearly necessary. Luckily, Jessica had opted not to have any bridesmaids—so my presence wasn't actually required.

Jessica ended up going minimal in all aspects of her wedding. They were having a simple ceremony at a chapel in Newport, then a luncheon for family and friends afterward. And that was it. Jessica had scratched having a reception about a month into her wedding planning. I think it was all just too overwhelming for her.

But regardless if my presence was necessary or not, I wanted to be there on time.

It had been about nine months since Luke and I had had our awkward relationship conversation and we had vowed to never force each other into another one again. Neither one of us could deal with that kind of discomfort.

Luckily, our relationship had been going strong ever since. We'd been able to balance each other out in a great way. I was there to make him more accountable in life, and he was there to help me relax a little more. He has also helped me gain more confidence.

Yes, you guessed it, I was writing my own cookbook. It took about two months of Luke's consistent pushing, but I finally reached out to Mariam and sent her a book query.

You can imagine my surprise when she agreed and asked for more samples.

Jenn's Sweets was also going strong, consistently building clientele. I hired two additional baking assistants and have begun to take more of a managerial role in the whole operation. My extra time had been spent mostly prepping and planning my cookbook. It's scheduled to print in about six months from now and I still can't believe it.

We pulled up to the wedding venue with a solid half hour to spare. Luke gave me the "I told you so look" that I pretended not to see. We had a good system.

We walked hand-in-hand into a chapel that was decorated with a beautiful array of white lilies and roses.

Bree and Christie weren't there yet and there weren't too many other people I recognized. Jessica's dad stood towards the front of the chapel, he was chatting with Jake and a few other men dressed in black tuxedos.

Luke and I found seats near the front of the room. I figured if you made the effort to arrive early, you deserved a good seat.

I told Luke I'd be right back and set off to find the bride. Jessica came from a family of four girls so she had plenty of women helping her get ready. I didn't want to intrude on their family time, but I didn't think she'd mind me peeking my head in for a minute. I found an usher who directed me towards a back room where the ladies were.

I tapped on the door then opened it to find a flurry of women doing last minute preparations.

Jessica sat in a chair in front of a giant mirror, looking absolutely gorgeous in a floor-length white dress. It was made of an antiqued lace material but was cut in a modern mermaid style that showed off her perfect figure. She had her hair arranged half up and half down, loose curls floating around her face.

"Jessica," I said rushing towards her, "you look absolutely beautiful! I'm so happy for you." And she did. I couldn't remember the last time I saw Jessica so happy. We spent five minutes chatting about last-minute gossip before I left so she could finish getting ready for the ceremony.

Everything went off perfectly from there. The service was beautiful; I swear I even saw Luke tearing up for a moment. Jessica and Jake were elated the whole time. Afterward, we all walked across the street to a site they had reserved for the luncheon.

The thought that kept popping into my head throughout the whole day was: Was this the future I wanted? Could I see this for Luke and me?

I wasn't sure what his thoughts were throughout the day, but he seemed much more subdued than usual.

When the eating and mingling began dying down Luke took my hand. "Let's go for a walk," he said, leading me out a set of French doors to an open balcony. It was a beautiful view of the Newport Back Bay, with the ocean in the distance.

Luke led me over to the railing where he turned and faced me. "Jenn, I know we promised each other we wouldn't have relationship conversations," he gave me a slight grin, "but there's something I need to tell you."

He looked me in the eyes for a minute, as if gauging my reaction. I held my breath, not sure what I was hoping for.

"I think I want what Jake and Jessica have. I think I want a happily ever after with you. I am sick of the dating scene, I'm sick of having to drive over to your apartment every time I want to see you." His smile warmed and he brought me closer. "I want to wake up with you snuggled next to me, knowing you'll be there every morning. Knowing you'll be there when I come home from work." He combed his fingers lightly through my hair as he spoke. "I know this isn't official, I don't have a ring, or anything prepared. But can we do this Jenn? Can we be the next ones to have a happily ever after?"

I looked at him for a second, trying to soak in the moment. I was so happy I could burst. "Well, I can't guarantee I'll be there every morning when you wake up," I said with a sly smile, "the bakery does open at 4 AM and you don't usually roll out of bed until at least 7 AM."

He matched my smile with his own.

"But yes. I can't remember the last time I've ever wanted something so much. Yes, yes, yes!" I wrapped my arms around his neck and kissed him with every feeling in my body.

The only reason we finally broke apart was because we heard the DJ announce Jessica and Jake were about to toss the bouquet and garter.

We got there just as Jake was chucking the garter into a swarm of single guys. A blonde kid that looked to be about 16 was the lucky recipient. Everyone cheered and slapped him on the back.

Next Jessica took her place center stage and motioned for all the single girls to gather together.

Luke gently shoved me forward and whispered, "Get up there, it might better my odds."

I laughed and walked towards the group, even though I felt a little ridiculous doing it.

Jessica lined us all up with her gaze then turned around so her back was to us. In a loud voice she hollered, "3-2-1...!" and chucked the flowers with all her might.

Next thing I knew I was standing there with a giant bouquet of white roses in my arms. When I looked up there was only one set of eyes that caught mine. Luke's.

THE END

Before You Go:

Wondering about the backstory of Jessica and Jake?
Find out how their perfect relationship got off to a rocky
start in my novella, A Run at Love:

"Jessica is done with dating. As a matter of fact she is
done with men as a whole.
Fueled by the bitterness of her last breakup, as well as
the ridiculousness number of blind dates she's been on,
Jessica is ready to lock her heart away for good. Somehow
her best friend and roommate Jenn convinces her to give
love one last shot with online dating.
And Jessica does, but will it end up just being another
mistake? Will the guy she's found turn out to be Prince
Charming, or just another heartbreak?"

*****

Note From the Author: Reviews are gold to me! If you've
enjoyed this book, I'd love if you'd consider rating it and
reviewing it on www.Amazon.com!

*****

To hear about my latest books first, sign up for my
exclusive New Release
Mailing List here: www.summerspen.com

Made in the USA
Columbia, SC
18 December 2018